The Spontiak Enigma

A.L. Wildman

ISBN: 978-0-244-01433-9

PublishNation
www.publishnation.co.uk

Dedicated to
Mum, Dad and my wonderful boys:
Patch, Benjamin, Jacob and Steed

Margaret

With love and best
wishes

Ann (the author)

December 1979

Wilson struggled on through the blinding snow. The blizzard tore at his clothes and skin like a rabid dog. There was no feeling in his legs from the knees down causing him to frequently stumble into the soft, thick carpet of freezing crystals.

Once again, he fumbled in his pocket for the compass but his gloves had become inflexible from the bitter frost. The relentless onslaught of white flakes was becoming thicker by the minute. After several attempts he looked down to see a glimpse of the compass in his palm but suddenly the blizzard took it from him, the swirling wind encompassing him as he frantically bent down to try to locate it. Flailing his arms around in the drifts, he dropped to his knees and rummaged around in a frenzy. Minutes passed by.

Wilson struggled back up onto his feet. Through the luminous sheet of white he caught sight of a dark shadow. Lifting his forearm to his forehead, in a hopeless attempt to shield his eyes, he stared at the amorphous figure as it fleetingly vanished then reappeared behind the flurry of the snowstorm.

Before he was aware it had hit him, he was dead, the bullet passing straight through his forearm, shattering his radius and boring straight through the middle of his forehead to burst his cerebrum before flying out the other side. The impact sent him falling backwards like a felled tree, his blood soaking into the sparkling white snow to form a vinaceous stain.

The dark shadow came forward joined by others. Wilson was lifted up and carried away. Within seconds his staring, glassy eyes were covered with the snow that was to be his final white shroud.

'They don't appeal to everyone. I've never been to Montreal, have you?'

The plane began to coast the runway and the familiar feeling of nausea bubbled in the pit of Professor Elling's stomach.

'Yes,' he managed to utter, 'quite a few times.'

'Are you going for a holiday?'

'No. No, I'm giving a lecture at the Carlsdown University, Montreal.'

'Really! How exciting. What is the lecture about?'

'Re-cycled energy,' he answered, glancing nervously out of the window at the moving ground.

Professor Elling smiled and leaned back again knowing that this was always a conversation stopper.

'That sounds fascinating,' said the elderly lady.

They always said that, of course, but there was something in her tone that caught his attention and he looked at her again. The plane gathered speed and the seats vibrated as the engines gathered force along the runway.

'Does it?' said Professor Elling.

'Oh yes! Of course, I'm not very knowledgeable about such things but what would be the point of that...?'

'Vehicles that would save on fuel consumption.'

'But, how would that work? Oh, don't mind me. I'm sure it's far too complicated for me to understand.'

'No. No, not at all,' said Professor Elling, whose great thirst to pass on knowledge had now begun to overtake the nervous effects of take-off. 'Just think of what happens when you strike a match,' he explained. 'Two materials come together in a frictional action that produces a spark, i.e., energy. Now, imagine if that energy could convert a fuel that was constantly recycled within the vehicle itself.'

'I was with you up until the recycling bit,' admitted the elderly lady.

Touched by her eagerness to learn, Professor Elling continued as the plane rocketed forward towards the end of the runway.

'Imagine a water feature in the garden, say a fountain. There is a constant waterfall that looks as if it is coming straight up from the earth, but beneath the water feature we know there is a pump and it is the same water going round and round. That's the type of thing I'm talking about.'

'Oh, I see what you mean. So the car could use the same recycled fuel? The tank would never have to be filled again?'

'That's correct.'

'How much room would it take inside the vehicle?' asked the elderly lady.

'Very little, because the constant recycling would require the minimum of raw matters and the brain of the outfit would be a tiny microchip – a miniature, electronic circuitry manufactured from silicon.'

'You mean like having a whole oil refinery in your own car?'

'That's exactly it!' said Professor Elling. 'It would be like having an oil refinery and petrol station together in one small unit that could fit into your car.'

'But wouldn't it be dangerous?'

'No more dangerous than switching on a light bulb.'

'And you really believe that is possible?'

'Yes definitely, in time. We already do it with metal, we do it with plastic, there's no reason we can't do it with fuel. I doubt the raw material would be petrol though. The reprocessing of raw materials is constantly progressing.'

The plane engines roared and the DC10 rose smoothly, leaving the ground streaking away behind it.

'That's absolutely fascinating. I can't wait to tell my daughter all about it,' she said. 'How lucky I was to have met you and the way you explained it to me made it sound so simple.'

'Well, obviously the process is far more detailed and complicated but I have found to strip to the basics and use simple language is the best way to teach my students, even university professors.'

'My name is Violet by the way,' she smiled, offering her hand, 'Violet Morcomb.'

'Professor Jeremy Elling.'

Professor Elling shook her hand warmly.

'What a nice name,' said Violet. 'It sounds like a poet's.'

Professor Elling chuckled.

The vibration had stopped and an announcement was made that passengers could now remove their safety belts.

'No son, they're not planes,' a paternal voice replied.

Professor Elling began to feel a little uneasy, for although his mind was racing with possibilities they were all logically dismissed until he was left with no possible explanation.

'Excuse me!' Professor Elling managed to catch the attention of an air stewardess.

'Yes, sir?' she enquired with a smile though the tone was taut.

'I'm Professor Elling from the Oxford Institute of Flexible Science. I wonder if I may have a word with the captain?'

'I'll just check for you, professor,' she replied.

Professor Elling sat tense in his seat, awaiting the stewardess's return.

'Are you going to ask him about the lights?' Violet enquired.

Professor Elling just smiled in reply.

The stewardess returned and whispered, 'Yes, sir. The captain will see you. Would you like to follow me?'

Professor Elling squeezed past Violet and the teenager to follow the stewardess up to the cockpit where he entered and introduced himself.

'I wondered if you had an explanation for those lights. I've never seen anything like that before,' Professor Elling addressed the captain.

Captain Mark Svelthart turned round and said, 'In truth, professor, neither have we. I've radioed in that we have unidentified phenomena'.

As he spoke a blinding light appeared suddenly in front of the plane.

'Whooa!' shouted the first officer. 'What the hell is that?'

Captain Svelthart spoke to air traffic control.

'This is Flight GA359. There is a very bright, unidentified light now directly in front of us. I may need to take evasive action. Have you any identification?'

'There is nothing showing on radar and we have no identification at this stage. We believe it could be freak weather conditions but we are diverting flights away from the area for you, captain,' the controller replied.

'What do we do?' asked the first officer. 'Lose height?'

'No,' said the captain, 'we don't have the speed yet. We could stall.'

'Hey! That can't be right,' said the flight engineer, pointing to the controls. 'We can't be at that height.'

Just then an alarm sounded and a red light flashed on and off.

'Damn it! We've lost the auto-pilot!' cursed the captain. 'What's happening, Mike?'

The flight engineer shook his head.

'Are we losing height?' asked the first officer.

'We can't be,' said the captain.

'Go up! Up!' argued the first officer.

Just then the white light vanished and what looked like bright, green arrows came flying towards the plane. There was a fizzing noise as each one flew past.

'What the hell...?' gasped the first officer.

'I'm holding course,' replied the captain.

'Are you sure?' asked the first officer, warily.

'Yes,' insisted the captain.

Professor Elling stood frozen as the green lights now disappeared and the white lights returned growing larger in the blackness of space. The tension in the cockpit became intense. Slowly, the lights became bigger and bigger until they were the size of large plates.

'Captain, I think we should take evasive action,' insisted the first officer.

'No. I'm holding this position until I know what's happening,' the captain answered firmly.

Professor Elling's fingers were like claws on the back of the flight engineer's seat. The lights became larger: shining, vibrating and growing. Suddenly, the lights disappeared completely.

'They've gone!' exclaimed the first officer.

'Look!' said the flight engineer. 'The auto-pilot's recovered.'

'We're too high!' shouted the first officer. 'Down, down!'

'Damn it! What's happening?' asked the captain.

'We had a temporary equipment malfunction,' explained the flight engineer. 'For a while we were being given false readings.'

'Julie, see if you can see those lights from back there,' the captain instructed the stewardess. Then, turning to Elling, he asked, 'How do you explain that, professor?'

Professor Elling remained staring out of the cockpit feeling a little shaken.

'I can't,' he said.

The stewardess returned a couple of minutes later.

'There's no sign of any lights now,' she said.

The captain radioed in their position and advised that the unidentified lights had disappeared as mysteriously as they had arrived. Control radioed back they had logged it.

'What happens now?' asked Professor Elling.

'It will just be recorded along with all the other sightings,' explained the captain.

'Other sightings? How many others have there been?' asked Elling.

'Quite a few, going way back to the fifties, but they've been few and far between. Recently, however, there have been reports about these specific lights. I have heard of other pilots seeing three, oval shaped lights but I had never had the experience myself until tonight,' admitted the captain. 'It would be best if you return to your seat now, Professor Elling. Please say nothing about what happened here. We don't want any panic among the passengers.'

'Of course,' agreed the professor.

As Professor Elling returned to his seat the captain announced an apology for the unexpected turbulence. The professor noted that Violet appeared to be the centre of attention from the other passengers as he came back down the aisle and he guessed she had given some indication of his profession and his request to see the captain. Expectant faces turned towards him as he arrived at his seat.

'Did he say what the lights were?' Violet asked him.

'I just wanted to see some flight deck equipment,' the professor stated in a slightly louder voice than usual. 'The lights? We think they are reflections bouncing off the aurora,' he answered casually. 'We may be lucky enough to see it soon.'

A certain feeling of anxiety within the cabin that he had sensed on returning to his seat immediately evaporated. From the back he heard a man explaining to someone he was with, 'That professor said it was just lights reflecting off the aurora'.

The passengers all seemed satisfied with the explanation and Professor Elling eased back into his seat with a sense of relief countered by the uneasy feeling that whatever those lights were, they remained unexplained and may not have completely deserted them.

'I'm glad you found an explanation for those lights,' Violet whispered in confidence. 'I was quite nervous back there. It reminded me of something odd that happened to my late husband, Albert, during the Second World War.'

'Really?' said Elling.

'Oh yes. There was a very strange tale that he recalled. They had been requested to go to the aid of an American pilot who had reported unexplained lights surrounding his ship...oh, that is, his aircraft. The Americans sometimes referred to their planes as ships, you know. Anyway, they located the craft by which time it was on the ground. When they got close to the plane, they saw it was blackened as if it had been burnt and yet it was still intact and totally undamaged so it couldn't have crashed. The pilot was still in his seat, dead, but his flesh was singed all down one side of his body. That plane was taken by the Americans for tests but neither Albert nor any of his colleagues heard any more, even though they enquired about it quite a few times.'

'That is odd,' agreed Professor Elling.

'It's certainly food for thought, isn't it?' she said.

Around them, a few of the passengers had given up on the aurora borealis, or had faith in their fellow passengers to awaken them if it was seen, as blankets were requested and blinds were pulled down over some of the windows. The stewardesses served tea, coffee and drinks. Professor Elling had coffee and a whisky. Violet decided to play dangerous and join him. Switching on the light above her head she took a magazine and began to thumb through the pages.

'Oh look!' she pointed out to the professor. 'There's a picture of the Rocky Mountains. Isn't that a beautiful photograph?'

Professor Elling took the corner of the magazine and turned the picture slightly towards him. Pointing to the name "Nathan King" he said, 'You see that name? He's the one who took the photo and he happens to be a friend of mine'.

'Oh really? You *are* an interesting person,' she told him. 'I'm so pleased that I sat next to you.'

'I'm pleased I sat next to you too,' he confided. 'I found take-off much easier with your *cure*.'

Violet smiled and continued to enjoy her coffee, whisky and magazine pictures. Professor Elling stared out into the darkness and thought of the lights, the captain's comments and a pilot in World War II.

CHAPTER TWO

CARNAGE

Nathan King stopped and slid the rucksack from his broad shoulders. A trickle of sweat ran down his throat and onto his chest. The open-necked shirt was damp with perspiration that covered his whole body. As he stood surveying his surroundings, a single bead of sweat ran down his long, straight nose to generous lips and his wavy, black hair stuck to his neck. Shaking each leg in turn, attempting to loosen the cotton from his damp skin, he noted the volatile wind across the plain that rose like an angry woman and abated just as quickly.

The land was arid. The dust clung to Nathan's clothes and the two-day stubble on his face, invading the pores of his skin and parching his tongue. It appeared he was the only soul for miles.

The sun blazed from a clear blue sky, reflecting the yellow-brown grass beneath his boots, golden streaks reclining across its surface. The white mountains glistened in the background. Only the hills refused to conform, appearing as dark, undulate shadows.

Nathan unzipped his rucksack and took out his camera. A freelance photographer, currently on an assignment for a well-known magazine, his work was a passion more than a job. Nathan King was well known as a professional prepared to go to enormous lengths, sometimes at the risk of his own safety, to procure the most stunning and powerful shots. Earlier that day, he had set out for this isolated place and had walked the last two miles across barren land, only the dead, brown moss that clung to some boulders giving any indication that heavy rain came to the area on occasions. Nathan had offered his Sherpa extra money to come the last two miles but the man had adamantly refused without explanation and taken the horses back with him. The Tibetans had certain superstitions and this area, Nathan guessed, was connected to one of them.

Nathan's forefinger pushed up the front of his brown, terai hat and he wiped his forehead with the side of his hand. It was warm and there was no shelter in this vast valley.

13

The lens moved slowly over the landscape. There were written rules about obtaining a good photograph but Nathan had never read them; he worked from pure instinct, knowing when the scene filling the lens had all the ingredients he wanted.

Nathan took his time. There was no hurry and perfection could not be rushed. The movement of the camera was steady but aware like a hawk's eye seeking its prey and then he had it. Where jagged mountain tops covered shadowy slopes that gave way to sweeping land beneath and the sky, peering between the mountains, in startling contrast to the earth below. Nathan had balance here: yin and yang, darkness and light, vividness and monotony, colour and starkness. It was a magnetic scene with its elements all coming together to form the ultimate shot.

Nathan clicked the camera, two, three, four times and then began the process over again. Gliding the camera very gently to his left, his eye caught something and he paused, blinked, moved back the frame just a touch and there it was.

Nathan adjusted the zoom to bring the image into sharper focus. Even enlarged, he could not quite make out what it was. It was a building of some description: a crude but large building that had actually been cut into the side of a mountain.

Nathan studied the coarse stonework with admiration. What an incredible work of art, he thought and what a back-breaking and arduous task it must have been to have hewn that mighty structure from the mountain itself. It was unlike the temples he had seen with their ornate roofs and oriental trimmings. This more resembled a prison.

Working with the camera to draw it closer to his vision, it became clear it was constructed of harsh squares and rectangles that resembled some type of ancient fortress. Nathan studied every detail of the outline but it was not sharp enough. Pulling his attention away from the structure for a few minutes, he changed the lens and refocused. Now he was able to see far more intimate details of the building. The image was larger and sharper. How cold and isolated it looked.

Nathan moved the lens across the walls until he spotted a familiar symbol carved into the stone. It was the padma – the lotus flower that rises from muddy roots, representing purity and detachment.

Further along on the same wall the lapidary showed the dharma wheel and further along still, Sakyamuni, the historic Buddha seated cross-legged on a lotus flower throne.

As Nathan realized he was, indeed, looking at an ancient monastery, he marvelled at how cold and bleak the place would be in winter and even at night when the temperature dropped sharply. It came as no surprise to him that the place appeared to have been long deserted, for there was no sign of life and its presence reflected a vacant loneliness.

Nathan put down the camera and stood akimbo, his lithe, taut physique poised like a bird watching its prey as his dark brown eyes viewed the distance, but the strange building was now a small, almost indiscernible mark.

Tired from his long walk and with hunger beginning to bite at the pit of his stomach, Nathan knew he could rest and eat or solve the mystery of the monastery. It took him only a few seconds to decide. Nathan picked up the camera, heaved the rucksack over his shoulders and resolutely began to walk towards the enigma of a distant mountain.

The feeling of excitement and curiosity, that had overcome the tiredness Nathan had been experiencing, became modulated by the realization that the ancient monastery that reared up before him was cut higher into the mountain than he had thought. It would be a long, uphill trek.

The building was an incredible structure. It was very basic, the emblems on the wall that he had viewed through the camera being its only external form of decoration. There was, however, something awe-inspiring about its isolation and its tenacity to exist in a world that was no longer of its time. There was also something substantial and permanent about the thickness of its solid stone walls and humbleness in its sacred eminence.

There was something else too, quite apart from the monastery itself and it had bothered Nathan for the last half-mile of his journey. Everything here was totally devoid of life. No birds flew, no moss grew, no insect crawled or animal stirred. Everything was dead.

The absolute silence disturbed him. It was so eerily and totally silent that he was aware of the pounding of his own heart and the subtle booming of the pulse within his ears as the blood surged around his body. This was an unnatural quietness like the silence of oblivion. Twice before he had come across it in war-torn areas, in the aftermath of battle, when survivors had fled and the slain left behind to rot though, even then, there had been some evidence of life: the whisper of a soft breeze that touched the faces of the dead like the blessing of an angel, the confused and erratic hurrying of insects, the movement of wary soldiers surveying the scene.

Nathan paused to survey the surrounding area before kneeling down to touch some odd tufts of grass that had withered and died. The blades shattered like crisps in his hand.

As he began to climb the long winding track that led up to the monastery Nathan noticed that some of the monastery walls were discoloured and the terrain beneath his feet had changed to grey.

Coldness gripped him. Although the track he was ascending was steep his exertion was producing an icy perspiration. Aware of goose-flesh on his arms he paused to catch his breath and glance back at the plain before casting his eyes across the varicoloured mountains. Uncannily, they appeared to be secretly observing and as he looked back up towards the monastery a feeling of dread suddenly enveloped him. It felt as if a blanket had been dredged from a grey sea and unexpectedly cast about his shoulders. Like a fishing line, cast into the depths of his memory, it hooked and presented him with a flashback from his childhood. Nathan had been six years old and playing in the sea when a freak wave had washed right over his head. It had come without warning, blocking everything from sight, knocking him off balance and catching him up into an overpowering, frightening world far removed from his own. For a few terrifying seconds he had been tossed and churned about, blind and choking, in a wet, dark chasm before the wave released him and retracted, leaving him screaming with fear. The recall unnerved Nathan as he had completely forgotten the incident until that moment.

The altitude was high and Nathan found the thinness of the air suffocating. Slowly he continued on his way, following the track, each arduous step bringing him closer to removing the cover from the sealed book ahead of him, for he already knew that fate had brought him here but he did not know why.

Halfway up the track, Nathan stopped. Tired and breathless, he was now aware that his brain had picked something up on a subconscious level.

With trepidation, he glanced all around him. All was too still. All was too silent. There was something inexplicable here that he did not like. The whimsical wind that had followed him across the valley had long since deserted him. Was it still down there flowing silently over that barren landscape or had it retracted and dispersed?

There were spiritual energies here, he thought, caught up around these monastic walls to survive forever as invisible prisoners shackled to the past.

Following the small, rugged track that stretched and spiralled upward to the holy structure, Nathan's unease grew with each advancing step. It was as if every sense he possessed was silently screaming at him to turn back. Was it danger he could sense, he wondered? What dangers could an ancient, deserted monastery hold?

Still he went on and still his wariness grew, gradually wrapping itself around him, until he felt smothered by some invisible force that was all the more frightening because he knew it was emanating from within himself.

The monastery was close now and he noticed the stark structure had no expression. Nathan found that disturbing. Every building had an expression that told the observer something about itself by its outer appearance. This one, however, gave nothing away. It had character but did not express it, as if purposely wearing a blank look to protect itself from the outside world. Contemplating the impermeable walls now just ahead of him, he wondered if this monastery was calling his bluff? Did its inner secrets contain nothing more than shadows and dust?

Nathan slowed his steps as he reached a rudimentary forecourt, the primitive walls almost within his reach. Clearly now, he could see the gaping holes that served as windows and the stout, cedarwood doors, weathered and battered by the elements, that would give entrance to the monastery itself. Originally there would have been outer gates to give access to the forecourt but these, Nathan noted, had been lost a long time ago, the remains of the stone walls that would have supported them long since broken and destroyed. Nathan assumed these had been victims of the Cultural

Revolution in which many thousands of people died and thousands of monasteries and temples had been destroyed.

As he approached the doors, he felt the flesh at the back of his neck begin to tingle. What was the strange stirring within him like a floating memory that vaporized when he tried to reach out for it? Nathan stood still. Although there was no breeze, he felt ghostly fingers brushing against his skin. All he had to do was walk forward and push the huge chunk of old cedarwood for the monastery to disclose its mysteries to him but he hesitated. An inexplicable nausea rose in his throat while, at the back of his mind, distant images loomed like half-forgotten shadows. There was a door in his subconscious waiting to open but he had lost the key. The solid doors in front of him creaked like old men's bones as they succumbed to his force. Nathan stepped into the interior of the monastery and blinked to adjust his eyes to the half-light. Everything was in shadow, the private interiors shunning the outside world. Upon entering, he immediately recognized what had teased but so far eluded him. Now he knew what he had sensed halfway up the track, why his steps had faltered, why his skin had crawled. It was the smell: subtle further away because there had been no wind to carry it, but stronger now even though it was mixed with other, less fetid, aromas.

Palms moist, chest heavy, heart racing as he lifted his chin to sniff the air, he discerned an overall musty smell from the weathered walls and the old wood along with the distinct aromas of sandalwood and candle grease, but above and beyond these was a sickening, unmistakable odour – the smell of dead, human flesh.

Nathan placed a hand on the hard, stone wall. It felt cold and rough. Memories flooded his brain with vivid, unwelcome pictures that returned in kaleidoscopic sharpness of bodies flung carelessly onto trucks and into pits, dark-skinned men with cotton scarves covering their faces (poor masks against the abysmal stench of death), weeping women, children crying in fear or silent in their frozen horror with minds numbed by their terror, old people with soulful eyes, their spirits broken by the helplessness of their situation and human carcasses with hollow cheeks and staring eyes, racked and ravaged by a disease long since eliminated in the Western world. It had been one of Nathan's worst assignments as a freelancer. For some years the memories had remained dormant in some dark recess of his mind but now they had re-emerged, awoken from a deep sleep by the haunting aroma of the monastery.

As his eyes adjusted to the half-light, he saw before him a large central figure of Sakyamuni, built from stone, before a backdrop of mystical beasts. Nathan crossed the solid, stone floor and took a door to his left that led him along a passageway lined with prayer wheels that opened into the main chanting hall. The sickening reek of dead flesh was more noticeable here and he instinctively placed a hand over his nose. Dominating one of the walls was an image of lung-ta, the wind horse, represented as an elephant with three jewels on his back, taking prayers to heaven by wind. There were columns made from whole cedarwood trunks and before the altar stood artefacts of porcelain, wood and marble.

Nathan took a short passageway from here that led him to another room. This one was larger and far more ornate with open wooden shutters in the windows. Large volumes of the Tengyur decorated the shelves along with copper stupas filled with ancient script. Lines of unlit candles paid silent homage to Sakyamuni who appeared, this time, as a grandiose figure decorated with splendid robes of rich red and gold. Religious statues in oriental wooden cabinets were placed each side of the Buddha and drapes of green and red hung from the ceiling, partly concealing the murals and thangkas on the walls.

The hues of red, gold and green displayed in this chapel appeared garish compared to the simplicity of what had gone before. The almond-shaped eyes of Sakyamuni seemed to study Nathan with interest.

Noticing a doorway to the right, where a mural of a dragon guarded the entrance, Nathan walked through and beyond to a small chamber where steps led to the monks' living quarters on an upper storey. The offensive smell faded here so Nathan decided to backtrack through the ornate chapel and into the small passageway. This time he noticed a small door halfway along. Slowly he turned the handle and pushed.

The stench sent Nathan reeling backwards. The air was disgusting here but nothing compared to the scene that met his eyes. Nathan entered in a daze. Dead monks, their own robes acting as shrouds, were scattered like debris around what appeared to be the eating hall.

The corpse nearest him was face up with one hand in a claw-like gesture. The mauve and black tongue hung from the mouth with dried blood crusted around the lips. Nathan surmised he had been throttled to death. Another corpse lay halfway across the first with a gaping wound to the throat.

Nathan's stomach turned over as he stepped cautiously over the bodies. Some were still in their seats, slumped over their upturned bowls, their shocked faces expressing the full horror of their final moments. Everywhere Nathan looked were limbs covered in congealed blood and pallid faces gazing up at him with sightless eyes. Some looked as if they had been shot, others tortured. Now, his initial shock and disgust had given way to a wave of anger. These gentle men who had practised ahimsa had not deserved to die this way. It was not a fit end for these monks whose way of life was the seeking of inner peace and tranquillity, whose faith forbade them to kill even the smallest of living creatures because, to them, all life was precious. The scene before him was an outrage, this one room reflecting all that was evil, sick and disenchanting about the world.

Without consciously knowing why, Nathan set his rucksack down and pulled out his camera. It was an instinctive action impelled by a photographer's thirst for proof and knowledge that could only be captured on film. Nathan was the professional now. The camera was what he knew, what he felt secure with; he could not handle the scene before him but he knew how to use it as an image in the lens.

Lining up the shots, he quickly and efficiently captured the ugliness and horror of it all. When he finally put the camera away he was finding it difficult to breathe. Whether it was shallow breathing or an emotional response he was not sure. All he knew was that he had to get out of that room. Leaving by a door opposite the one he had entered by, he found himself in a small antechamber. Here, he noticed that he had used up the last of the film. In the dim light of the antechamber he took out the used film and replaced it with a new one, placing the used one into a back pocket of his trousers. There was a door facing him. Opening it, he found himself in a paved courtyard surrounded by three walls about three feet in height. The open air came as a relief. There was a wooden form around the walls and in a corner of the yard another statue of Sakyamuni, this time holding a bowl. In the centre of the yard was a well.

Nathan slumped down onto the form, removed his hat and ran his fingers through his tousled, black hair. Although he felt sick, his stomach was too empty to enable him to vomit. After retching a couple of times, he concentrated on taking deep breaths. The air was still but at least the pungent smell had lessened, though it still trailed around his nostrils like a stalker. As he became calmer he noticed the beauty of the scenery and began to comprehend why this particular spot had been chosen to build the monastery. The mountains were like dormant dragons, the jagged peaks of their scaly backs tipped with the whiteness of snow. They appeared live and yet sleeping, absorbing nature's energies, confident in their glory, morose in their loneliness. Nathan knew he should take a photograph of the land from this aspect but it seemed wrong to capture these images after what he had just seen inside the monastery. With the high altitude the thin air was also beginning to take its toll.

Replacing his hat on his head, he suddenly felt very weary. To eat was out of the question but he felt thirsty. There was water in his rucksack but he had a long walk back to where the Sherpa would be waiting for him, so he stretched his legs and wandered over to the well. Nathan picked up a stone from the courtyard, dropped it down the well and listened. Hearing a faint splash he began to unwind the rope to lower the wooden tub attached. It was then that a weak cry disturbed the eerie silence.

Nathan grabbed back the rope he had let slip in surprise and swung round, his eyes sweeping the empty courtyard. For a moment he wondered if his imagination was playing tricks on him, but the faint sound came again and this time there was no doubt it was real.

Nathan leaned over the wall of the well. Peering down into the dark interior he could just make out the shape of a human about halfway down. Moving around the well to get a clearer view, he saw a monk who looked very old and frail. Nathan lowered the water tub hoping the monk would understand what he had to do.

'Climb on,' Nathan told him.

Feeling the weight yank the rope, he then pulled down on it to ascend the monk. Although the old man was not very big it took all of Nathan's strength to bring him up. When the monk's head appeared clear of the well, Nathan was perspiring heavily. It was clear the old man was far from well and Nathan quickly hooked up the rope and grabbed the monk who collapsed on him. Half-lifting, half-dragging, Nathan pulled him clear of the well and onto the ground. The old man's almond eyes were half-closed with pain. There was stubble on his shaved head and his wrinkled face was dehydrated, his lips swollen, cracked and dry from thirst. Nathan grabbed at his rucksack to find the bottle of water. Raising the old monk's head up gently, Nathan held the bottle to the old man's lips. The monk's eyes searched Nathan's face as he drank and Nathan wondered how long he had been trapped on the ledge down the well, hungry, thirsty and cold at night.

The monk spluttered and Nathan pulled the bottle away.

'American?' enquired the monk.

'You speak English,' said Nathan.

'You…English?' the monk replied.

'Yes. I'm an English photographer. What happened here?'

'The others…?' enquired the monk.

'Dead,' said Nathan.

'All...?'

'Yes, they are all dead,' Nathan confirmed. 'I'm sorry. Who did this? What happened?'

'They came to seek The Wise One,' croaked the monk.

Nathan did not understand but he could see the old man was fading. Nevertheless, questions needed to be asked and answers given.

'Please. What happened here?' Nathan pleaded with him. 'You must tell me.'

The monk struggled to speak.

'They came at dusk, three days ago. I was hit... pushed down well, but...'

'The ledge saved you,' Nathan finished for him.

The old man paused to fight for breath before continuing.

'The others were…'

'It was quick,' said Nathan, seeing the torture in the old man's eyes.

The monk moved his head slowly from side to side.

'Not quick. I heard screams. I heard…'

'Is there anything I can get you?' asked Nathan. 'Any medication?'

'No,' the monk replied. 'I have delayed too long. I will move on before sunset.'

'Who were they?' Nathan asked again. 'Who wanted to murder you?'

The old man gasped. Breathing was becoming difficult for him.

'They are followers of darkness. You...' smiled the old monk, '...are Sign of the Light. You are the one we hoped for.'

The old man closed his eyes, a rasping sound came from his chest and his breathing was heavy and erratic.

'I don't understand,' said Nathan. 'Who is The Wise One?'

The monk slowly opened his eyes and pointed to the statue of the Buddah then he lifted a gnarled hand and grasped Nathan's shirt.

'Darkness will follow you now, but you will overcome, Sign of the Light!'

It was the last thing the monk ever said. The hand slipped down. As his lips turned blue, a deep guttural sound came from his throat and he closed his eyes.

Nathan placed his ear close to the old man's mouth. There was a wheezing sound issuing from his lips that changed to a death rattle. The monk turned his head to one side before going into a deep sleep from which his body would never awaken.

Staggering away from the pathetic figure that had a dead finger still pointing towards Sakyamuni, Nathan turned and beat the stone walls with the sides of his fists. As he knelt and placed his forehead against the cool, stone wall, he felt a throbbing in his temples and nausea, once again, filling his chest. Nathan knew he had to leave the mountain at once and get to lower ground. As he took another look at the dead monk with the top half of his robe open, something incongruous caught Nathan's attention. There was a chain around the old monk's neck that he had not seen on the other monks. Kneeling down, Nathan grasped the chain and pulled gently to reveal a rectangular, metal tag. On it was an inscription. Nathan gently supported the old monk's head and removed the tag. Standing up, he turned it over in his hand and read the inscription:

SPONTIAK
David J.
3249-701-685
USN A Pos
BAPTIST

23

Amazed, Nathan realized it was an ID tag and, if he was not mistaken, it was an issue of the US Navy. The old monk had asked if he was American. Nathan's head whirled. What the hell was an old monk in Tibet doing with an American naval ID tag?

Nathan picked up the bottle of water, took a few gulps and put it in his rucksack. Placing the tag carefully down the side of his left boot, he took one final, sorrowful look at the monk, slipped on his rucksack and left the monastery as quickly as possible. As he started off down the track he felt light-headed but he would not rest in this place a moment longer and would walk until he could, once again, feel the wind dance across his face.

The skies had turned to a reddish purple and the sun, though still high in the sky, would later begin its descent behind the mountains. The old man had been right, thought Nathan, he had moved on before sunset.

CHAPTER THREE

DANGEROUS ENCOUNTERS

It was the early hours of the morning. Nathan groaned and stretched; his limbs and head felt heavy from the long trek and the events of the previous day. It had been an arduous walk back from the monastery and he had rested only briefly to use up another film on spectacular shots of the ever-changing skies. As agreed, the Sherpa had met him to take him the last two miles back to Lhasa. Back at the hotel, Nathan ate sha phaley then went to his room and fell backwards onto the bed too tired to remove his hat or boots. Within minutes he was sound asleep.

Slowly he became aware of the chill of the night and the distant howling of a dog: a hollow, lonely sound that echoed through the deserted streets. The kerosene lamp by his bed cast a dull glow on the wall beyond. Nathan's eyelids flickered then closed; his head and legs felt like lead weights that refused to move. Sleep slowly crept upon him again, cradling him in its nurturing blackness.

Nathan was awoken, heart pounding, by a cacophony of vicious barking. Outside the hotel the street dogs were having a fight. It was a horrible sound as, with strident and coarse vocals, they tore into one another, biting, snarling, yelping and growling. Nathan let out an audible moan and then something moved against his leg. The material of his trousers, he thought. Slowly, distant memories came flowing back into his mind. They were unpleasant memories and he was so tired he tried to close the door on them, but they burst it open and became more vivid. Nathan groaned again. Outside, the noisy and raucous fighting had reached a crescendo. Something nudged his leg and this time he moved his head to see what it was.

Nathan froze. A large snake was gliding slowly over his right calf. In the dull light, he saw its shadowy gleam weaving leisurely but resolutely. The cotton of his trousers creased beneath the weight of the flowing reptile as it slithered between his legs and along his left calf. Nathan swallowed but even this subtle movement alerted the predator and its head reared up, eyes cold and glassy in the lamplight, as it fixed him with an antagonistic stare. A low hissing sound came from its mouth as its tongue flicked in and out. Nathan remained still, trying to reason how a snake could have entered his room when he always kept the door closed. The snake stared at him for a long time before lowering its head and slithering along his inner thigh then over and alongside his left hip. Nathan gently moved the fingers of his right hand. The snake raised its head again, pulling it back into the shape of a question mark that hissed and spat.

Outside, a long, blood-curdling howl pierced the night and died slowly on the wind along with its owner. It was a weird, unearthly sound as the soul was wrenched prematurely from the body. Another dog had met his fate on the dark streets of Lhasa.

Nathan's right fingers slowly undid the pocket where he kept his knife. Feeling the handle he attempted to pull it gently from its sheath. The snake slid slowly over his left arm, then reared up, its eyes fixed on Nathan's head. Every muscle in Nathan's body was tense. Aware the snake would sense it, he tried to relax as his right fingers still gently attempted to slide the knife out. Once it was free he would have to act with the speed of light. Nathan had lightning reflexes but he would have to be faster than the snake for it would be a matter of life or death.

The snake spat and jerked its head forward. Nathan froze. It would have to be one fell swoop, slicing the snake's head from its body and he would only get one chance. Before he could free the knife, the snake took a sudden lunge at his head. Nathan sprang off the bed and onto the floor. As he looked up, he saw the snake's true prey caught in its jaws – a scorpion, its tail curled over, legs moving violently as it tried to free itself from the predator's jaws. There was a crunch as the snake bit through the scorpion's armour. With the snake distracted, Nathan crept up behind it. With one swift movement he grabbed it and slung it out of the open window, the scorpion still caught firmly in its mouth.

Leaning against the wall, Nathan took deep breaths. Although he was no snake expert he was almost certain it was a Russell's Viper, one of the most deadliest snakes. It had not got into his room by itself and neither, he suspected, had the scorpion. Someone wanted him dead. Nathan carefully checked through his rucksack. The camera was missing.

Cursing, he quickly felt in his back pocket. The film was still there. A victorious smile crossed his broad lips but evaporated quickly. How long, he wondered, before the thief developed the film and discovered it was not what he was looking for? More to the point, who was the thief and who did he work for? Nathan was beginning to suspect the Chinese authorities. What the hell had happened in that monastery? Had *they* killed the monks? If so, why?

There were many questions going through his brain, interlinking, stopping, reattaching and dividing like an underground railway, but there was no time to stop and find the answers now. Clearly he was in danger and he did not know who from so he packed his rucksack, tucked the film inside his right sock on the inside of his leg and waited for first light before he cautiously went downstairs. Nobody was around so he left money on the table and surreptitiously glanced outside. Dawn was breaking. The rectangular, white and sand-coloured buildings were in contrast to the wafts of dark pink and lavender streaking the skies above. Just outside the hotel were two street dogs from the previous night's dogfight. They appeared to be eating the remains of some small animal. One was a small, brown and white dog, the other a larger, sandy dog, with a chunk out of his right ear. Occasionally they would silently snap at one another, both possessive of the tiny amount of nutrition that remained. The sandy dog suddenly turned and looked at Nathan. The animal's eyes reflected the uncertainty that Nathan felt himself. They were two souls meeting in passing, yet sharing a moment of divine and mutual understanding. As the dog turned away, Nathan prepared to go. These were simple people, with a simple way of life, but there were darker forces at work and he was no longer safe here. It was time to leave Tibet.

Nathan was suddenly surrounded by four, armed, Chinese policemen as he walked through Lhasa. Speaking their native tongue and using gestures, they appeared to be requesting him to get into the back of a jeep. Although Nathan felt reticent about this bleak encounter, he could see no immediate option than to do as requested.

Two of the police joined him in the back of the jeep, watching him with piercing eyes and stony faces. Nathan avoided their gaze. After a short, bumpy ride, the jeep came to a halt. One of the men flung open the rear door and Nathan found himself outside a stark, grey stone building in the Chinese quarter of the city. A poke in the back directed him towards the entrance. Further along the street, he noticed the main entrance to the Public Security Bureau. Once inside, three of the police remained with him whilst the fourth relieved Nathan of his rucksack and disappeared with it through a doorway. One of the men checked Nathan's pockets. Minutes later the fourth man reappeared. With the back of his hand facing Nathan, he pulled his fingers inwards in a gesture for Nathan to come forward. Waving him through the doorway he closed the door behind him and Nathan found himself in a small room with grey, crumbling walls. There was no furniture except for a desk and three chairs. The two chairs behind the desk were occupied by a middle-aged military policeman who, by his uniform, Nathan guessed to be of much higher rank than the ones who had brought him in and a young Chinese woman, with long, silky black hair and wearing a white dress patterned with black orchids over black leggings. The middle-aged man, who had a flat face and jet-black eyes, gestured for Nathan to sit in the chair facing them.

The man, Nathan noticed, had a bad case of body odour.

As Nathan sat down, the middle-aged authoritarian said something in Chinese to the young woman who then addressed Nathan.

'Thank you for coming,' she told him with a deadpan expression.

Nathan gave a sardonic smile.

'Did I have any choice?' he enquired.

The official looked at the woman but she did not relay the comment. The official produced Nathan's passport from his rucksack, which had already evidently been thoroughly searched. Opening the passport the man then proceeded to say something in Chinese while scanning Nathan's face with suspicious eyes.

'You are Nathan King?' interpreted the woman.

'Yes,' replied Nathan.

Again, she interpreted for the official.

'What is your occupation?'

28

'I'm a photographer.'

'You are not a journalist?'

'No. I'm a photographer,' Nathan reiterated.

'What do you photograph, Mister King?'

'Life, scenery, wildlife for magazines.'

The predatory eyes of the official uncomfortably reminded Nathan of the snake he had encountered earlier and he wondered if this was the demon who had arranged for it to pay him a visit. The young woman continued to relay questions asked by the authoritative figure next to her.

'You visited a monastery yesterday.'

'Yes.'

'Why did you do that? What were you hoping to find there?'

'I wasn't hoping or expecting to find anything,' said Nathan. 'I just happened upon the monastery when I was photographing the mountains.'

'Does a photographer not need to travel with a camera, Mister King? Where is yours?'

Nathan felt his muscles tense. So, he thought, they did not have the camera.

'It was stolen from my room while I was sleeping.'

A long verbal encounter then took place between the official and the woman. Nathan was becoming increasingly aware of the disagreeable smell of the Chinese man's sweat. It was a cross between fusty linen and stale soy sauce.

The official produced three reels of unopened film.

'Do you have any more films?' the woman asked Nathan.

'No,' said Nathan, sighing and looking as casual as he could manage. 'Apart from the one in the camera. I'd taken shots of the mountains.'

Another long discussion took place between the two Chinese before the woman addressed Nathan again.

'You saw the dead monks at the monastery?'

'Yes, of course I did. What happened there?'

'We ask the questions, Mister King. Were all the monks dead when you arrived?'

'Yes,' said Nathan. 'Just bodies everywhere.'

29

Nathan's mind was racing now. There had been no one out there in that barren landscape. Could someone have been spying from the mountains? Did they see him help the dying monk?

'Why did you not report the incident, Mister King?'

Nathan was silent for a moment as his brain urgently sought an answer.

'To be honest, I like to keep my nose out of things that aren't my business. Besides, it shook me up a bit. I wasn't thinking straight,' he replied.

'Did you take photos of the dead monks?'

'No. I got out of there as quickly as possible. It scared me.'

'Did you take anything from the monastery?'

Nathan's toes instinctively curled inside his boots and he felt the hard edges of the dog tag inside one and the film inside the sock in the other.

Nathan fixed the Chinese official with a stern look of his own.

'I'm a photographer,' he stated firmly, 'not a thief.'

The official leaned back in his chair and lifted his chin, fixing Nathan with a judgemental look. There were a few moments of tense silence. Nathan could hear the thumping of his own pulse in his ears and the ticking of his watch.

Unexpectedly, the authoritarian's face relaxed into a smile.

'A bad thing has happened at the monastery,' the man told him through the interpreter. 'Rebels. Bad men. We will be certain to find them and they will pay the price. This is a very bad reflection on Tibet and her people. The Chinese are honourable people. We do not want such bad publicity in the western world.'

Handing Nathan back his passport and rucksack, but keeping the new films, he gave a quick nod. Nathan remained seated; uncertain.

'You may go, Mister King,' the woman told him.

Nathan nodded his head, turned and left the room.

Outside, it was quiet. Lhasa's skies were now a stunning cool blue. Nathan made his way back through the Chinese quarter to the Tibetan quarter of the inner city and to the Barkhor, the street that surrounded the Jokhang Temple. Here there were pilgrims lying in reverence, strewn like litter. Nathan continued through small alleyways until he reached the rough and inadequate building that called itself a hotel. Inside, Yeshe, an elderly Tibetan man who ran the hotel, was sweeping the floor as if his life depended on it. Looking up as Nathan entered, he smiled showing a black gap where one of his front teeth should have been.

'Ah! Mister King. You decide stay longer?'

Nathan found the broken English endearing and the smile was welcome after that of the Chinese official who had resembled a hungry shark.

'Yes, a little longer.'

'Chinese police find you?' Yeshe asked, the smile now wiped from his face.

Nathan studied him carefully.

'That's right. How did you know that?'

'They come after you go. Ask questions. I know nothing.'

'Did anyone come here earlier yesterday after I left with the Sherpa and before I returned to the hotel?'

The Tibetan shook his head.

'No. I see no one.'

'I need another Sherpa. Could you find me one?'

'Sherpa? I find.'

Nathan thanked him, then turned to mount the stairs to his room but changed his mind. Turning back to the old man he asked him a question.

'Where did you learn to speak English?'

Yeshe leaned on his broomstick and gave a grin.

'Englishman teach me. Long time ago.'

'What kind of an Englishman?' enquired Nathan.

The Tibetan frowned and shook his head as if he did not understand the question.

'Who was he?' asked Nathan.

'Good man. Kind man.'

'What happened to him?'

'Not know. Think he die. Was long time ago.'

'What was his name?'

Yeshe shrugged.

'No know name. Just Englishman.'

Nathan reached into his rucksack to find a piece of paper and a pen. Leaning on a rough, wooden table he drew a map. The old man came alongside to watch.

'I need to go back to this place,' Nathan informed him, pointing to where he had found the monastery. 'Here there is a monastery, very old, cut into the mountainside.'

Nathan studied the old man's face but found it difficult to interpret his reaction.

'I need a Sherpa to take me all the way. It's too far on foot,' Nathan informed him.

Yeshe shook his head.

'No Sherpa go there. Bad place.'

'Why?'

'Something happen, long time ago. Place cursed. People not like. Bad spirits there.'

'What happened?' Nathan insisted.

'Fog come. Bring bad spirits. Everything die. Bad place.'

'OK,' said Nathan.

Picking up the map and tucking it into his pocket he went upstairs to his room.

CHAPTER FOUR

THE DARK STRANGER

Nathan left the hotel in the afternoon to take a wander around Lhasa. All morning he had tried to find a Sherpa, or someone with transport, who would be willing to take him to the site of the deserted monastery but had at last given up. Like before, he would have to pay someone to take him part of the way and walk the rest. Rubbing the stubble on his face and the untidy tangle of dark hair around his collar he wondered if he was going a little mad. All he had were an old monk's dying words and a dog tag tucked inside his boot, yet he felt he was on a quest. The only clue he had was what had happened at that monastery and like a child presented with a gift, he could not rest until he had unwrapped it.

As he walked idly through the overcast streets, where Tibetans relied on candles and kerosene, he passed Tibetan men in felt boots, black bowler hats and chubas. Some who worked and were housed in Chinese units wore cropped hair and tunics. The Tibetan women with large smiles, friendly eyes and jet-black hair, sporting turquoise or coral beads and braids, wrestled with their boyfriends or laughed in groups.

Finding himself back at the Barkhor, where pilgrims wandered clockwise or lie prostrate, he studied the Jokhang Temple, the religious centre of the Tibetan quarter, when he was suddenly surrounded and jostled by Khampas. They were swarthy men who originated from Kham in Eastern Tibet. They dressed in mao pants and white shirts over which they wore chubas. Their shoes had high heels with buttons or colourful patches of corduroy. Around their waists, beneath their chubas, they wore ornate red and black belts made from leather with pockets, studs and chains. Their long black hair was worn wrapped around the head, secured with red tassels. At their waists were woven sashes holding long knives in silver sheaths. Most were traders. They would trade anything but mostly silver, turquoise and God's eye beads. The tallest, swarthiest of the group nudged Nathan hard on the shoulder sending him bumping into another of his comrades. They enjoyed agitating foreigners.

'Hey, hey, you buy. Yes?' said the Khampa.

From his belt he swiftly produced a small, ornate silver charm.

'You like. Yes?'

Another shove to the back knocked Nathan forward again. Nathan turned to look at the man who smelt of testosterone, sweat and dust. Large, black brows arched over even blacker eyes. A straight nose with a slight bump led down to a wide mouth with even teeth, slightly discoloured.

The Khampas' hassling of foreigners was usually done in a cheerful and playful way but there was something about this group that was more threatening. It made Nathan feel uncomfortable but he was aware that from one of these he could find the rebellious character he required.

'Here, good price,' said the Khampa, offering Nathan a God's eye bead on a leather string.

There was more shoving and pushing followed by raucous laughter. Nathan fixed his eyes upon the man who had last addressed him and pushed a finger into his chest. It was like hitting rock.

'You come with me. Get rid of these,' Nathan told him firmly, looking him sternly straight in the eyes.

The man waved his companions away and Nathan led him into an alleyway that led off from the Barkhor. Nathan withdrew the map from his pocket and showed it to his swarthy companion.

'I want to be taken here,' he said, pointing to the site of the monastery. 'I want you to arrange transport there and back.'

Nathan took a wad of notes from his pocket to show the Khampa.

The Khampa suddenly looked wary. The confident, flashing eyes that had held humour just moments before now reflected suspicion.

'The dead valley. Why you wish go there?' he asked cautiously.

'That's my business. Your business is to get me there,' Nathan answered.

For a long moment the Khampa held Nathan's steady gaze with one of his own.

'You buy?' he asked, showing Nathan more trinkets.

Nathan gave a sneer.

'Forget the ornaments. I want transport.'

34

'No one go there,' said the Khampa.

'I know,' replied Nathan, 'but I'll make it worth your while.'

Nathan took more notes from his pocket and waved them in front of the Khampa.

The Khampa shook his head and turned to leave.

'Oh, I see. There is superstition attached to the place. You feel nervous about it,' Nathan taunted.

The Khampa turned, his face turning to steel.

'I understand,' Nathan continued. 'You're afraid. I must have got it wrong. I thought you chaps had courage.'

For a moment, the black eyes blazed and Nathan saw the lean, powerful fingers move towards the knife in the sheath. Clearly this man's eager need to trade with western tourists had produced a better understanding of English than Nathan had thought. Immediately, Nathan realized he had gone too far and that this Khampa may possibly not think twice about seriously harming him. All Nathan's muscles were tense but he kept his gaze steady. For a few icy moments, the Khampa's fingers toyed near the knife then a wide grin cast itself across his face.

'I take you.'

Nathan proffered his hand. The Khampa took it with a crushing grip and the deal was done.

'Meet me here. Seven,' he told Nathan.

'Seven? In the morning?'

'Yes. We leave then.'

'What's your name?' Nathan asked him.

'Sonam,' he said. 'You?'

'Nathan.'

'Seven, Nathan. I take you.'

The Khampa left the alley, his vulture-like shadow disappearing back into the Barkhor. Nathan remained for a few moments taking deep breaths. Before the Chinese had taken control the Khampas, evolved from warriors, had been the horsemen and rebels of the Tibetan hills. These were the people who had played a major role in the 1959 rebellion. Nathan felt uneasy in the man's presence and felt uncertain regarding his safety. Nevertheless, it was a chance he was prepared to take.

Nathan wandered casually back out into the Barkhor. The Khampas were now nowhere to be seen. Weaving his way down alleyways, he made his way out into the Chinese quarter of Lhasa where streets straightened and broadened out. The Chinese quarter was always brighter due to the straighter, wider streets and the mercury arc lamps. Nathan found a place to eat where he had stewed meat followed by chang, a beer made from rice or barley. Sated, he walked slowly back to the Barkhor and along alleyways now dim and silent except for the packs of wild dogs that roamed the streets.

As Nathan arrived at the alleyway leading out to his hotel, a horrifying sound of frenzied, blood-thirsty dogs hit the air. Nathan felt it rather than heard it, like a knife cutting through his nerves. As he came out of the alley, opposite the hotel, he witnessed a ring of mad dogs, snarling, biting and screeching. At the centre of the circle Nathan recognized the sandy dog with the missing piece of ear. The animal was on his back, desperately trying to defend himself. Without even thinking, Nathan suddenly waded into the canine furore using arms, fists and boots, shouting and growling so that he, himself, became like one of the growling pack he was challenging. When the largest dog, a black, ungainly type, showed subordination and galloped off down an alley, the rest followed and all was left in unearthly silence, save for the injured dog's whimpering and Nathan's laboured breathing. The dog, now turned onto his right side, struggled to get up. Once again, their eyes met and the dog's reflected wonderment and suspicion. In Nathan's the dog saw pity. Across a dusky side street in Tibet their souls touched, albeit briefly.

'You OK there, fellow?' Nathan spoke to the dog as he now stood on unsteady paws.

The dog looked around as if confused as to where he was or perhaps concerned the pack may return. Nathan saw bite marks on the dog's trunk and blood oozing from his back hip. The animal would somehow survive or limp away to die. Yeshe shuffled out.

'You brave man,' he told Nathan.

'No,' smiled Nathan, 'just a little crazy.'

Yeshe went inside while Nathan watched the dog. The animal stood still as if waiting for something that would never come. The animal's pack had left and now he was alone. That would be a dangerous existence. Dogs needed a pack to survive, even if that pack would occasionally turn on the weakest and kill a member of its own. Nathan felt a sudden sorrow for this dog who would never know the love of a dedicated owner and the security of a proper home. The dog's future was doubtful and Nathan wondered about the dog's past and whether he remembered his siblings and his mother.

Yeshe brought out a bowl and filled it with water from the outside pump, the hotel's only piece of plumbing. Placing it a couple of feet away from the dog, who thanked him with a baring of teeth and a guttural snarl, Yeshe then turned and went back inside. Nathan followed him.

'You find Sherpa?' Yeshe asked.

'I found Khampa!' announced Nathan.

The dubious look in Yeshe's eyes was not lost on him.

'I know, but I have to get to that place. I want to know more about it,' Nathan explained.

Yeshe nodded.

'You right. You crazy man,' he commented then, turning, he shuffled away to his room.

When Nathan reached his own room, he looked out of the window to see if the dog was still there. The empty water bowl was all he could see. The dog had gone. Nathan guessed that slowly, painfully, he had slunk off to some dark, quiet corner, perhaps near one of the monasteries, to recover or give up the ghost. It was at that point that Nathan began to feel his own wounds. On closer inspection he found a bite mark in the calf of his right leg, a slice wound inside his left thigh, probably from a sharp claw and a small chunk of flesh hanging from his right arm. Nathan remembered the bottle of lavender essential oil he had left on a shelf in the small cupboard against the wall. It was still there and he undid the lid, grabbed a mug and went downstairs to get some water from the pump to mix with it. As he reached the bottom of the stairs, he saw the dog just inside the doorway, licking at his wounds. Nathan filled the mug with water from the pump and added the lavender. Back inside, by the light of a kerosene lamp he applied some to his injuries.

'This is what you could do with,' he told the dog.

37

The dog leaned forward and sniffed with interest. Nathan cautiously moved his hand towards the dog. The creature looked up at him earnestly. Nathan emptied some of the fluid into his hand and carefully stroked it into the dog's wounds then went back up to his room where he did a quick search for unwanted visitors before dropping onto the bed.

What had made him wade into those dogs like that, he wondered? The sandy-coloured dog was one of hundreds roaming Lhasa. Theirs was an alien world to humans. Daytime they would doze or roam whilst night-time they would return to their roots of pack hunting for food. These dogs seemed hardly of this time but of a past age when humans were few and forests, mountains and plateaux lay raw and desolate. They belonged in history. Why had the world not changed for them? Why had he felt the unconsidered instinct to protect this particular animal? It bothered Nathan, as the old monk's final words bothered him, for they were both mysteries for which he could find no answer.

CHAPTER FIVE

RETURN TO THE MONASTERY

Nathan stole out of the hotel at 6.45a.m. The dog was wide awake just where he had left him the previous evening. Now seeing Nathan, he rose, his ears pricked and eyes alert. Nathan motioned for him to lie down again but he either did not understand or chose to ignore him and determinedly followed Nathan through the quiet alleyways. In one a Tibetan girl stood, legs apart, urinating in the street. Turning, she looked at Nathan, smiled and turned away again. Nathan continued on his way to the Barkhor. Once there, Nathan turned into the designated alleyway and there were three, giant shadows. The Khampa stepped forward, looking even more threatening and inhospitable in the raw half-light. Behind him were two horses: one jet black, the other chestnut. The Khampa said nothing, just fixed Nathan with his coal-black eyes and pulled him beside the chestnut horse, placing the rein in Nathan's hand. They walked on foot, the soft thud of the horses' hooves sounding dull and hollow in the stillness of the morning. A little way behind them walked the dog, his head bent, stalking like a tiger. There were Chinese checkpoints on the outskirts of the city but they covered the main routes in and out of Lhasa.

Once outside the city the Khampa mounted his horse and Nathan followed suit, easing himself onto the saddle of the chestnut stallion and taking up the rein. They walked for some time before Sonam took off into a canter and Nathan followed, keeping a few yards behind him. Nathan turned to check they were alone and saw the dog running behind them, eyes fixed firmly on Nathan like a guided missile. Nathan waved him away but he took no notice. Behind them Nathan could see the amazing view of the Potala Palace, once home of the Dalai Lama, in the distance. Nathan turned his head to the front. The Khampa was leaving a cloud of dust so Nathan pulled back a little on the rein.

Soon they had left the city far behind and pale-blue skies gradually materialised, stretching ahead of them like a giant canvas. Far away, Nathan spotted a drogpa with goats and yaks. They continued to canter over the plain with the jagged mountains in the background and a symphonic wind playing around their ears. Soon Nathan spotted it in the distance rearing up out of the mountain: a sacred relic of years gone by.

As they neared the monastery the Khampa pulled up his horse. Nathan did the same, turning his in a circle and bringing him up alongside Sonam. Turning quickly, Nathan saw the dog some distance behind, trotting steadily, his tongue hanging one side of his mouth.

'This is place?' enquired the Khampa.

'This is the place,' confirmed Nathan. 'That's where I'm going.'

Nathan pointed to the monastery.

'I wait here with horses. They need water,' said Sonam.

The Khampa nodded towards the dog as he walked towards them then stopped a few yards away, waiting.

'Friend?' he asked Nathan.

'It seems that way,' replied Nathan. 'I won't be long.'

Nathan dismounted, handed the rein to Sonam and walked towards the monastery, once again noting that the colour of the earth had changed and everything was lifeless as before. Nathan sensed the dog behind him and turned. The animal was following cautiously, sniffing at the ground. Nathan began to ascend the track that led to the monastery but something was different. The sensate atmosphere that had existed before had now vanished. Nathan stopped and looked about him. Below, some way off, he saw the Khampa remove a container that hung from a wide leather strap behind the saddle of the black horse. From it, he poured water into a wide tin dish and held it just under the horse's jaw. The horse began to drink. The dog watched Nathan thoughtfully.

Slowly, pensively, Nathan continued to climb the track, the dog now close at his heels. Following the twists and turns, he came at last to the forecourt with the cedarwood doors ahead of him closed firmly against the world. Now it dawned on Nathan. There was no aroma of death, just the smell of the Tibetan morning air.

Leaning his shoulder on one of the cedarwood doors, one hand firmly on the other, he pushed against them and they groaned open. The aroma of sandalwood met him, of old books and wood, candle grease and must. Nathan took the door to the left and walked along the passageway. The dog followed him, stopping briefly to sniff at the prayer wheels before rejoining Nathan as he entered the main chanting hall. Here, the image of lung-ta stared back at him, the cedarwood columns stood firm as before. The altar with its artefacts remained untouched. Here he took the short passageway and stopped at the door halfway along. Nathan was aware of his heart beating faster in his chest and the dog's hot breath against his leg. Bracing himself, Nathan turned the handle and opened the door.

Shock was the first feeling he had as he stood staring. This was not what he had expected. There were no bodies, no blood and no overwhelming stench of death. The eating hall was tidy, the wooden tables scrubbed and bare. The stone flagged floor was clean with just the faintest smell of disinfectant.

The dog entered the room, sniffing around and whining softly as if he sensed what had once been there. Nathan followed him in, walking around in a daze, unable to believe the difference that had come upon the place in such a short time. Someone had been very efficient. It would have been no easy task with blood to clean up, bodies to remove, tables to scrub, cutlery to clean and yet it had been done and achieved in a very short time. The dog continued to sniff beneath the tables and around the corners of the room.

Nathan walked back out into the small passageway. Suddenly aware of a shadow to his left, he looked up and started at the sight of a figure that stood silent in the shadows. The figure stepped forward and Nathan saw the red robe and sandals. The man was young, mid-twenties perhaps, with shaved black hair, dark-brown almond eyes and salient cheekbones and forehead. For a few, tense moments neither of them spoke. Nathan was suddenly aware of the dog by his side and he felt oddly reassured. When the figure did speak, it was in a soft, calm voice.

'What is it that you seek…?'

'I seek The Wise One.'

Nathan had answered intuitively. The words had left his lips before he had even been able to consciously gather them.

The young monk gazed at him in wonderment.

'Who are you?' questioned the monk.

Nathan was about to say his name, but realizing this would mean nothing to the monk he said instead, 'I am the Sign of the Light'.

Nathan's whole body was tense with expectation.

'I have been waiting for you,' said the monk in a gentle voice that even the dog seemed to find soothing. 'Follow me. I have what you seek.'

Obediently, unquestioningly, Nathan and the dog followed the robed figure through the eating hall to the door opposite, into the small antechamber, then through the door opposite again and into the courtyard with the well where Nathan had found the old monk. There was no old monk now, just an empty courtyard with the well and figure of Sakyamuni. Down below to the right, Nathan could see the Khampa seated cross-legged on the ground, the horses beside him. The monk turned.

'You have brought a friend?' he asked, regarding the figure below.

'No. He's no friend of mine, just a guide to get me here.'

The monk bowed his head to Nathan as if to communicate he understood and then went and stood before the statue of Sakyamuni. As the monk bowed low before the statue, Nathan noticed the monk's right foot slide forward and his toe press a small rim on the base. Nathan was alarmed by a harsh grating sound and he saw one of the flagstones just inside the antechamber opening up. The monk placed his palms together and bowed, once again, before Sakyamuni then he said, 'Come' and went back to the antechamber where Nathan joined him. Looking into the opening in the ground, Nathan saw steps leading downwards but it was too dark to see further. The monk led the way and Nathan followed. The dog hesitated but seeing Nathan disappear gave a whine and made up his mind to follow.

'Wait,' said the monk.

There was a sound like fingernails running down a blackboard as the flagstone scraped its way shut and Nathan found himself in total darkness. Feeling trapped and disorientated, Nathan ran his hands over the cold rough walls as he felt his way gingerly down the steps that had been crudely cut out of the rock. Behind him, the dog whined and suddenly let out a nervous yelp that put Nathan's nerves on edge. The smooth velvet voice of the monk came out of the darkness immediately quelling their fears.

'There is nothing to fear, my friends. Soon there will be light.'

Nathan continued to precariously feel his way in the dark, his senses alert and feet cautiously checking before each step until there came a command from the monk.

'Stop. Take my hand.'

Nathan reached out into the darkness and felt the monk's hand, warm and reassuring, claim his own.

'Just one more step,' instructed the monk.

Nathan took the step.

'Now you are on the ground,' came the sedate voice from the darkness.

Nathan slid his foot forward to feel. The monk kept a grip on his hand, gently guiding him forward until Nathan could see a flicker of light followed by another, until the darkness turned to shadows and then the walls came into view. They were in an underground passageway lit up by large candles that stood on shelves of jutting rock. The monk released his hand and smiled benignly at the panting and agitated dog.

'You are very brave, my friend,' the monk told him. Turning to Nathan he said, 'You have a good dog'.

'He's not my dog. I just got him out of a scrape. Isn't that right, mutt?'

The dog looked up at Nathan with a quizzical frown, his head held to one side and ears pricked.

'You are wrong,' smiled the monk. 'He has chosen you, therefore, he is yours.'

The monk turned and continued along the passageway. The odour of candle grease mingled with the smell of ancient crag and a faint aroma of jasmine that seemed to come from the monk's robe. Their footsteps sounded hollow. The candlelight flickered and eerie shadows danced around them like dark ghouls.

'Where are we?' Nathan asked the monk.

'Inside the mountain,' replied the steadfast voice.

They continued, silent and pensive with only an occasional, impatient complaint from the dog. At last, the flickering candlelight illuminated a small, square room with shelves. In the centre were two, large, oblong crates each on a wooden framework. The monk held out a hand towards the crate on the right and as Nathan entered the room he saw they were not crates but wooden coffins on biers. There was a scraping sound as the monk eased the lid across. In the alternately projecting and retracting light, Nathan looked inside and saw a decomposed body. Rotten clothes still clung to the skeletal bones like ivy to a trunk and the wispy hair, like a badly fitted wig, still covered part of the skull.

Nathan recoiled.

'Who is this?' he asked the monk.

The monk looked at him, uncertain.

'This is the man you seek. The Wise One.'

'Who is he?' Nathan asked again.

'His name is Price.'

'Price?'

'He is not who you sought?'

Nathan found this impossible to answer for he had not known what he was looking for. All he had were the old monk's words.

'I found an old monk still alive after the massacre in the monastery and he told me I was the Sign of the Light,' explained Nathan.

'Then that is who you are or he would not have told you so,' replied the monk.

'But I did not understand what he meant.'

'*He* understood. Now I have shown you.'

Nathan shook his head.

'How did this man come to be here?'

'He came to seek sanctuary. The darkness sought him.'

Nathan cupped his chin in his hand and rubbed his palm against the stubble of his jaw. Momentarily he was lost for words then he remembered and felt for the dog tag in his boot. Retrieving it and holding it up by the chain, he showed it to the monk.

'Where is this man? Spontiak.'

'Ah! Here.'

The monk pointed to the other coffin. Again, he pushed the lid aside to reveal a skeletal corpse. Nathan took up one of the candles and held it over the coffin. The unsteady light cast small, dancing shadows that made it look as if the skull were alive and making different expressions. The empty, black eye sockets stared up at him and the teeth grimaced. Nathan glanced up and down at what was left of David Spontiak's body. There was something strange about this one.

'How long has this body been here?' Nathan enquired.

'Thirty-six years,' the monk told him.

'The bones on this corpse are a strange colour,' Nathan noted, for some of the skeleton, mainly on the shin bones, was of a yellowish-green colour as opposed to a whitish-grey.

'This man came out of the fog. This man was different to us.'

'I don't understand,' said Nathan.

'This man was sent from the skies,' smiled the monk.

'This man was in the American Navy. Are you telling me he came here by plane? Where did it land? Can you show me this plane?'

'There was no plane,' smiled the monk. 'The man came out of the sky.'

'You mean he parachuted in?'

'Sorry...I don't know...parachute?' queried the monk.

'A parachute is a large piece of cloth that floats.'

'I was told of no parachute, only of fog and man from the sky.'

The monk, years younger than Nathan, looked at him now like a father would a son.

'You must seek the light and all will become clear to you,' he said gently.

'But you said this man,' pointing to Price, 'was the one that I sought.'

'But the light does not shine clear to you, so you must seek further. Price knew one day you would come. This was entrusted to us...'

The monk raised a hand to one of the shelves and removed a dusty, red covered A4 notebook that had faded to a dull scarlet. Handing it to Nathan he continued, 'The master knew you were the sign. Trust him. Others have come but they were of the darkness. We made a promise to Price.'

'You were too young to have known him,' said Nathan.

'The promise and the words have been passed down,' the monk assured him.

Nathan flicked through the book. The pages, all handwritten, were yellow with age. There were pages of number sequences, charts, maps of the world with lines all over them, numbers and what looked like calculations as well as strange signs.

'This belonged to Price?' asked Nathan, for confirmation.

'Yes.'

'He left nothing else?'

'Nothing. He said one day someone good would come to seek the truth and the book was all that he would need.'

'What am I supposed to do with this?' Nathan asked him.

The monk contemplated for a moment and then smiled.

'That I cannot answer for you. The darkness will come upon you. Price said that would happen. The darkness will come upon he who seeks the truth and to those who would help him. The book is all you need to see the light.'

Carefully, Nathan tucked the notebook under his shirt easing the bottom half of it below his belt and into his underpants.

'Price,' said Nathan. 'He came out of the skies too?'

'No,' smiled the monk. 'He came much later, on foot.'

As Nathan reached the cedarwood doors of the monastery, he turned and shook the monk's hand.

'Your English is excellent,' Nathan told him. 'How did you learn it so well?'

'My master taught me. Price taught him.'

'Is your master still alive?'

'Sadly, no.'

'Do you live here? Alone?' Nathan asked him.

'I was sent from another monastery when we heard what had happened to the monks here. The promise had to be kept. I will return now. The promise made to Price has been fulfilled.'

'Who killed the monks and who cleaned up here?' Nathan asked him.

'I do not know,' the monk told him. 'When I arrived, it was as it is now.'

They parted and Nathan left the monastery, closing the heavy, whining doors behind him. The dog went ahead down the path, relieved to be out of the confined space. As Nathan approached

46

Sonam he saw he was drinking. From a tin mug he sipped yak's milk. Nathan sat beside him and Sonam offered Nathan the mug. The dog helped himself to water the Khampa had placed in a mug in a hole in the ground.

Slyly, Sonam glanced over at Nathan.

'You visit monastery before?' he asked.

'Yes,' Nathan replied.

'Why you come back?'

'I lost something. I was sure I'd left it there.'

'What you lose?' asked Sonam.

'It doesn't matter,' replied Nathan, casting it aside with a jerk of the head. 'It wasn't there.'

'You don't find?'

Nathan turned and their eyes met. Nathan could not read the look in the Khampa's eyes but there was something that made him feel uneasy.

'That's right,' Nathan replied with solemn-faced mendacity.

'Here!' said Sonam, offering him a slice of dry, salted meat from one of the pockets in his belt.

'Thanks,' said Nathan. 'What is it?'

'Yak. Here!'

The Khampa threw a slice to the dog who pounced on it and ripped it apart with bared teeth.

'Do you know why this place has a bad reputation?' enquired Nathan.

Sonam chewed at the meat then took up the milk that Nathan had put down and drank some of it before he answered.

'It long ago. My grandfather saw. From there.'

Sonam pointed ahead to the right of the monastery.

'He say it come in thick, green mist. From nowhere. Sky empty, then mist and in mist, a ship. It bring men. Not real men. Only half men.'

'Half men? What do you mean?'

'Not real men. They make bad sound. Whole place in mist. When mist clear, ship gone, half men gone.'

'And that's why nobody comes here?'

'My grandfather say bad thing to see. It come in dreams many years. People say place cursed.'

47

'This ship... did your grandfather say what it looked like?' asked Nathan.

The Khampa shrugged.

'Big. Very big and float in sky. You know this. This why you come,' Sonam stated emphatically.

Nathan threw his head back and laughed.

'You think I'm a UFO enthusiast, seeking little green men roaming around a Tibetan plain!'

The Khampa was up, the knife released from his belt within a second, but the dog was quicker, clamping his jaws around Sonam's wrist, snarling and twisting. Sonam screamed out in pain and dropped the knife, by which time Nathan was up to seize it. Sonam grabbed the dog's ear with his free arm, causing the animal to squeal, but it was Nathan who grasped the dog's jaws and forced them free of Sonam's wrist. The Khampa's eyes were ablaze as he stood flailing his arms, like a huge bird of prey, the blood running freely from his wrist and dropping onto the ground below. The dog remained by Nathan, poised, his head low and teeth bared.

'My grandfather not lie! Khampas not lie! The ship here! The half men here!'

'It's OK,' said Nathan, his voice steady and his tone cordial. 'I wasn't saying your grandfather was a liar. I just think there's an explanation for what he saw, that's all.'

'You not see. Half men! Half men! He saw! Crazy men. Half men!'

'I meant no insult to your grandfather or the Khampas,' said Nathan. 'I understand your grandfather saw something very unusual that day.'

The Khampa shook his head and strutted around like some great beast, the primal energy that sparked from him like a piece of dynamite about to explode.

'Sonam, forget what I said,' requested Nathan.

The Khampa's eyes held him with a dark, brooding contempt.

'I'd do something about that wrist if I were you,' Nathan suggested.

The Khampa seemed to notice his injury for the first time. Ripping a piece of cloth from his chuba, he wound it roughly around the wound and tied it with his teeth. Nathan approached Sonam and the dog stalked right beside him, every muscle rippling in readiness.

'Let's finish our milk. I meant no insult,' Nathan assured him.

The Khampa lifted his head proudly and defiantly. Nathan offered him the knife.

'Keep it 'til we back,' the Khampa told him, 'or, I swear, I slice your throat with it.'

There was a tension that chilled the air between them. Nathan nodded and placed the knife carefully in his belt. They finished their milk in silence. Nathan attempted conversation, asking about Sonam's grandfather, but the Khampa ignored him, saying nothing. The ride back seemed long and arduous with an unpleasant strain in the air. When they reached the city, Nathan gave Sonam the money and returned the knife. They parted in silence. Nathan walked slowly and thoughtfully back to the hotel with the dog at his heels. It was a while before Nathan came out of his reverie and noticed the faithful companion by his side. Nathan looked down at him and the dog looked up expectantly.

'Thanks,' said Nathan.

The dog looked away again and continued walking in his awkward gait down the alleyway towards the hotel.

Nathan awoke suddenly. A low, guttural growl was coming from inside the room and Nathan realized the dog was by his bed. The clear night sky was covered in stars. In the distance, howling dogs disturbed the peace.

'You heard your friends, did you?' Nathan said to the dog, but it was then that he heard a sound in the passageway outside his door. Nathan sat up, rigid and cautious. A low laugh came from the passage and Nathan strained his ears.

'Yeshe...? Is that you?'

Yeshe entered the room but the dog immediately rose to his feet, crouching low with his hackles raised, head dipped forward and ears back.

'I sorry. Heard noise but it only dog. He your friend now?'

'Yes,' said Nathan, 'he's my friend.'

'Good. You sleep well.'

'I will. Goodnight Yeshe.'

Yeshe gently closed the door but the dog crept forward, ears now pricked but hackles still raised as he sniffed the bottom of the doorway. A threatening snarl came from deep within his chest. For some minutes Nathan remained sitting up in bed, his body tense as the dog guarded the doorway. When the dog did lie down he placed himself between the bed and the door, as if protecting Nathan from any further intruders, but even before that, thoughts had started to enter Nathan's head: Someone accessing his room to steal the camera and the pick up by the Chinese police. Yeshe's remark came back to him: *'Chinese Police find you?'* Then there was the snake and the scorpion. How easy it would have been for someone already in the hotel to access his room. Yeshe had to be the spy in the camp and what had he been about to do, creeping outside his room like that? The dog must have surprised him. If the dog had not been there…?

Nathan studied the dog and the dog looked back at him, wide awake, alert to sounds Nathan could not hear, his eyes glowing in the darkness. Nathan was aware that the dog might have just saved his life and a heavy weight pulled on Nathan's heart, for tomorrow he knew there was something he had to do.

CHAPTER SIX

THE ATTACK

Nathan awoke early to a cerulean sky. Already dressed, he put on his rucksack and with the dog at his heels went down the alleyways of Lhasa towards the Barkhor. There was a temple a few streets away from the Barkhor that Nathan wished to visit for a very special reason. Soon he would return home, but he would have to leave the dog behind to his fate and that disturbed him.

Just seconds away from his destination, three Khampas suddenly appeared from an alleyway. Two were holding sticks and waved them at the dog whilst the third grabbed Nathan by the throat, pushing him against a wall. Nathan struck a blow to the Khampa's throat. For a second the attacker's grasp loosened, just long enough for Nathan to strike him in the neck with his elbow. Above the frantic snarling and growling of the dog rose the Khampa's cry of pain as he fell to the ground. Stealthily, out of the alleyways, came two more Khampas. They stood facing him, their features like stone, eyes glinting like ice. One of them Nathan recognized for he had seen him with Sonam the afternoon he had arranged for Sonam to guide him to the monastery. Now that Khampa came forward, ranting in Tibetan through gritted teeth. Nathan could understand little of what he was saying except that he mentioned Sonam and something about the Chinese police.

'I know nothing about that,' Nathan told him.

The Khampa smirked. It was the grin of a tiger about to eat its prey. From the corner of his eye Nathan saw the dog in a frenzy, trying to ward off the sticks that were taunting him and holding him back. The Khampas exchanged glances and one lunged at Nathan. As Nathan brought up his arms to protect himself, another Khampa sprung his knife from his belt and plunged it at Nathan's stomach. As Nathan fell forward, the Khampa swiftly sliced Nathan's leg as another Khampa punched him in the head then they all left as quickly as they had appeared, the last Khampa fighting the dog off with a stick as the canine followed them, growling with fury, into an alleyway. Nathan slid down the wall, one hand holding his thigh now flowing with blood. The dog reappeared seconds later with one of the sticks in his mouth. Tearing into it with ferocity and anger, he broke it and tore it into strips, pouncing on the splintered fragments as if they were alive, teeth wrenching and grinding. When the stick was totally demolished and lay in splinters he abandoned it with a final warning growl, plodded up to Nathan and sniffed at the fingers that were covering the wound. Licking the blood, he let out a low-pitched whine. Nathan tried to stand, finding the wall with one hand and grabbing at the hard, rough stone.

Once on his feet he made his way slowly along the alleyway, the blood soaking into his trousers. The blow to his head had made him feel dizzy. In the distance, moving towards him, was a figure in red but it was nebulous and wavy like a mirage. The way ahead began to dim. Nathan clung to the harsh wall, willing his legs forward, but his head felt as if it were leaving his body and floating slowly upwards. The alleyway began to get narrower and darker until Nathan could hardly see at all.

Nathan aimed his camera at the wrinkled face before him. The old woman, squatting on the ground, wiped her eyes with a piece of dirty cloth as she rocked back and forth, wailing and muttering. All around him, soldiers and voluntary workers collected bodies to take away on stretchers and place blankets over them. Others worked on digging out the recently filled 6' by 20' hole piled up with human beings killed by the rebels. The air was filled with the stench of death as the corpses were dug up, carried and laid out. The old lady had lost her entire family. Overcome with grief she seemed to be holding onto her mind by a very fine thread.

'Nathan!' shouted an urgent voice from out of the chaos.

Nathan lowered the camera. From amongst the soldiers, the workers and the dead, a man came running and shouting, his countenance one of anxiety and horror. It was Henri, one of the French voluntary workers.

'Nathan! They've attacked the camp!'

Nathan sprang up and hurried towards Henri. As he joined him, Henri turned direction and they both ran towards the jeep.

'It's Nicole,' shouted Henri as they ran.

'Oh no! What happened?' demanded Nathan.

'They attacked out of the blue,' Henri yelled.

As they reached the truck, Henri placed both hands on Nathan's shoulders and his eyes held both fear and pain.

'Nicole,' he said and the brief pause that followed sent a shaft of ice through Nathan's heart. 'She's in a bad way. They don't think she'll make it...'

Nathan felt as if all the blood had suddenly evacuated his body. Shaking, he leaped into the jeep beside Henri, his left hand grabbing hold of the window frame and clutching it for all he was worth. Henri put his foot down, guiding the jeep through the confusion of bodies, both alive and dead, until they were on the open track. Fields of dried grass swayed gently in the breeze under the burning sun as the jeep tumbled along the track, lurching left then right to avoid boulders, bumping over stones, churning their insides until Nathan felt a nausea rise in his stomach and enter his throat. It was quiet save for the groan of the engine and the constant clanging of the pebbles as they hit the underside of the vehicle. Fifteen minutes later, they arrived at the desolate camp. Bloodied bodies were sprawled over the ground, limbs contorted and eyes half-closed, unseeing. Henri rushed towards one of two tents. Nathan ran behind him, heart thumping and silent screams filling his head.

Nicole lie on the ground, limp, vulnerable, soaked in blood from wounds to her stomach, her hands covered and fair hair matted with the sticky red substance. One of the voluntary doctors was kneeling next to her, leaning over her, inspecting the bullet wounds. Seeing Henri and Nathan he shook his head at them, his eyes full of sympathy and sorrow.

'No!' Nathan pleaded with him. 'No! Not her! Not her!'

The doctor shrugged and held out his hands in a gesture of helplessness, rising to his feet as Nathan took his place beside her. Gently sliding his left hand under her head, his right hand rubbed her left forearm before sliding around her waist and pulling her towards him. The stethoscope around her neck pressed hard into his chest, a remnant of her compassion. At twenty-five she had given up a comfortable lifestyle to risk her life to save others. Cradling her head between his shoulder and arm he gently kissed her cheek. It was soft and still warm, but her eyes were half-closed. It reminded him of how she looked when they made love, when he brought her to that final pleasure, but now the light in them was fading as if they were already seeing another world: a world where he was unable to join her and where she would have to venture alone.

'Nicole,' he whispered in her ear, 'I love you.'

Rubbing her head with his cheek, he then kissed her lips, pressing the soft mounds of flesh against his own, but they were cool and unresponsive. Nathan felt a hand come on his shoulder and the doctor's voice, deep and sympathetic, addressed him.

'She's gone, Nathan.'

Those three words were like arrows into his heart.

Clutching her fiercely, he rocked back and forth like the old lady he had only shortly before been photographing. Grief racked his body and stabbed at his chest like a sharp knife. Tears ran down his face and dropped onto Nicole's hair.

'Nathan... let her go.'

It was Henri at his side, his voice flat and tired.

Nathan held her tighter, angry now, defiant, crushing her body against his own as if the power of his energy would somehow spark life back into hers. For some minutes he remained that way as the shock and emptiness flooded over him in cold, irrepressible waves then he loosened his grip, moving his arm so her head fell gently back and he could look into her face. Pushing her hair tenderly back from her forehead, he kissed her cheek, smearing it with salty tears that mingled with the blood then he reverently laid her down.

Outside the tent, volunteers hurried back and forth. Nathan did not see them. Standing staring into the distance, suddenly lost and alone, he saw nothing and felt nothing except a deep, hollow emptiness that overcame him and swallowed him up into a frightening cataclysm. It was then that a memory came to him. Nicole had once said to him, 'Nathan, there is something I want you to remember. No matter where I go, or whatever happens, I will always love you. Always. Believe me, Nathan. Believe me'.

Nathan had replied, 'I do' and she had said, 'I know you do'.

Had Nicole had a premonition of their parting?

Suddenly Nathan felt bitter for it was as if she had chosen the path that would inevitably lead to it.

From the darkness came a voice.

'Hello!'

The darkness had been familiar but now it felt weird and hostile. Nathan fought the darkness.

'Hello!'

Nathan struggled to open his eyes, the lids flickering as he tried to take in an uncertain world.

'Hello!'

From out of the darkness appeared an angular face with shaven hair, mahogany eyes, a wide, retroussé nose and well-shaped mouth. The lips broadened into an open smile and Nathan saw even white teeth with a gap between the front incisors. Nathan moved his head sideways and immediately saw a sandy muzzle and pink tongue coming towards him. The dog licked his cheek and Nathan drew in his lips and closed his eyes as the long, wet tongue made its way over the whole of his face. When Nathan opened his eyes again the monk was laughing. Placing a hand on the dog's head, he rubbed his ear and the dog responded with a lick to the monk's wrist. The red-robed figure stood up and walked away. A memory came back to Nathan: the alley, the figure in red and then the darkness. Nathan took in his surroundings. It was the cloister of a temple with tiled floor and an open colonnade that overlooked a private, high-walled garden. The gentle tinkling of wind chimes came to his ears. From the inner sanctum could be heard the muted beating of drums, blowing of horns, clanging of cymbals and chanting. The monk reappeared. Placing a hand behind Nathan's head, he drew him up and placed a small cup to his lips. Nathan drank the herbal tea and nodded his thank you. The monk made him comfortable again and Nathan noticed the monks had changed his trousers for him.

'You speak English?' asked Nathan.

The monk replied in Tibetan and Nathan could not understand him. The monk left him again but shortly returned with a small, elderly, round-faced monk with kind, twinkling eyes.

'Westerner?' asked the old monk.

'English,' Nathan told him.

'You injure. We care,' the old monk told him. 'Wound not deep.'

'I have to get out of Lhasa. I'm in danger,' Nathan informed him.

'Out Lhasa?' queried the old monk.

'Yes. I'm in danger. Do you understand?'

The old monk looked confused.

'Harm, kill,' Nathan said.

'You kill?' said the old monk, his eyes widening.

'No. Me. They want to kill me,' Nathan explained, pointing to his injuries.

'Ah!' smiled the old monk.

The old man seemed to understand.

Nathan felt his stomach and realized the book was not there.

'Book,' he told the monk. 'I had a book with me.'

'Book. Yes.'

The old man turned and said something to the young monk who quickly left.

'You go out Lhasa?' queried the old monk.

'Yes. I need to fly home,' Nathan told him, moving his hand flat across the air like an aircraft. 'Will you help me?' he asked him.

'Out Lhasa. Home,' said the old monk, miming Nathan's hand movement of a plane. 'Yes, help.'

Nathan had no idea if the elderly monk was just repeating or understood what he was saying. The young monk rejoined them, holding the faded notebook which he gave to Nathan who noticed the slit where the knife had gone in. The book had saved him from having a more serious injury to his stomach. The knife had only bruised the muscle. Also handed to him were his passport, papers and wallet. Since the theft of his camera, Nathan had taken to carrying these around on his person. The old man turned to the young monk and they began to talk, slowly walking down the garden. Their exchange seemed complicated. A couple of times the young monk glanced back at Nathan. When they had finished their talk they walked back and rejoined their guest.

'Men try kill. You go out Lhasa?' said the old monk.

'Yes,' said Nathan.

'We take...' said the old monk, pointing to Nathan then away to the distance, 'other temple. You go...' he pointed again to Nathan, then away, 'Gonggar...Kathmandu.'

Nathan understood. They were going to transfer him from monastery to monastery to the airport south of Lhasa where he could catch a flight to Nepal. Nathan thanked the monk then leaned forward confidingly.

'There was a film...' he whispered, leaving the sentence unfinished.

The old monk frowned and shook his head. Nathan made a square of his hands and peeped through the gap, moving his hands slowly round the room before pressing down on an invisible button with his forefinger and clicking with his tongue. Nathan then rolled his forefingers around each other before using a forefinger and thumb to give an indication of the size of the film. The old monk looked confused but the young monk made a sound of recognition, smiled and left. Soon he reappeared with Nathan's rucksack. Nathan retrieved the film and the ID tag.

Taking the book, film and dog tag, Nathan placed them in the old monk's hands.

'These are important,' he told the monks, but their expressions were blank.

'Monastery near fog. Monks dead on this film,' Nathan explained.

There was a sharp intake of breath from both monks. Clearly word had travelled.

'Chinese must not have these,' said Nathan, shaking his head and pointing to the three items. 'Not for Chinese,' he reiterated.

The monks exchanged words then studied Nathan with new respect. Nodding his comprehension the old monk asked Nathan, 'You want out of Tibet in secret?'

'Yes. Out of Tibet to home,' Nathan replied.

The old monk nodded and indicated for the young monk to come and converse. They remained in earnest conversation for a couple of minutes before the young monk left and the old monk said simply, 'Aadesh'.

Nathan did not understand and shook his head.

'Aadesh take,' said the monk. 'Over pass. Meet Aadesh, Kathmandu.'

Nathan's mouth eased into a broad grin. Now he understood. There were mountain passes over the borders between Tibet and Nepal. Clearly the monks had a trusted messenger in this Aadesh. It was dangerous but he guessed that Aadesh had made this trip before, possibly a few times. Nathan placed his hands together and bowed to the monk in reverence and thanks. Looking up into his eyes he gave a sincere thank you.

The monk held up both hands and spread his fingers.

'Days,' said the monk. 'Aadesh. Kumari Ghar.'

'Meet Aadesh at the House of Kumari in ten days,' confirmed Nathan.

The old monk nodded and smiled. The young monk returned and he and the elder monk appeared to be confirming arrangements.

Nathan was aware of the Kumari Ghar in Kathmandu which housed the living goddess.

'The dog,' Nathan said. 'Will you look after him. Keep him here?'

'Keep dog?' the old monk asked the young monk.

The young monk smiled and nodded.

Nathan relaxed.

'You sleep now. Later eat,' the old monk told him.

'Thank you,' said Nathan.

As he sank back into idle reverie, the dog joined him, stretching out his body next to Nathan's own and placing his chin on Nathan's arm. The monks looked down and smiled before turning into the inner sanctum of the temple.

Nathan's robe reached to the floor. It was extra long to cover the boots he was wearing. The monks had ensured no western clothes could be seen underneath. Outside the temple the cart was being prepared, the monks busy decking it with prayer flags. The rucksack had already been concealed safely beneath one of the seats. The young monk who had looked after Nathan brought him butter tea. Pointing to the dog, who sat watching Nathan, he announced, 'Chu'. Nathan understood. The name meant running water such as a stream or river. Water was one of the eight trigrams of the I Ching. It made sense that the monk would choose a name that would represent an element of nature. It suited the dog who was fluid and strong.

'It's a good name,' said Nathan, smiling and nodding his head.

The monk understood from the smile that Nathan was pleased with the name.

'Chu!' called the monk.

The dog stood up, looked uncertainly at Nathan and then followed his new friend. Nathan sipped the tea slowly. The bruising to his head and the wound to his leg were sore but healing well. When he had finished the tea, Nathan wandered through the temple where the smell of smoke was forever present as it rose in wafts from the incense burners, twisting upwards towards the ceiling. The floor was slippery with butter from the lamps and the hem of his robe became quickly soiled. Passing the prayer wheels and chanting monks, Nathan stood in the entrance hall looking out to the front courtyard where monks were decorating the cart. Pilgrims were muttering over strings of prayer beads, swaying and chanting, lying prostrate or bringing offerings to the altars. The old monk made his way over the paving stones between two large prayer wheels at the entrance to join Nathan. Placing a hand on his shoulder he said simply, 'It time'.

Nathan nodded. As he turned round, he saw the young monk standing behind him. Chu sat at his side, ears pricked, eyes intense and expectant. Nathan shook the young monk's hand then stroked the dog's head. Nose pointed upwards, Chu's eyes looked at him entreatingly and Nathan felt a stab in his chest and a strange feeling of desolation.

'Farewell, Chu. I'll never forget you. Thanks friend,' he whispered.

The dog's eyes lingered on him and never moved. As Nathan raised his hood over his head and left the temple, head down, to climb into the cart and sit among the other monks, Chu attempted to follow him. With sadness, Nathan rubbed his ears and sent him back. Chu returned to the young monk's side. As Nathan took one final look back, the dog's eyes were fixed on him. Chu had become an ally who had shared part of this adventure with him. Fate had brought them together to form a special tie and now fate was about to tear them apart. There was a haunting bewilderment in the dog's eyes at Nathan's desertion and an emotion rose within Nathan's chest knowing this was the last time on this earth they would see each other's faces. They remained looking at each other as the cart moved off, their gaze, like an invisible elastic cord, reaching out, stretching by their will until they lost each other from sight and the cord snapped. It was a moment Nathan would remember for the rest of his life.

Nathan was grateful that at least the Khampas had not stolen his belongings. After the kind hospitality of two more temples he was able to take a flight from Gonggar to Nepal. The wait at the airport had been nerve-racking. A Chinese customs official had thoroughly checked his person and his belongings, even to the point of ripping out the lining of his rucksack. Nathan could barely believe his luck when the plane left the runway and he was airborne. Only then did he allow himself to relax. Now his whole mind was on Aadesh, the mysterious messenger of whom he knew nothing but a name. Aadesh had to get through. How could Nathan repay him? What do you give a man for risking his life?

After three juddering rides on rickety buses and long walks past fields with sparse vegetation and buildings in disrepair, he eventually arrived in the colourful city of Kathmandu. Passing rickshaws, bell-ringing trishaws, the odd car, street sellers with their wares sprawled across the ground, stupas, wandering cows, beggars, scavenging dogs and women carrying wicker baskets on their backs, he came to the Kumari Ghar, a large, brick building on Durba Square with its three-storey, wood-carved reliefs of religious symbols. Further on, past the square he came across a hotel with basic amenities and booked in.

Nathan slept a lot for the first couple of days or wandered around the square, studying the stupas: domed structures representing the five purified elements and containing the ashes of dead monks or religious relics. From just outside the courtyard of the Kumari Ghar, he caught sight of the living goddess. To photograph her was strictly forbidden and anyway Nathan did not have his camera. Not for the first time, he wondered who did.

The following days he spent more time exploring the streets, narrow lanes and maze of alleyways, smiling at the women, avoiding the beggars and shaking off the bare-footed children who followed him like packs of dogs. Nathan thought of Chu and wondered how he was faring. The people were friendly and the days relaxed and long.

At night, his sleep was disturbed by strange dreams which he only vaguely recalled when awake. Faces came and went in the shadows of his sleep. One night he dreamt he was being chased by Chinese soldiers and awoke, perspiring and trembling in the darkness.

As time went by, Nathan's initial anxiety and impatience began to slow to the way of life in the peculiar and lively city of Kathmandu which always seemed to smell of dust and smoking wood. The women with long sticks on their shoulders and baskets either end became a familiar sight to him. The wandering cows did not seem out of place. The earthenware pots everywhere became like old, familiar friends. The women, sweeping with brooms made from bound straw and even the stench from the mounds of rubbish on the streets and lack of a proper sewage system, had become comfortable and reassuring to him.

On the arranged day Nathan spent all day in the Durba Square where he constantly kept a surreptitious watch on the Kumari Ghar. At 2.00p.m. Nathan noticed a young man, about eighteen to twenty years of age, wandering back and forth outside the building. Nathan approached and enquired, 'Aadesh...?'

The young Tibetan man with a square face, jet black hair, wide eyebrows and perfect teeth, smiled warmly. So, this was the young man who had risked his life to do a westerner a favour.

'Nathan? Yes, they described you to me.'

The accent was not typical Tibetan. Nathan sensed a hint of Indian also.

'Your English is excellent,' Nathan complimented him.

'My father speaks English.'

'Do you have my belongings?' Nathan asked him.

Aadesh went to feel in his jacket but Nathan stopped him. Although he had kept a keen eye during his stay in the city, his sense of survival and suspicion was still strong.

'Wait. Not here. You look very weary and dusty. I'm staying in a hotel just along from here. It's basic but you can at least get a jug of water and a bowl to wash, then we will go somewhere to eat. There's a place just off the square.'

The young man looked relieved.

'Thank you,' he said.

'No,' said Nathan earnestly. 'Thank you, Aadesh. Thank you so very much.'

The young man heard the sincerity in the tone and acknowledged it with a smile.

Inside the hotel, Aadesh handed over the book, film and ID tag. Nathan gave Aadesh an odd amount of money as custom dictated then presented him with a new watch as a token of lasting friendship.

Nathan knew that hundreds, sometimes thousands, of people crossed a person's path in life. Most of them left no mark, like footprints in sand washed away by the tide, but occasionally a very special soul entered the sphere and what they left would be everlasting. The favour was done and Aadesh's watch would not last a lifetime, but the remembrance of the mutual goodwill would never fade.

CHAPTER SEVEN

THE MYSTERIOUS LODGER

The small, withdrawn figure that wandered along a grimy street in Kensal Rise appeared insignificant: dark brown shoes, brown trousers, beige mackintosh and a face that was blue-eyed and impish with rosy cheeks and aquiline nose. The sixty-four-year-old man had sandy hair, turning silver-white at the temples and thinning on top.

Sidney Roche paused just outside his lodgings. Three steps led up to a Victorian house with faded blue and white paintwork. Sidney leaned over the chipped black railings and peered at the dusty window below to see the faded, yellowish net curtains blocking the light of day from its interior.

The impish face gave a smile. Sidney was fond of that room. It had been his best sanctuary in years. Although he had only spent a few months there, he had become extremely contented. The landlady, Mrs Edwina Robertson, was a tall, middle-aged, Jamaican widow of ample proportions and a sense of humour who had given his life a down to earth comfort that had been absent for the last twenty-eight years. For the first time, since his life-changing experience, Sidney felt truly at home.

Sidney walked up the steps to the front door. It was a grey, overcast day and as he put his key in the lock he contemplated the possibility of rain. Not that it mattered to him for he would not be venturing out again that evening. Sidney was an avid reader and he was looking forward to enjoying his evening meal and then settling down in the worn armchair in his room with a good book. It was purely a theoretical book, of course, because Sidney enjoyed theories. It was a quirk of mind he had carried with him from youth and it had never left him. The nature of cause and effect had particularly interested him. At one stage he had considered studying philosophy but he had decided on science and engineering instead. It was that decision that had caused his life to take a completely different turn. Sidney often wondered what type of life he would be leading had it not been for that fateful day when, after a career in the Merchant Navy, he had followed a friend into aeronautics and then been approached by a certain man from a certain organization. How callous life was. From birth, life was the hunter; the born the prey. Life had little respect for beauty, or brain, for wealth or poverty. Like a shark, it was indifferent. It attacked randomly, with resoluteness but without justice.

The door opened suddenly and the beaming, oval face of Edwina Robertson met his haunted expression with just a hint of kindly indulgence.

'Why, Mister Roche! I thought that was you I saw coming up the steps. When the door didn't open I thought you had mislaid your key. Come in, I think it's going to rain.'

Sidney placed the key back in his pocket.

'Yes, it has turned a bit murky hasn't it?' Sidney replied as he entered the hallway and the smell of cumin and coriander met him like an old acquaintance.

An open door to the left revealed Sidney was not Edwina's only present company. An angular black face and brown eyes with a cold gaze looked back at him.

'You know my friend, Thelma,' said Edwina.

Sidney looked a little uncomfortable. The shapely Jamaican figure, with short, straightened dark hair that was curled under, moved a cat-like arm and Sidney almost expected her to purr and lick her wrist. A hand with blood red fingernails gave the briefest of acknowledgements as if she were waving away a fly.

Edwina gave her friend a reproachful look.

'Yes, indeed, good evening,' said Sidney to the feline-like figure.

Edwina turned her look of contempt away from Thelma and smiled at Sidney.

'I'm doing your favourite meal. Jamaican chicken with a spicy sauce,' she informed him.

'Lovely, Mrs Robertson,' said Sidney. 'That's very kind of you, very kind indeed. Thank you.'

'It's no trouble. There's some tea in the pot if you'd like some?' invited Edwina but Sidney declined.

'It's very kind of you but I think I'll just freshen up and go to my room for a while until dinner's ready.'

'I'll bring the tea down for you,' insisted Edwina. 'It's no trouble.'

'Thank you so much,' said Sidney then, nodding briefly at Thelma, he went downstairs to his basement room.

Thelma leaned back and gave a low, scornful whine.

'It seems nothing is too much trouble for the wonderful Mister Roche. I don't know how you can bear that man in the house, he gives me the creeps.'

Edwina was aware of a slight flush to her cheeks. The resentment in her voice was clear when she replied, 'Mister Roche is a gentleman. He's quiet and well-mannered'.

'Edwina,' said Thelma, 'I do believe you have a crush on that man.'

The saucepan came down so hard on the hob it made Thelma jump.

'Now don't you go talking that way,' Edwina warned her. 'Careless talk like that. I got no time for it, woman! Mister Roche is the ideal lodger. He's pleasant and no trouble.'

'I dare say his neighbours said the same about Crippen,' Thelma hissed.

'What are you saying?' demanded Edwina.

'I'm saying that there's something not right about the man, that's all,' replied Thelma defensively.

'What do you mean? Not right?'

'Well...' said Thelma, leaning forward and placing her slim, feline-like arms across the table, '...for a start, who is he exactly? Where does he come from? You know nothing about him.'

'Don't you think that's his private business?' argued Edwina. 'I don't need to know his life history to know he's a decent man.'

'So you think he's a decent, upright member of the community?' smiled Thelma cattily.

'Of course he is.'

'Then tell me this,' said Thelma, licking her lips like the cat that's just had the cream. 'How come he doesn't collect his pension?'

'What!' exclaimed Edwina.

'The man doesn't collect a pension. I know because Sheila in the post office told me.'

'Then maybe he goes to another post office or it goes direct into his bank account. You don't know Mister Roche. He's a good man,' insisted Edwina.

Thelma watched shrewdly as her friend busied herself preparing the sauce to go with Mister Roche's piece of chicken.

'OK, have it your way. I'm just warning you to be careful, that's all,' said Thelma as with a crossing of sleek arms across her chest she closed the conversation.

CHAPTER EIGHT

A FRIEND IN NEED

It was a busy night at The Dog and Duck in the village of Masterton, just outside Blandford Forum. The cosy country inn with beams and log fire was almost bursting at the seams, not just with locals but off-duty soldiers from the nearby barracks. The popularity of the public house was not just down to its convenient location and good atmosphere. The natural friendliness and warmth of its middle-aged proprietors, Tom and Ellen McCarthy, created a jovial and homely welcome that was hard to resist.

Ellen served drinks to the groups of soldiers in laughing banter and the locals in earnest conversation or fluent chat, but one lone figure was very quiet this evening. Using frequent, sideways glances she studied the young man, seated at a table near the door, who had been distracted for the last thirty minutes. Ellen saw the broad face, the fair hair, the slight crease on the wide forehead and the green eyes that flitted abstractedly from one person to another and she also noticed the closely bitten nails on strong, fair-skinned fingers that turned a beer mat over and over. At a convenient break, Ellen wandered over to the young man.

'Richard! You haven't said a word to anyone. What's the matter with you tonight?' she smiled.

Richard Paulton looked up, surprised and slightly irritated she thought.

'Oh nothing, Ellen. I'm just waiting for a mate.'

'Shall I fill that up for you?' she enquired, nodding towards his empty pint glass.

'Yes, thanks,' he replied half-heartedly.

Ellen took the glass and as she was filling it Richard wandered over to the bar. As she took his money, a young man with dark hair in a crew cut entered the pub. The new arrival, dressed in combat gear, joined Richard.

'Make that two,' Richard told Ellen.

Ellen obliged and the two men wandered back to the table near the door. Richard had been a regular for over a year and Ellen knew there was something troubling him, but there were lots of customers to serve so she forgot about Richard Paulton for the time being and carried on serving drinks, chatting and harmlessly flirting with the other customers.

'Well, have you thought about it?' Richard asked Jason Turner.

The dark brown eyes looked about furtively and the firm jaw clenched.

'Crikey, Rich! I just don't know.'

'Look mate, I know there's something not right about this.'

'What bothers me is we've only got this other bloke's word for it. How can we be sure they are never coming back?'

'One of them came back,' Richard corrected him, 'and he was stark, raving mad.'

'But again, it's only hearsay isn't it? Where's the proof? I mean…going AWOL. It's a bit drastic, isn't it?' Jason reasoned.

'You know what they say about the ones that went. None of them had families. They were loners, just like us,' Richard reminded him.

'I'm not a loner. I've got mates.'

'Yeah, army mates. Mates who'll be kept in the dark and believe what they're told. Think about it, Jase. Come on. Why aren't they sending anyone who has a family?'

Jason did not reply.

'Something really terrible must have happened,' Richard reasoned.

'It's just rumours, Rich. Come on. You know how things get exaggerated.'

'Something sent that bloke loopy. What kind of thing has he witnessed to turn his brain like that?'

'Your mind's made up then?' said Jason.

'Yeah, I'm going AWOL for sure.'

'It could be your career over and think of the shame of it. Are you sure that's what you want?'

'Yes it is because, do you know what? I don't think any of you lot will be coming back.'

'You're just chicken, mate. This is exactly what you've been trained for. You should be up for it with the rest of us, Rich. I can't understand you.'

'I am not going to end up in some mental home having food fed to me on a spoon, not knowing what day it is or what year I'm in,' Richard rasped.

'How are you going to manage? Have you thought of that?'

'Liz will help me out.'

'That skirt sniffer. Come on, Rich. Why should she?'

'Don't call her that. Liz is all right. She's a mate. I can trust her.'

Jason leaned back and shook his head.

'Please, Jase, think about it,' Richard pleaded.

'I have thought about it, mate. I'm sorry. You're on your own.'

Jason finished his pint.

'Do you want another?' Jason enquired.

'No thanks, I'm out of here.'

Jason watched Richard as he left the pub then he went up to the bar to get another pint. Ellen McCarthy commented, 'Your friend's very quiet this evening. Is there something on his mind?'

Jason hesitated for a moment then said, 'No, he's all right'.

Ellen McCarthy gave a knowing look, continued to pull the pint and said no more.

Liz was just coming into the pub forecourt as Richard came out of the door. Dressed in denim jeans, boots and a short brown jacket she fingered her cropped black hair and sucked on a cigarette which she then chucked onto the ground and stamped out. A single, silver loop earring adorned her right ear.

'Hiya, Rich! All right?' she called to him.

Richard approached her and acknowledged her with a nod.

'Lizzie, I need a word. I've got a favour to ask you,' he said.

'Come on then, I'll buy you a pint,' she suggested.

'No, I've just had a couple.'

Liz made her way over to a stone wall that surrounded the forecourt and sat on it, legs crossed, boots swinging. Richard leaned on the wall next to her.

'What's up, matey? You look right miserable,' she commented.

'I'm being sent away,' he blurted out.

'You mean they're posting you?'

Richard gave a nod.

'When?'

'Tomorrow.'

'Where?'

'That's just it, Liz. I don't know. They won't tell us.'

Liz remained silent for a moment.

'So, it's one of those secret missions, is it?' she ventured.

'I suppose so. They've told us sweet F.A. about it.'

'How long are you going for?' she asked.

'Don't know that either. It's a special. We won't know anything until we get to wherever they're taking us.'

Liz scanned the tense features and the clenched jaw.

'We've been mates a long time, Rich. There's something you're not telling me.'

Richard reached into his pocket for a packet of cigarettes. Taking one out he lit it then offered one to Liz who politely refused. Leaning back, he took a long draw on the cigarette and blew out slowly. Liz remained silent as he drew on the cigarette, savouring the flavour.

'I feel uneasy about it, Liz. I don't want to go.'

'But you've got to go. You're in the army, Rich. That's what happens. You're given an order and you follow it. This isn't like you.'

'I know. Jason senses something as well; he'll be drunk before he leaves here. I'm sure he's scared but he doesn't want to let on.'

'Scared of what? You must know something if you feel uneasy about it,' she persisted.

'All I know is what someone else has told me. Apparently ten months ago twenty others went on a similar operation.'

'There you are then. You can locate one of them, surely. Get the gist of what happened?'

'I can't do that, Liz. They never came back. Except one and we've heard he's in a psychiatric hospital.'

Liz glanced all around as if searching the air for an answer.

'Perhaps they're still out there, wherever that is. Maybe they will come back.'

Richard fixed her with a desperate look.

'Listen to what I'm saying, Liz. I don't think they're ever coming back. Some of them were younger than me. There are all sorts of rumours going around. There are whispers it was some type of suicide mission. The latest rumour suggests they were guinea pigs for chemical warfare.'

'Rich, they're just rumours. You can't be sure those men aren't coming back.'

Richard shook his head.

'They seem to be choosing men who don't have any close relatives. I think they are sending us out to die. This isn't like fighting an enemy, Liz. It's different.'

Richard threw the cigarette away and clasped both her hands in his.

'I'm going AWOL, Liz. I need help and you're the only one I can trust.'

'Hell, Rich!' she exclaimed. 'AWOL? Desert the army? You'll never get away with it.'

'I will, if you help me.'

'If you're caught it could mean detention, Rich. Maybe even prison or dishonourable discharge,' she reminded him.

'I don't care. At least I'll still be alive.'

Liz slipped her hands from his and placed them over her face, blowing out a long whistle as she did so. Raucous laughter came from inside the pub, the smell of ale hung heavy in the air. After a few seconds she turned to face him.

'So, what do you want me to do?' she asked.

'I need money. I'll get it back to you when I've sorted myself out. I promise.'

'OK, no problem, but I haven't got much, Rich.'

'I know. Could you manage five hundred?'

Liz pursed her lips and blew, then she slapped him on the back and said, 'Don't worry. I'll get it. When do you need it by?'

'Midnight. I'm going to make a run for it in the early hours. You know the graveyard that backs onto the woods here?'

'Yeah, I know.'

'There's a big, marble grave right at the back partly shaded by a weeping willow.'

'Yeah, I've seen it,' Liz told him.

71

'Leave it behind there in a plastic bag.'

'OK.'

'Thanks, Liz,' and the tone of his voice, a mixture of relief and gratefulness, said it all.

'Where will you go, Rich?' she asked him.

'I can't say, Liz. I'm not sure myself yet, but I promise I'll get your money back to you.'

'I won't let you down. Are you sure you don't want that pint?' she asked him.

'No, I'm going back to camp,' then, turning, he placed a kiss on her lips.

'Thanks, Liz,' he said again.

'Good luck,' she told him.

Liz sat on the wall watching the solitary figure disappear into the distance then she went into The Dog and Duck.

'Hey, it's Liz the lez!' called out one of the soldiers.

Liz stuck a forefinger up at him and leaned on the bar.

'The usual, Liz?' smiled Tom McCarthy.

'Please, Tom.'

An arm came around her shoulder and Jason Turner whispered in her ear.

'Have you seen Rich?'

'Leave it, Jase. You don't stand a chance with that one!' shouted one of the soldiers.

They both ignored him.

'What's it to you?' she asked.

'Has he told you he's going AWOL?'

'Yeah, right,' she sneered.

'Did you talk him out of it?' he asked.

'Out of what?' she replied.

'Going AWOL. He's got some idea into his head this posting's a bit weird. He said he was going to ask for your help? So, did he?'

Liz handed her money over to Tom and sipped her rum and coke.

'Get lost. You don't know what you're talking about,' she said.

Jason's arm slid from her shoulder and he skulked back to one of the groups. So, thought Liz, Richard had confided in Jason Turner.

'You fool,' she muttered to herself.

Liz arrived back at her flat at ten o'clock and pulled open a chest drawer. Quickly, she fingered through the notes that were kept in the far corner. There was only three-hundred pounds. Liz bit her lip. Damn, she thought. Somehow she would have to get the money but where could she get it without being asked questions? The McCarthy's who owned The Dog and Duck were good sorts. No, she decided. Word could get out and it might look suspicious her borrowing money the night Richard went missing. That divvy she worked with in the café might lend it to her, she reasoned, but she was a gossip. There were friends but they would want to know what it was for. Mentally she crossed off a list of names that popped into her head and then vaporized with the realization that, for one reason or another, they would not be suitable. Only one remained.

Liz alighted from her car in a back street of Weymouth and approached an ex-fisheries building that had been imaginatively turned into a nightclub. The gentle swash of the sea rhythmically joined the sound of the music emanating from the building and the air was fresh with the smell of brine. Purple lights shone lambently from inside the large, square structure and bold, artistic, mauve lettering read "The Depot" above double doors where a smartly dressed bouncer guarded the entrance. Stealing down a Dickensian alleyway she pushed on the side door. It failed to open so she rang the bell. Some moments later it was opened by Rene Gates, an attractive woman in her mid-forties with long brown hair done up in a French roll. Rene wore heavy eye make-up and a coral-coloured lipstick. Warm brown eyes flickered momentarily and a smile crossed the sensuous mouth.

'Well, well, if it isn't the bad penny dropped on my doorstep. You'd better come in,' she invited.

Liz went inside and followed a pair of shapely legs up a flight of stairs and into a living room that smelt of rose petals. The room was adorned with pale pink and lemon furniture and curtains.

'It's a rum and coke if I remember right,' said Rene, who was the owner of the club.

'Thanks Rene,' said Liz, standing awkwardly in the middle of the room and wondering whether she should just blurt out that she needed two-hundred pounds or lead up to it gently. Liz need not have worried. As Rene handed her the drink she commented, 'I'm assuming you're not just paying me a social visit so you must be in some sort of trouble. What is it?'

'I need a loan. Two-hundred pounds,' said Liz, swallowing hard and taking a gulp of rum and coke.

'There. That wasn't so difficult was it?' smiled Rene, lowering herself into an armchair. 'Sit down and tell me what you've been doing with yourself. I've missed you. Fancy coming back?'

'To the club?'

'Why not? Where are you working now? Don't tell me you're still in that grotty café?'

Liz shifted awkwardly.

'You are! You're still in that awful café. What a waste!'

Liz shrugged.

'There's been a change of staff you know,' Rene told her.

'I know.'

'Then what's stopping you? You'll be looked after here, you know that. There's a spare room in the attic. Think about it.'

'I wouldn't want to give up my flat,' said Liz.

'You wouldn't have to. The room's there if ever you need it. Come on, what do you say? I need extra staff.'

Liz beamed.

'OK. Thanks Rene.'

'That calls for a glass of champagne then!' Rene announced.

'No!' Liz protested. 'I'm driving. I've probably already had too much.'

'All right. We'll open it the day you start. Is next Monday OK for you?'

'That's great.'

'I won't be a minute,' Rene told her as she placed her drink on a side table and left the room.

Liz leaned back in the armchair and sighed with relief. Finishing her drink she stood up as Rene re-entered the room with a wad of notes.

'There you go,' she said, offering it to Liz.

As Liz went to take it, Rene's carefully manicured fingers wrapped themselves around hers.

'Tell me this is nothing to do with drugs,' she said, her brown eyes penetrating Liz's hazel ones like sharpened knives.

'No, it's nothing like that Rene, honestly.'

Rene nodded, satisfied and released the money.

'You can take it out of my wages,' Liz suggested.

Rene laughed.

'I know I can, but I won't. Think of it as a welcome back gift.'

'Thanks, Rene. I don't know what to say,' said Liz, pushing the money into her jeans pocket.

'Don't say anything. Just turn up the usual time next Monday. I lost a lot of my punters when you left.'

Rene kissed her and Liz left, holding her jeans pocket tightly as if she expected the money to evaporate.

Rene stood watching from the window as the slight figure below ran across the road and got into a red Mini. Rene had first encountered Liz in the club when Liz was seventeen. That same year Rene had offered her a job behind the bar.

Watching Liz now, as she drove off out of sight, Rene could not help but wonder what the money was for and why it was so urgent, but she would not have asked. Rene had her own secrets and she respected those of others.

CHAPTER NINE

THE SIGHTING

Martha Kemp poured milk into the saucepan for her nightly cup of cocoa. At seventy-one she was still sprightly and her brain showed no sign of the usual senility that accompanies the destruction of the brain cells by the natural ageing process. Martha still managed to complete the most difficult of crosswords in ten minutes or under, knew where she kept her keys and never mislaid her slippers. Martha's only encumbrance was the annoying inability to have a good night's sleep. Martha was a chronic insomniac.

Every night she went through the same punctual routine. After watching the ten o'clock news, ensuring the doors and windows were locked, the switches turned off and her teeth cleaned, she would make her favourite nightcap and then mount the stairs of her small cottage to her bedroom. There, with the light off, she would sit in an armchair by her bedroom window overlooking the woodland owned by the MOD. From this window, at night, Martha had discovered a world very different from her own: the mysterious lives of the nocturnal creatures. Foxes, badgers, cats, owls, bats and deer were all to be seen rummaging or wheeling around the Dorset woodland. Over the years Martha had become fascinated by their antics and the sphere of darkness in which they ate, hunted and played.

This particular night Martha sat down in her usual chair with the hot cup of cocoa held ceremoniously in her hand. Outside the window darkness had fallen onto a clear autumn day, marking the end of one phase and the beginning of another. The light at the back of The Foresters public house lent a lambent glow to the edge of the dusky wood, creating a touch of fantasy. A few last stragglers from The Foresters made their way home and then complete silence settled over the woodland. Martha sipped her cocoa and waited.

Elwood, Mrs Treeb's cat from the bakery, was the first to make an appearance, his lithe black and white body slinking along towards the ferns, his paws lightly finding their way across the ground. Martha smiled to herself as he paused before the oak for a quick wash before disappearing into the cover of the undergrowth.

'There's Elwood,' mused Martha, 'up to no good, I dare say. After the poor field mice I expect.'

There was a quiet, rustling noise in the room. At the sound of Martha's voice, her hamster, Henry, had awoken from sleep and was now venturing out of his nest. Henry stretched, yawned and proceeded to wash, paying particular attention to his ears.

'Ah, if only humans were as careful about cleanliness as you animals. Three empty crisp packets I saw scattered in the woods yesterday,' she tutted disapprovingly.

Henry came to the bars of the cage and poked his nose through, his little elfin face alert with eager anticipation.

'I know, I know,' said Martha. 'You want your treat.'

Martha rose from the chair and removed a small packet of yoghurt drops from a drawer in her bedside table. An aroma of sweet milk emerged from the packet as she opened it up and offered one of the drops to Henry, who grabbed it with his tiny paws and swiftly stuffed it into his pouch.

'I see you're saving it for later,' she observed, returning the packet to the drawer.

Martha took another sip of cocoa then let Henry out for his usual run around the room. After forty minutes smiling at his antics, she settled him back into his cage and resumed her seat by the window. The night was yet young for her. The stars were out in all their glory, crystal clear, scattered like thrown diamonds across a black velvet gown. Martha's eyes followed their familiar patterns. Nights like this were a treasure to her for between the periods of woodland activity she could study the small, diamond-like speckles above that seemed to wink as if acknowledging her as an old friend.

Something down below caught her attention.

'Ah, there's the vixen, if I'm not mistaken,' she informed Henry as she observed the movement of the ginger brush moving stealthily between the silver birches.

Martha leaned across and picked up her binoculars from the window sill.

'Now, let me see...'

The vixen came sharply into focus, stealing surreptitiously along the edge of the trees. Martha watched carefully, admiring the pretty pointed face, alert ears, watchful eyes and white fur collar until, without warning, the vixen shot off into the cover of the ferns.

'Tut,' muttered Martha. 'I wonder what startled her?'

A familiar call gave her the answer. Martha trained the binoculars on one of the enormous oak trees that stood solid like a monumental guard. Martha moved the lens over the branches, checking every one carefully until she found what she was looking for. The rattling warble belonged to a nightjar. As she watched, it swooped skilfully between the trees and out of sight.

Inside the room, Martha was aware of the regular click-click of Henry's exercise wheel as he ran enthusiastically inside it. Martha looked at her watch. It had just turned midnight.

The constant sound of Henry's wheel and continuous ticking of the clock sent Martha into a light doze. It was always disappointing for Martha when she awoke from one of these naps to find she had only slept for five or ten minutes. Tonight, however, as her eyes opened wide and the window came back into focus, she blinked and moved her gaze to the clock on her bedside table to discover it was almost 2.00a.m.

'Goodness,' muttered Martha. 'Have I slept that long?'

Closing her eyes, she tried to regain sleep but as usual it ran from her so she resigned herself, once more, to gazing out of the window. The moon was full and the stars sparkled. Elwood, a surly little figure in the moonlight, was sloping off home.

Martha then became aware of a major disturbance in the undergrowth and suddenly three figures emerged from amongst the tall, woodland ferns. Two of them appeared to be attempting to restrain a third. They stumbled into a clearing near the front of the woods and Martha saw all three of them were soldiers, two in combat gear. One looked as if he had another's hands forced behind his back. Another appeared to be threatening the man who was restrained. Martha took up the binoculars from her lap and pointed the lens in the direction of the men. It took her a couple of moments but then she had them in clear focus. One of the captors pushed the restrained man onto his knees but the captive, a fair-haired man with a broad forehead, managed to break away. The other two pounced on him but the man fought back hard and managed to push them off. One of the pursuer's grabbed him as he fled, his arm came up and Martha saw something glint in the moonlight as the arm came straight down onto the escapee who doubled up and then keeled over onto the ground. The third soldier came up and gave a swift blow with the back of his arm to the victim's head.

Martha was wide awake now attempting to concentrate on the faces of the men. One soldier leaned over the felled man. There appeared to be an urgent exchange of words between this soldier and the other, who appeared to be holding something that Martha could not quite see. Spellbound, she watched as the two soldiers dragged the third from the ground and carried the limp body back through the undergrowth, disappearing into the black obscurity of the woodland.

Stunned, Martha sat still and silent for a moment, her mind in turmoil. It could have been nothing more than a training exercise of course. There were often night-time manoeuvres and she desperately wanted to believe that was what she had seen, but her reason argued with that. There had been something so desperate in the young, fair-haired man's attempts to ward off his captors and he was so still after slumping to the ground. There was a nasty feeling creeping up on Martha. Something had glinted: something that had the appearance of metal. Steel, she wondered? The fair-haired man had been felled instantly by something the other man had held in his hand. The more she thought about it, the more Martha became convinced that it had been a knife. In her mind she could see the scene again. Such a young man, his head slumped forward, his limp limbs trailing along the ground.

Martha suddenly felt very cold. A frosty finger slid down her spine as she realized if it had not been an exercise then she had, in fact, possibly witnessed a murder.

Martha checked the time: 2.20a.m.

'Oh dear,' she muttered to herself. 'I don't want to make a fool of myself but…I'm sure. Yes, I *am* sure.'

Martha put her hand to her mouth. It had been so long and yet the memories came flooding back. How she wished she could erase those memories! How young she had been and how passionate! There had been a duty to carry out and she had done it, but it had been at such a high price and she had since paid for it every day of her life.

Martha gently whispered his name before going downstairs to the telephone. By the time she picked up the receiver, she was very calm and collected. When she was put through to the police she told them simply, 'This is Martha Kemp of Number Two, Honeydew Lane, Masterton. I believe I have just witnessed a stabbing. Possibly a murder...'

CHAPTER TEN

UNEXPLAINED EVENTS

Liz walked along Alderney Gardens towards the graveyard. It was a pleasant afternoon in Dorset with bright skies, cool temperature and a late autumn freshness. Liz did not notice what kind of day it was; neither did she notice Mrs Earl when she said, 'Good afternoon' as she crossed to the park with her Pekingese dog. Liz's thoughts were elsewhere.

Liz reached the end of Alderney Gardens and turned onto the small track that led up to the church. As she passed through the lich-gate she glanced all about her but it was silent and empty. The grass needed a cut. Some of the taller blades stirred in the gentle breeze: a soft, green carpet, interspersed with grey stones that looked as if they too had grown from the earth. Liz cast her eyes over various inscriptions, pausing only briefly to glance wistfully at her Uncle Sam's grave. The stones looked peaceful in the daylight. The previous night they had seemed very different as she had made her way tentatively, with just the light of a small and inadequate torch, to the marble tombstone at the back. They had seemed alive then, lurking in the shadows, jumping out at her as the torchlight disturbed them, waking them from their deep slumber.

Liz approached the eminent marble monument, pushing away willow branches that reached down like long, ghostly fingers, to survey the ground at the back of the tombstone. The plastic bag was still there. It looked just as she had left it. As Liz touched it she realized it was not empty. Stunned, she felt the roll of money inside and opened it to check. Placing her hand inside, she withdrew the five hundred pounds in notes.

Liz's head reeled. What had happened? Why hadn't Richard taken it?

Liz ran her hands through her cropped hair.

'Oh hell!' she murmured.

Keeping a tight grip on the money, she slumped to the ground. There had to be an explanation and she had to think logically. Either he had not had the chance to take it or he had decided not to. Perhaps he had changed his mind. Richard's face came back to her from the night before, pale and desperate with a haunted look in his eyes. Never before had she seen him like that and she had decided to help him for that reason.

There was only one way to find out. Liz got up and walked back to her car as fast as she could, weaving her way around the gravestones and through the lich-gate, her mind racing and her thoughts muddled. The grey paving stones passed by beneath her feet as head down, fingers tightly gripped around the money, she marched swiftly back down to the very end of Alderney Gardens where her red Mini was parked.

Once back inside her flat she went to the telephone directory, found the number she was looking for and dialled.

Liz sat biting her nails and staring at the wall. The loud ticking of the kitchen clock was beginning to annoy her. Strangely, she had never noticed it before. A constant drip from the kitchen tap joined with the ticking to create a rhythm.

'For an assignment that's supposed to be top secret he gave that information out very easily,' Liz remarked out loud.

Liz had been informed that Richard was fine and had left for Northern Ireland but would be back in twelve weeks. Liz's restless fingers strummed the table, joining with the tap and the clock to form a crescendo that seemed to bubble up and suddenly spill over. Leaping up from the chair she lunged at the kitchen tap, turning it round hard until the dripping ceased, then she turned and leaned her back against the cold rim of the sink, feeling its coolness along the top of her hip and the breadth of her waist. Something was not right and Liz felt frustrated that there was absolutely nothing she could do about it.

Martha Kemp wandered around her garden with a pair of secateurs that could have been for decorative purposes only, for she was not using them but merely holding them aloft whilst her mind was elsewhere.

The Commanding Officer had been a pleasant man. Yes, very pleasant. The police, he informed her, had contacted him concerning the training exercise she had unfortunately witnessed. They had to make these exercises realistic to prepare their men for the real thing. It was unusual, he maintained, for anyone to see their night exercises, apologized profusely for causing her any alarm and had been kind in reassuring her she had been perfectly correct in reporting the incident to the police.

Martha pursed her lips. The blood had thrown him of course. There had been a definite twitch of the moustache and glazing of the eyes when she had mentioned that for, that very morning, Martha had ventured across to the woods to painstakingly inspect the grass and had found what she had been looking for: a dark red, sticky substance. Not much. After all, the man had been dragged away too swiftly to leave much blood. The CO, however, had been most definite that it would not have been a real knife used and had explained the blood was probably from an animal. Possibly a fox had caught a rabbit. Private Harris, he had assured her, had not so much as a bruise to discolour his lily-white skin. In fact, because he could tell the matter had obviously shaken her, he had insisted on fetching Private Harris to put her mind at rest.

Private Harris had been brought to her doorstep and ordered to stand at ease.

'I'm so relieved you're all right,' Martha had told him. 'In the dark...and so realistic.'

Private Harris had smiled but said nothing.

'It's meant to be realistic, madam,' the CO had informed her kindly.

'Yes,' she had told him. 'I have clearly wasted your time.'

The CO had insisted it was of no consequence at all. Private Harris had been dismissed and with a polite departure from the charming CO the army truck had been driven away and the little lane left silent once more.

Where to go from here was the problem facing her now because she knew, from the moment she saw Private Harris, that he was not the man she had seen and the CO was a barefaced liar. Obviously taking the darkness and an old lady's failing eyesight for granted, an army officer had just told her a pack of lies. Unknown to him, however, Martha had very keen eyesight. The Private Harris presented to her on her doorstep was stocky, whereas the man she had seen that night had been lofty. Furthermore, Private Harris, if that was, indeed, his name, had brown hair whereas the victim she had seen had fair hair. Why was it, she wondered, that once you turned a certain age people automatically assumed you were half-blind and half-deaf? There was the awful woman from the fishmonger's, for instance, who was always shouting and mouthing words at her as if Martha was not only considered hard of hearing but stupid as well.

Martha tut-tutted to herself as she realized she had just accidentally pruned the fully bloomed head off one of her best chrysanthemums. Sighing, she wandered back into the cottage. This situation, she knew, could open a Pandora's box and she would have to think things through very carefully: very carefully indeed.

Edwina Robertson was ironing and watching television when she heard the familiar sound of the key in the front door. The news had just started and Edwina smiled to herself. Mister Roche was always punctual. Edwina had never enquired where he went during the day but he had mentioned he enjoyed visiting places and going for long walks. Almost, as an afterthought, he had mentioned a sister in Bayswater.

Edwina was alone and called out as she heard her lodger enter the hallway.

'Hello, Mister Roche! Did you enjoy your day?'

The amiable face appeared from behind the door.

'Good afternoon, Mrs Robertson. Yes, thank you. I had a lovely walk around Regent's Park.'

'I've done you a nice piece of yellow haddock with a poached egg. Will you join me now? The news has just started.'

Sidney Roche hesitatingly entered the room.

'That sounds delightful,' he murmured. 'Thank you very much.'

Sidney hovered self-consciously. Edwina put the iron down and came forward to tap the back of an armchair.

'Here, Mister Roche, take the weight off your feet. I'll just finish ironing this top and I'll serve our meal.'

'Thank you,' said Sidney, removing his mackintosh and sitting down to savour the smell of hot, buttered haddock from the kitchen.

'Turn the television up if you like,' she told him. 'I was only half-listening to it.'

Sidney did so, vaguely aware of Edwina humming in the background. It was the second news item that stunned him. It was as if the cold hand of death had suddenly touched him on the shoulder, which was ironic, he thought, because he was already dead.

Edwina was saying something to him but Sidney was not listening and she saw he was leaning forward, mesmerized, his eyes fixed firmly on the screen. Realizing he was concentrating intently on the news item, she stopped ironing and listened herself to the newscaster.

'The luxury cruise liner was thirty miles off the Icelandic coast when all electricity aboard was lost. Passengers were plunged into darkness and there are claims that some watches stopped working. The ship's captain said that strange lights had been spotted in the sky shortly before the loss of power and following the incident some passengers suffered with headaches,' the newsreader announced. 'A spokesman from The Institute of Meteorology said it could have been flash lightening caused by an unusual mix of atmospheric conditions.'

'Nature is a mystery,' muttered Edwina.

The figure in the armchair did not respond. Sidney continued to listen carefully to the report.

'...and it was only last week that a fishing boat went missing in the same area. The boat has never been traced and no bodies have been found,' the newsreader concluded.

'I hope Thelma isn't watching,' said Edwina. 'She'll be convinced the aliens have landed. She swears she saw a panther loose near the railway line last year. That woman has a very vivid imagination. I said to her: "Woman, it was probably an overweight cat or a prowling black Labrador. You've got an overactive mind".'

Sidney Roche looked across at his landlady and smiled wanly. Edwina noticed his face had visibly drained of colour and there was a certain tenseness about him that had not been evident when he had first entered the house.

'You've gone a little pale, Mister Roche,' she observed. 'Are you feeling OK?'

'Yes. Yes, I'm fine,' he assured her.

Nevertheless, she noticed the slight tremor in his voice and the nervous agitation of his hands.

'I hope you don't mind me asking but have you ever seen anything like those lights?' she enquired.

'What? Oh! No, thankfully, never.'

Sidney said no more and after a moment's hesitation, Edwina told him, 'If I'm not mistaken, you're coming down with something. I'll fetch you a brandy'.

'That's very kind of you,' he replied.

Edwina handed him the brandy and asked, 'Would you like me to make an appointment for you with the doctor, Mister Roche?'

'No!'

The swift and defensive tone of his voice momentarily startled her.

'I don't like doctors,' he followed up quickly by way of explanation.

'Who is your doctor?' she asked him.

There was a hesitation before he commented, 'Do you know, I don't believe I've signed on with one. I'm never ill'.

'Sign on at my surgery, Mister Roche,' suggested Edwina. 'Doctor Richmond is very nice. You'd like him.'

'No. No, that won't be necessary. I've always found doctors a complete waste of time.'

'But in an emergency…'

'In an emergency, you would have to call an ambulance, Mrs Robertson.'

An impish smile crossed his face and they both laughed.

'Seriously though, Mister Roche, it might be a good idea to give me your sister's number in Bayswater, just in case you were suddenly taken ill or something.'

'Really, Mrs Robertson, you are very pessimistic this evening. It isn't like you at all. As for my poor sister, I'm afraid she is very prone to depression. There would be no point in making contact with her because she wouldn't be able to handle anything like that. I've always tried to protect her from the uglier things in life.'

Edwina smiled at him.

'You are a kind man, Mister Roche,' she told him, but at the back of her mind discomforting thoughts were beginning to stir.

CHAPTER ELEVEN

THE ICE GLOBE

Jason placed a cigarette between his lips and looked out at the fine layer of snow beyond the ten foot, chain link fencing. Even with thermal underwear beneath his uniform it was cold and he stamped heavy boots to try and bring the circulation back to his feet. Martin Foster joined him, wiping his nose with the back of his hand and cursing.

'Where the hell do you think we are?' Jason asked him.

Foster shrugged, his thinner and smaller frame feeling the cold more than Jason's.

'Northern Canada? I don't know.'

'It's freezing, I know that. My privates are like icicles. If I scratched them, they'd snap.'

Jason offered Foster a cigarette and he took it, his red, raw hands trembling as Jason held the lighter steady for him.

'What do you reckon happened to Rich?' Foster asked him.

Jason's stomach muscles contracted and his jaw stiffened.

'Don't know.'

'I heard you told Witchell he was going to do a runner.'

'Rubbish,' snarled Jason.

'That's what I heard.'

'I don't care what you heard.'

'Yeah, well, I just thought it weird that's all because he seemed fine the night before, didn't he?'

'That's what happens sometimes. People just get sick, that's all.'

'You don't reckon he tried doing a runner then?' queried Foster.

'Look, forget what Witchell said!' Jason replied irritably. 'Rich was taken ill and that's that. There's nothing we can do about it, is there?'

Foster shrugged again.

'The Yanks are organizing a match with us tomorrow.'

'What kind of a match? Ice hockey?' Jason sneered.

'No, football I think.'

'Only the Yanks would think of that one – football on ice – great!'

Foster, keenly feeling the chill, stamped his feet and rubbed his hands together.

'What do you reckon we're here for then? I mean, there's nothing here is there? This isn't a war zone or anything,' Foster observed.

'Training.'

'What kind of training?'

'How to survive frostbite? How the hell do I know? Like you said, this is no war zone so it's got to be training of some sort.'

'Why all the secrecy though, that's what I don't get. Making us sign that Official Secrets Act document. I mean, what was all that about?'

'You're all questions, aren't you?' said Jason.

'Well, it's getting to me all this waiting around. We've done sod all since we got here.'

'Perhaps that's part of the training. To see who cracks first.'

'Do you reckon?' asked Foster.

Jason hesitated. The silence between them bit like the wind.

'I think they're getting us ready for something and whatever it is, it's going to be tough. That's what all these medical tests are for. Blood tests, lung capacity, strength, power. They're preparing us.'

Foster surveyed the bleak white landscape and shook his head.

'Preparing us for what, though?'

'Well, whatever it is, we're here now and we've got no choice but to go through with it so, sod it, why worry?' replied Jason as he threw his cigarette onto the icy ground and walked away.

Foster watched him like a mouse watching a cat. There was something odd going on and he felt sure it was something to do with Jason and Richard Paulton.

Glen Witchell wandered across the yard to join Foster. Clapping his hands together, he gave a cheery greeting.

'All right, mate?'

'He's a miserable so-and-so,' muttered Foster, still watching Jason as he disappeared into the barracks.

'Why, what's up?' asked Witchell.

'I just mentioned Rich and he nearly bit my head off.'

Witchell leaned against the wire fence and gazed up at the pale sky that reflected the haunting whiteness of the snow. Tall and lean he gave the impression if he bent too far one way the cold would cause him to snap like a twig.

'What do you reckon about that? Strange none of us woke up or heard anything. One minute Rich was with us, next minute he wasn't,' said Witchell.

'He's in sick bay, Jase reckons.'

'Jason told me he was ready to make a run for it,' said Witchell.

'Do you really think he bottled it?' queried Foster.

'Yeah, I reckon he wanted out.'

'You really think he's gone AWOL?'

'Either that, or they caught him,' Witchell replied.

'He must have done a runner or he'd be here with us, wouldn't he?'

'Or he could be on a charge back home,' Witchell suggested.

'Well, wherever he is,' said Foster, 'it's got to be a damn sight better than here.'

Jason ignored the two Americans playing pool and sat on a table. Looking out of the window, he witnessed the exchange between Martin and Glen. The cold and the atmosphere were getting to him. The Americans were cocky and relaxed but his own comrades were tense and edgy. Reluctantly he had to admit, if only to himself, that a certain uneasiness was creeping up on him. Any questions were blanked by the officers and Jason was beginning to sense an intimidation that pervaded the air, as if something formidable but invisible were present. It drifted between them during the day and haunted them at night: a spectre of untold fear. They were all aware it was there, though no one spoke of it as if the mention of its name would release some unspeakable curse on them. It was alien and insidious. It issued from the walls and seeped up from the ground. It was everywhere – a sense of unspoken dread. A half-told story, the ending of which, nobody wished to contemplate.

Jason sighed. In the distance the snow and sky became one and he remembered, from his childhood, a glass globe with a little boy inside it dressed in winter clothing. When he turned the globe upside down, shook it and stood it upright again, the snow would swirl around the child and slowly fall to the ground about his feet. Right now Jason felt like that boy, trapped inside a dome of white nothingness, feeling empty and alone waiting for fate to turn his world upside down.

An unexpected, raucous bout of laughter from the Americans broke the bonds of memory and brought Jason back to the present with a jolt. Where the hell was Richard? Stupidly, he had confided in Witchell. What the hell had happened? Witchell had obviously passed the information on. Probably it was common knowledge now that Rich had bottled it. Had some psychiatrist announced him unfit for the task? Had Richard kept his word and gone AWOL? No one would tell him. Pieces of their conversation in The Dog and Duck came alive then died in his mind like fireworks in the night. Impulsively, Jason addressed the two Americans.

'Hey! Are either of you married? Got families?'

'Na!' answered the taller of the two. 'I was brought up in a kids' home.'

'What about you?' asked Jason, addressing the other man.

'I had a misspent youth, buddy. Mother was an alcoholic. Came home from school one day and found her dead in the bath with an empty bottle of gin for company. Never had a clue who my father was.'

'No cousins or uncles, anything like that?' persisted Jason.

'Are you kidding? Nobody wanted to know us – a gin-fuelled waster and her arsonist son. The army put me straight, man. It was the best thing that ever happened to me. What about you? Got a little woman at home?'

Jason shook his head and turned back to the window. The Americans resumed their game. Large flakes of snow had begun to fall like lost souls from heaven, landing gently on the rooftops of the tin huts and concrete blocks. Jason felt as if someone had just picked up his globe, turned it upside down and shaken it.

CHAPTER TWELVE

OLD ACQUAINTANCE

Martha Kemp sat at her kitchen table with a notepad and pen. The small, cottage kitchen had a cooker, a small fridge-freezer, a Welsh dresser and a stone sink behind which was a window, framed by red and white chequered curtains, that overlooked the lane.

Martha wondered if there would be any point to what she was about to do. It had been such a long time, she thought. There was a strong possibility he could be dead, or in a home suffering with dementia, or sunning himself on some Spanish island. Nevertheless, she had to try. The vision of the lofty, fair-haired soldier was haunting her night and day. No matter how much she busied herself he simply refused to go away. How odd, she thought. Why should it bother her so much, with her past...?

Well, she decided, it was no good trying to reason it out. Perhaps it was simply that she was approaching the final phase of her life. Maybe, when one got older, one got that way – soft like a rotting peach.

Placing the pen on the paper, she wrote: *The Nightingale is in Berkeley Square.*

Martha studied the words carefully. Had she got it exactly right? Yes, she was certain. Making up her mind, she completed the letter, tucked it with her cheque inside the envelope addressed to The Daily Telegraph and put a stamp on it.

Old fool, she thought to herself. Did she really expect a reply? Did he even read that particular paper any more? There were so many odds against a response that she was dumbstruck three days later when she saw the ad in the designated column of The Daily Telegraph: *Will the Nightingale sing for two or four?*

A strange excitement filled her as she studied those words. It was just like old times, as if the last thirty-five years had been a dream and suddenly she was reunited with her past. So, he had remembered. Two o'clock on the fourth day – tomorrow. Of course, it would not be Berkeley Square. One notable London landmark always stood for another. They had been a devil to remember, even when she was young, but one had no choice but to learn and remember them. Berkeley Square was, in fact, their old meeting place on the Embankment. Martha would be there and so, she knew, would he. What a peculiar reunion it would be. Would she even recognize him? Would he recognize her? Martha felt a thrill through her veins and it dawned on her, for the first time in years, how much she actually missed the danger and had done for a very long time.

There he was, waiting. Martha would have known him anywhere. As he removed his trilby, she saw the brown hair, now turned to silver, had virtually disappeared on the top of his head and he had put on weight, but the familiar awkward gait and turning in of the shoulders, as if he were always trying to shelter himself from something, was still very evident. A heavyset face with hazel eyes, slightly bulbous nose and broad jaw, now displaying heavier jowls, was as unmistakable to her now as it had been all those years ago. Immaculately dressed in a navy-blue striped suit and long black coat he could easily have been mistaken for a retired banker. People of all ages and descriptions walked past him, unaware that this man had been the top operator of a very secret organization that had played a major part in winning the Second World War.

Bertram Tanner watched in fascination as she came towards him: A small, slightly built, still lithe and agile woman with short, wavy, silver-grey hair, twinkling blue eyes, small nose and gentle smile who had sent her own lover to his death to save the lives of many soldiers – an ex-undercover agent, fondly nicknamed 'Sparrow' by her comrades, who spoke fluent French and German, had been tortured by the Gestapo and had lived to tell the tale. Bertram's admiration and respect for her had not been watered down by the years. The prim figure in grey jacket and skirt, matching grey coat, grey shoes and a pink silk scarf, still had a certain air of distinction.

'Bertram!' she gasped, offering her hand.

Bertram kissed it and placed in it a bunch of red roses. The smile on his face was indulgent.

'Sparrow! How good to see you again.'

The voice was deep and warm with a kind tone.

Bertram sat down beside her on a bench. The River Thames flowed sullenly by: a massive, grey snake that rippled and ebbed its way along to time eternal. Martha pulled up the collar of her coat against the fresh breeze that blew along the Embankment and studied the roses.

'You remembered,' she said.

Martha's old comrade gazed at her fondly.

'They were always your favourites.'

Martha turned her head to face him.

'How are you Bertram? It's been an age.'

'I know, dear girl. We are now in the twilight.'

'Is Cynthia...?'

'Died fourteen years ago. Cancer.'

'I'm so sorry. What about David?'

'Happily married to Marie. I have two grandchildren. Giles is at Cambridge. Amanda is studying music and is a wonderful harpist. What about you, dear Sparrow?'

'I never married. I have a wonderful hamster called Henry!'

Martha gave a rich but mischievous laugh. Bertram had always loved her laugh which was deep and genuine but with a hint of naughtiness.

'Lucky Henry,' he commented and his mind went back to the days of her specialist training when she had refused outright to kill a rabbit. When she had been called before her superior she had looked him straight in the eye and informed him she would kill nothing that could not fight back or present itself as a danger. When he had asked her how she would survive, if she had to, without anything to eat, she had given him an informative lecture on a wide variety of roots and plants and their nutrients. Astounded, he had let the matter drop.

There was a short but comfortable silence as they both contemplated the years they had shared in the past and the alien years in between. It was as if they both existed in two separate worlds at the same time.

'I was surprised to receive your communication,' he told her. 'Is there anything I can do for you, Sparrow?'

'If you still have contacts, then yes,' she informed him.

'I see. What is it you think I may be able to help you with?' he enquired.

'I may have witnessed a murder,' she told him simply.

'Ah,' he responded, as if this was an everyday occurrence which, in their world, of course, it had been.

'A young soldier on MOD land. I saw it happen. They tried to trick me with an impostor.'

'More fool them,' he remarked dryly.

'He was a young man,' she commented and the sad tinge to her voice was not lost on him.

'It must have haunted you all these years,' he observed.

Martha gave a wan smile. That had always been one of the comforting things about Bertram. It was as if he had known what she was thinking and feeling even before she knew it herself. That was one of the reasons she felt their relationship had been so successful.

'Not a day goes by...' she lamented.

'You had a choice to make. You made it,' he told her simply.

'But did I make the right choice?' she asked and there was a hollow compunction in her tone that stung at his heart.

'It was your *pis aller*. You saved many by sacrificing the one. You were professional in your decision. Gaston would have done the same.'

'Would he?'

'My dear, we all knew our duty...our place.'

'Oh yes,' she sighed. 'We all knew that.'

A silence fell between them like the fall of an autumn leaf.

'What is going down, Bertram?' she demanded.

'Do you think it wise to know?' he asked with a hint of anxiety.

'My young soldier reminded me so much of Gaston. I let Gaston down, but this one I will make it my personal business to find out about.'

Bertram Tanner drew in his cheeks. This was not the answer that he had wanted but it had been the one he was expecting. The moment she had mentioned contacts, he realized that whatever she knew, she would not rest until she knew more.

'You have heard of the TIDI of course?' he enquired.

'Ah! That old turkey.'

'The old turkey has been resurrected. The Japanese forced the hand, I'm afraid.'

'I see. You are still actively in touch. Do tell more...'

'We have a deal with the Americans.'

'Just the Americans?'

Bertram gave a smile and shook his head.

'Dear old Sparrow, as canny as ever. We are also playing ball with the Germans,' he admitted. 'We felt it…sensible…considering the circumstances. Their programme is technically complementary to our own. Like a jigsaw, some of our pieces fitted into their missing picture and vice versa, though their input is mainly financial.'

Martha gave a tired, cynical smile.

'Odd isn't it. We fight them, we murder them, they murder us then we shake hands and work with them.'

'War isn't murder, my dear,' protested Bertram. 'It is the survival of the fittest. You, of all people, should know that.'

'Yes, I should know,' replied Martha, 'but I'm not sure I do any more. Is it old age that makes the world seem upside down?' she asked him.

'The world has always been upside down,' he assured her, 'and we hang on as best we can. That's how it has always been. How it always will be.'

'By working with the Germans?' she remarked cynically.

The bitter edge to her tone implied a far deeper emotion than she was daring to express. Although she held nothing against individual Germans, she was wary of them as a nation.

'By sometimes working with the Germans, by undertaking projects with the Americans, by sharing certain technical knowledge with the Japanese, by supplying arms to the Middle East and by doing deals with the Russians. You know the score. Sometimes we work with them to forward our own interests. Sometimes we work to mislead them or slow them down, again to further our own interests. The world is a casino, my dear. You have to cover all the odds and Britain, as you know, has learnt to cover its back well. We never know who will stab us next, so we merely keep ourselves in a state of preparation. All are enemies, all are friends, for it's all down to timing isn't it?'

'I know, but it so goes against the grain with me.'

'Yes, I'm aware of that,' he said softly.

'So, there are sacrifices to be made. Why my young soldier I wonder?'

'I will make certain enquiries,' he told her.

'And how many more die in the meantime?' she asked him.

'You know, being older and closer to death brings it home more, Martha, but don't let it cloud your judgement. You know what can happen if the solution to the magician's trick is revealed – the show is over. Actually, it may be a member of the public who could destroy the show.'

'What do you mean?' she asked, intrigued.

'Name of Nathan King. A freelance photographer. He wandered into the Tibetan square mile, by accident it is believed, but it's caused quite a stir I can tell you.'

'Is he still alive?' she enquired.

'Oh yes, very much so. They aren't sure how much he knows or what he found there. The Chinese authorities picked him up shortly afterwards.'

'Interesting,' she mused. 'Will he be disposed of, do you think?'

'He's averted one mishap. It would seem he's a rather discerning and invincible man.'

'He will need to be, won't he…?'

Martha stared at Bertram and it was as if an invisible exchange passed between them. There was almost an accusation in her tone and a sudden coldness in her eyes that left him perturbed. Martha observed a sad acceptance in Bertram's return gaze. A cold wind suddenly whipped up along the Embankment causing a rippling of the Thames. A piece of litter blew past their feet and somersaulted along the pavement. Soft, light-grey clouds moved slowly overhead, focused on some invisible destination. Martha shivered.

'Time for coffee?' he enquired.

'Yes, I think so, don't you?'

They ambled along and turned up a side street where the smell of fresh ground coffee wafted across an invitation.

'It's some time since I came to London,' Martha remarked as they settled into a seat by the window of a 1960's retro coffee bar.

A waiter, who looked about seventeen with a dark moustache and Italian accent, took their order for coffee and persuaded them to partake of the strawberry flan before hurrying away, a hem of his white shirt hanging unceremoniously from the back of his black trousers. For some reason it made Martha smile.

'Will you be coming again?' Bertram asked with caution.

'Oh yes,' came the definite reply, almost challenging in its connotation. 'I will need to get your answer concerning my young soldier, won't I, Bertram?'

Martha's blue eyes, now slightly faded with age, still shone. The eyebrows were raised and so was the chin in a gesture of defiance.

'Yes, of course,' said Bertram, smiling benevolently. 'Shall I contact you?'

'I will wait to hear,' she smiled.

The service was quick. Over coffee and flan they reminisced about certain people and events, saying little about the alien years since as if they both appreciated and understood that those years had little to do with their partnership of the past. Later, they wandered back to where they had met. Bertram took Martha's hand into his own. Squeezing it gently and looking earnestly into her eyes he said, 'You know, Martha, Gaston's end was not your fault'.

Sighing, she slipped her hand from his and replied, 'I never said it was'.

For a long moment they stood looking at each other as old comrades from another time and another place.

'I have to tell you, Bertram,' said Martha, 'my torture should have ended with the Gestapo but I feel an inner torture now. Will mankind never learn?'

Bertram did not reply. There was no need for words. Martha held out a hand to shake his. As they touched, once again, Bertram felt the same tug as he had first felt all those years ago.

'Goodbye, Bertram,' she said, then turned and walked away.

As he stood and watched the slight figure distance herself along the Embankment he wondered if she had known that he loved her. Perhaps she did for women tended to know these things didn't they? Bertram had married Cynthia and reared a wonderful son. It had been a happy marriage but deep down there had always been the feeling of something missing. The love had been different. Martha had been the only woman he had deeply loved, not just with his heart but with his soul...just as she, in turn, had loved Gaston.

CHAPTER THIRTEEN

THE REUNION

Joseph Veldman had been so busy working on his account books at the back of his antiques shop, Veldman's Victoriana, in a small side street in Ealing, that he had lost track of time. As he heard the tinkle of the bell to announce a customer he checked his watch and realized it had turned 5.00p.m. Muttering to himself, he stood up, slid his hands down grey trousers that had become creased and briskly straightened his waistcoat. Round-faced and rotund with receding, dark-grey hair that curled at the nape of his neck, he wiped tired brown eyes with dumpy fingers adorned with three exceptionally expensive gold rings.

As he stepped out into the shop he took a sudden step backwards as he caught sight of the small, innocuous figure just inside the doorway.

'Good grief!' exclaimed Joseph. 'Hoffman! It can't be! I thought you were dead!'

Stanley Hoffman, the man known as Sidney Roche, stepped forward a couple of paces, a sad smile crossing his innocent face.

'They all think I'm dead,' he replied. 'Sometimes, I feel as if I am dead or perhaps in a dream from which I may never awaken.'

Joseph stepped forward, shaking his head in disbelief.

'They would kill you if they knew you were alive,' he uttered.

'Do you think I don't know that?' Stanley responded in a voice tinged with bitterness. 'Why else do you think I have had to hide myself all these years, living like a rat, moving from one place to another?'

'How? How have you managed to survive?' asked Joseph.

'Financially? I made contingency plans before I disappeared. It's nearly all gone now.'

Joseph held up a hand.

'Wait,' he said. 'I have some money…'

98

Stanley moved forward and restrained him by placing a hand on his elbow.

'No, Joe. That isn't why I'm here.'

'But food, clothes?' argued Joseph.

'At present I have an extremely kind landlady,' smiled Stanley. 'It's all right. I can pay my rent for another year or so. After that I'm not sure it will matter any more...'

Stanley's voice trailed off, leaving behind an uncomfortable silence.

'Come into the back,' suggested Joseph. 'I'll just lock up.'

Settled into the back office, Joseph made them tea.

'You must let me help you,' Joseph insisted.

'You can,' Stanley told him, 'but not by giving me money.'

'Then how?' shrugged Joseph.

'Information.'

'Information?' enquired Joseph in a suspicious tone.

'I think you know what I mean,' said Stanley. 'It has started again. Look...'

From his mackintosh pocket, Stanley produced a newspaper and showed Joseph a headline.

'No,' Joseph muttered, shaking his head. 'It is a coincidence, nothing more.'

'Ah, but there *is* more to it, Joe, both you and I know that.'

'Not this time. It can't be. Unexplained incidents happen all the time,' Joseph replied nervously.

Angrily, Stanley shoved the paper right beneath Joseph's nose.

'Don't deny it! We both know what this is about, Joe! I knew it would only be a matter of time.'

Joseph slumped down in his chair.

'What if there is more to it?' he argued, his hands open in a gesture of helplessness. 'What could you and I possibly do?'

'We can't let it happen again.'

'I don't know what you want from me,' Joseph pleaded with frustration.

'You still have contacts. You left because of health reasons. There is no stain on your record, Joe. Use your contacts. Find out anything you can,' Stanley implored.

'Even if I could, do you think they would tell *me* anything? Do you realize what you are asking of me? I could be putting my life in danger,' Joseph reminded him.

'But I am asking you to save many more lives, Joe,' Stanley remonstrated.

'You are a fool if you think you or I could do that,' Joseph told him vehemently.

'I have to try,' Stanley told him with remorseful acceptance. 'What if the lives lost are the *wrong* lives?'

'Stanley...' began Joseph, but Stanley quickly corrected him.

'There is no Stanley Hoffman now. I had to change my name.'

'Ah well, what does a name matter?' mused Joseph. 'It makes no difference. You and I both know that we cannot change the world. These matters are beyond you and me. Go back to wherever you came from, my friend. Keep your head down and live out the rest of your days as best you can. It is the wisest way. The *only* way. Believe me. You and I were just puppets. The powers that pull the strings, they are too great for us.'

'You are wrong,' argued Stanley. 'I refused to be their puppet and so did Price.'

'Price?' The name seemed to stun Joseph. 'Is Price still alive? Have you seen him?' he asked urgently.

There was a silence as Stanley suddenly regarded his old comrade with shrewd eyes. A certain tension had seeped into the atmosphere and Stanley's usual amiable face turned to stone as he continued to gaze at Joseph, noting the slight trembling of the fingers and nervousness of manner. The taut silence was broken by Stanley's strained voice.

'You are still working for them,' he said flatly.

The words fell like ice on concrete.

Joseph closed his eyes but did not reply.

'You are!' accused Stanley. 'You, of all people!'

Joseph looked physically shaken and Stanley noted the beads of perspiration appearing on his forehead.

'For pity's sake! Why?' pleaded Stanley, an agony in his voice that seemed to tear through both of them.

Joseph got up and paced the floor shaking his head then he flared up.

'Me, of all people!' he shouted. 'You, of all people, should know the answer to that! They know everything about me, everything about my family. They know where my grandchildren go to school, what care home my mother-in-law is in. They probably know what I had for breakfast this morning! You know, Stanley, they will stop at nothing. Go back and forget about this,' he spat, throwing the newspaper back at him. 'Remain dead. At least, that way, they can't get to you like they can me!'

'I have remained dead long enough,' Stanley told him. 'They stole my life. They took it and destroyed it. For years now I have had to live like a stray dog, lying, cheating, deceiving, finding shelter where I could, never making friends, forever looking over my shoulder, imagining footsteps behind me. You think being dead is to find peace?' he asked in amazement. 'I am proof of the living dead, Joe. I can't live and yet I can't find the peace of death either. I merely exist. What have I to lose?'

'Nothing!' rasped Joseph between gritted teeth. 'That is exactly my point. I, on the other hand, have everything to lose. Surely you can understand that?'

'I know,' replied Stanley and as he stood up the two men suddenly came together, tears in both their eyes, arms clasped firmly around each other. Two souls sharing the same torture, bound together by their bitter memories of the past.

When they parted, Joseph slumped down in his chair like an exhausted boxer who had gone one too many rounds. Stanley felt a strong surge of pity for him but an equally vehement hatred of the men who controlled him.

'I cannot turn away now,' Stanley said gently.

A defeated Joseph nodded his head.

'What can I tell you?' he whispered.

'All that you know,' said Stanley. 'I promise, Joe. It will never get back to them – not from me.'

Joseph continued to nod his head for a moment then asked, 'And when I have done that, what will you do?'

'That will be my problem, Joe. Not yours.'

Joseph gave a sad and weary smile.

'Let us hope so,' he murmured.

Stanley waited, watching the crumpled, dejected face full of lines that told of a chequered past. At last Joseph began to talk.

'They use me as a consultant. I am only in the background. I know very little.'

Stanley waited patiently as Joseph sighed and then continued.

'You are correct in your assumption,' he informed Stanley. 'The programme has been resurrected.'

'I knew it!' exclaimed Stanley, hitting a fist into the palm of his other hand.

'But they had no choice. They discovered the Japanese were beginning to take an interest. They have two of the Swiss who worked on the sixties' programme. So, they had no option but to begin again.'

'The nightmare continues,' murmured Stanley pensively.

'I do not know any details. As I said, I am kept very much in the background. They use me only for past reference.'

'You know nothing of dates or times?' queried Stanley.

'No. All I know is that it is not yet perfected. They are having major problems, I believe.'

'What of Price? No news?' queried Stanley.

'No, he disappeared without trace. You haven't...?'

'No,' said Stanley. 'I've no idea what happened to him.'

'Then there is some top secret information floating about somewhere,' said Joseph.

'You can tell me nothing more?' coaxed Stanley.

'The Chinese appear to be taking an interest in the Tibetan square mile.'

'Now, how did they get onto that I wonder? Do you think they know what is going on?'

'It is believed they are fumbling in the dark. Fortunately, they are more interested in building up their armaments at the current time.'

'Let us hope they remain preoccupied,' said Stanley.

'There is another concern – a photographer by the name of Nathan King.'

'What of him?'

'They don't know. He came upon the monastery in the Tibetan square mile.' Joseph hesitated. 'The Americans believe the monks there know something about Price. I don't know why. It was imperative the west got the information first, but the Chinese got wind of something. I believe there were discussions about agents being sent in. I don't know if they managed to infiltrate. I don't know what happened. What does King know? Did he photograph something? Who knows? TIDI is very nervous. They don't want media interest. It is better no attention is brought to the Tibetan square mile.'

'What are they intending to do about King?' enquired Stanley.

'I believe they are monitoring him for the time being.'

'Just tell me one more thing. Are the powers that be totally convinced that I am dead?'

'I believe so. It has been such a long time without news.'

'Yes,' pondered Stanley. 'It has been a long time. Far too long...'

Stanley prepared to leave and held out his hand. Joe shook it warmly.

'Goodbye, Joe. I doubt we shall see each other again,' said Stanley.

'May God go with you,' muttered Joseph.

Stanley sneaked from the back door of Veldman's Victoriana with great trepidation. For someone who was supposed to be kept on the outside, Joseph seemed to know more than a member of the outer circle would be aware of.

CHAPTER FOURTEEN

A VISIT TO THE CORPSE

Bertram's footsteps clicked crisply on the tiled floor but were silenced as he ascended the polished oak staircase with thick olive-green carpet. At the top of the staircase he passed an arched stained-glass window of vivid greens and reds and turned right along the hallway to the end door. Here he pressed a buzzer and placed a thumb on a small dark circle encased in a panel. Moments later, the door opened and Bertram entered a roomy office dominated by a large oak desk. Old oil paintings of horses, with legs far too thin for their bulky bodies, adorned the dark-panelled walls. The lighting was subdued, even with the run of wide windows on the opposite wall to the door. Outside, across a stretch of closely mowed lawn, a line of oak trees touched one another's bent boughs in some sort of tribal dance as the wind tickled their leaves and branches.

Bertram always sensed the atmosphere of this inner sanctum rather keenly. It was like entering an undertaker's, he always thought, with that smell of polish mixed with leather from an imposing black chair behind the desk and a brown one in front of it.

The man the other side of the desk, of average height and thin with mouse-coloured hair, sharp nose and liquid grey eyes, stood up in austere and formal greeting. Bertram, who towered over him, nevertheless always felt as if he were confronting a headmaster of some very distinguished, private boys' school. As Bertram took the man's pale, bony hand into his own large one he felt as if he were exchanging salutations with a corpse.

'Welcome Bertram,' said the corpse, attempting a smile that got lost in a lopsided twist.

'Alistair.'

'Take a seat. Would you like tea? Coffee?'

'Coffee, black, no sugar.'

The door opened. Like a genie from a lamp an elderly man, with a vacant expression and black hair either side of a shiny bald head, suddenly appeared. It seemed like magic but Alistair Milestone had a buzzer situated beneath his desk.

'Coffee, black, no sugar and tea for me, Squires,' Milestone instructed.

Squires left, silent, unobtrusive like a mouse that had burst in on a cats' party.

'Now, what can we do for you, Bertram. I take it we need to do something…?'

Bertram gave a broad smile.

'I met with a friend recently,' Bertram began by way of introduction.

'A friend who is known to us?'

The face of Alistair Milestone was of pallid complexion. Bertram always thought a few good meals and a month in the sun might make him look more human.

'Oh, undoubtedly I would say.'

'Name?'

'Martha Kemp.'

'Ah!'

There was a short silence.

'She…is known to you?' sought Bertram.

'Of course,' Alistair told him.

'Then you know her history, of course?'

'Oh yes,' said Alistair. 'We know her history.'

'All of her history I mean.'

'Yes, she resigned her lover to his death for the good of the whole. An admirable lady, I dare say.'

'And a personal friend of mine,' remarked Bertram and there was a distinct warning in the depth and tone of his voice.

Alistair contemplated the bold figure in front of him.

'As I understand,' he conceded.

'She witnessed a murder, she believes,' Bertram told him.

'Yes.'

This monosyllable was followed by a sharp click of the tongue.

'Very unfortunate,' Alistair added.

'Who was he?' asked Bertram.

'Now Bertram, you know we deal with information on a "needs must" basis. If there is no need, we must not tell.'

'Nevertheless, this lady *needs* to know and I *need* to tell her.'

'You are no longer in active service, Bertram. Indeed, you never have been an active member of this particular branch,' Alistair coolly reminded him.

'Oh, I know that,' smiled Bertram, but the smile was fixed and his comment contained a connotation. 'However, if you won't tell, I will make it my business to find out.'

'This is delicate. We can't have you blundering about, Bertram. I realize the high regard you are held in...'

'Oh yes. I think you would do well to remember that.'

Alistair wandered across to the window and took time to deliberate. At last, he turned back to Bertram who was seated calmly and confidently in the brown leather chair.

'Old ladies...their minds. One word to the wrong person. I need not tell you what impact it could have.'

'Mind sharp as a razor and if senility did eventually take over...the ramblings of an old woman...such outrageous claims. It would be dementia. No one would turn a hair.'

'Richard Paulton,' said Alistair laconically. 'Rumours had got back regarding the last "outing". It seems he got the wind up his backside.'

'Is he dead?' asked Bertram.

'No, just recovering from a small accident. The man was about to go AWOL. Something had to be done.'

Bertram unexpectedly stood up and crashed a fist down onto the desk, making papers jump and Alistair jolt.

'Good grief, man! What kind of a show are you running here? The bloody CO turned up on her doorstep with an impostor not remotely like the man she saw! What kind of an idiot is he?'

'I believe Commanding Officer Davis has...'

'Get rid of him. Pension him off for goodness sake. The man's a ruddy joke!' fumed Bertram.

Alistair's head fell slightly to one side, his face like stone.

'I'll deal with it, of course.'

Bertram sat down again, immediately calm, for his outburst had not been a sudden loss of control but a planned ruse to unsettle Alistair Milestone.

Alistair sat down opposite him. The buzzer went. A minute later, Squires entered with the coffee and tea.

'Thank you,' said Bertram in his most charming voice as Squires set about serving before leaving again like a shadow at sunrise.

Bertram sipped his coffee.

'Are the Chinese still sniffing?' Bertram enquired.

'We think so, thanks to that blasted photographer.'

'You'll deal with him?'

'We will try to avoid it. At the moment we are just keeping him under close observation.'

'How humane of you, Alistair.'

It was said with a note of sarcasm that went over Alistair's head.

'He's well-known. There would be a lot of media interest should he meet with a questionable accident.'

'Perhaps if the first effort had not been so careless...' remarked Bertram.

'I know, dismal. They had to rely on a Tibetan. Their own would have stood out a mile.'

'And you still believe Price to be there?'

Alistair threw out his hands.

'Who knows! We can only be sure that he went there. Did he stay? Did he leave? He could be anywhere in the world or have been dead years for all we know, like Hoffman.'

'I always wondered about Hoffman,' mused Bertram.

'You think there's a possibility?'

'Do you?'

'We never thought so, but Joseph Veldman had a visitor recently. The photographs, unfortunately, were not clear enough to tell. It was likely just an old friend who has no connection at all. However, no chances will be taken.'

The telephone rang: a sharp, shrill sound that seemed crude in the piousness of the room. Alistair picked up the receiver, listened for a few moments then said, 'Thank you,' and replaced it.

'That's interesting,' he said solemnly.

Bertram gave him a questioning look and he continued.

'The photographer has left Tibet, but before he left he hired a Khampa to take him back to the Tibetan square mile. Why, I wonder?'

'Whatever the reason, Alistair, you need to find out,' said Bertram.

There was a long silence as they both sipped their beverages.

'Your friend, Martha…' began Alistair.

Bertram glanced up, his cup poised in mid-air. The look was one of a stern father waiting for his child to make a very big mistake. Alistair noted it.

'…isn't likely to cause us any problems?'

Placing his cup back on the tray, Bertram leaned back in the leather armchair and placed his hands together, the tips of his fingers touching.

'Martha has always put her country first,' Bertram stated. 'She was one of the best agents we had.'

'That's what worries me,' murmured Alistair.

The room seemed to have turned colder. Outside, the wind had whipped up the trees. Like neighbours having a row they shook their boughs and wagged their branches at one another. Suddenly, into the austere silence, came the crashing, booming sound of Bertram's laughter. Alistair looked slighted as if this were a personal insult.

'Martha will be thrilled to know she has the powers that be, worried!' declared Bertram, between hearty guffaws. 'I am sure you will make that lady very happy.'

Still laughing at Alistair's shocked expression, he gamely took his leave.

As the door closed Alistair let out a deep sigh of relief and frustration. Visits from Bertram Tanner, that were, thankfully, few and far between, were always unnerving to him. If Bertram did not have such a distinguished record and the ear of such powerful people, he considered, an accident could easily be arranged, but the repercussions! Damn the cursed man, he thought. Damn him.

Bertram kept a smile on his face until he left the building then a cloud passed over his countenance. The deep lines that puckered on his forehead reflected his uneasy thoughts. It would have been preferable to him if Martha's name had been kept out of the conversation, but Bertram had been in the game long enough to know that his meeting with Martha would have eventually come to light. Safer this way, for both of them, that he had not attempted to conceal anything.

The powers that be now knew the situation and he hoped both his and Martha's reputations would speak for themselves, but Alistair Milestone was a cold and calculating individual. Bertram did not like him, neither did he trust him and he knew, deep within his heart, that Martha had pushed them onto a path that, without great caution and manipulation, may have no happy ending.

CHAPTER FIFTEEN

A FACE FROM THE PAST

Liz jerked up and down to music as she drove along the high street of Masterton village. Suddenly, she spotted a figure she was sure she recognized. Turning the car round to circle the village green, she passed the figure again and this time she was certain. A broad smile crossed her lips and she pulled the car into one of the spaces by the green then rushed over to the petite, slim figure that stood outside the grocery store.

Liz tapped the elderly lady on the shoulder and she looked round, her face blank but her eyes curious.

'Miss Kemp? It is you, isn't it?' asked Liz.

'Yes...?' Martha answered with reserved cordiality.

'It's Liz. Liz Stone. My Uncle Sam used to help you out sometimes with odd jobs. You looked after me once when he was in hospital.'

Martha marvelled at the face before her now.

'Not little Lizzie?' Martha smiled. 'Good heavens! Little Lizzie. How lovely to see you again.'

Martha placed a sympathetic hand on Liz's arm.

'I was so sorry to hear about your uncle. Such a kind man. Cancer wasn't it?'

'Yes. In the stomach,' Liz told her.

As Martha gazed at the cropped hair and the hazel eyes, an image of the young child she had known came vividly back to her: The orange juice, the grazed knee, the cheeky smile and the daring. Yes, she remembered little Lizzie very well.

Liz saw that Miss Kemp was recalling past days. It was then that some words of her uncle's came back to her, almost as if he had just spoken them: *'A clever woman that Miss Kemp. They reckon she worked for the Ministry during the war. They didn't entertain half-wits I can tell you. Our Miss Kemp probably knew more of what was going on than some of those colonels...'*

It suddenly seemed to Liz that her meeting with Miss Kemp was fatalistic.

'Lizzie, I must get my fruit and then...have you time for coffee? I'd love to hear how you've been getting on,' Martha told her.

'Yes, I'll wait here,' Liz agreed.

'I won't be a moment,' said Martha.

As she waited to be served, Martha considered the young woman outside. The child had not had an easy life as her parents had died in a car crash when she was ten and then her father's divorced brother had taken care of her until he died of cancer. Martha did the calculations in her head and realized Liz would only have been seventeen when her Uncle Sam had passed away and now she would be twenty.

Martha exchanged polite conversation with the grocer as he served her and then she rejoined Liz waiting outside the shop. Martha slipped her arm through her young companion's and they wandered along the street to The Whistling Kettle where they settled into seats by the window and ordered coffee and doughnuts. Martha listened as Liz told her how she had worked at a nightclub, then a café but was now returning to the nightclub. Liz talked fondly of a Rene Gates, Rene's brother and of the flat where she now lived. Martha was more guarded in her answers to Liz's questions, giving a humble description of her quiet life and bringing giggles from Liz when she told her about Henry's antics. When they had exhausted their conversation, Martha noticed Liz appeared a little on edge and pensive. The girl wanted to tell her something else, she was sure of it, but she was uncertain how to approach the subject.

'You decided not to stay in the village?' Martha queried. 'Was that through choice or...?'

'I wanted to leave the village,' Liz replied solemnly. 'There were too many gossips there.'

Martha knew to what she was referring. Whilst a teenager, Liz's close relationship with another girl had even managed to reach her ears and had been the subject of speculative gossip for months.

'Naturally,' said Martha, 'but, my dear, that's because they haven't *lived*.'

Martha had lived. Martha had not gone to work at nine and returned at five, worrying about bills and where to go on holidays.

Martha had not married and had a family and fretted over teenage rebelliousness, university education or a husband's affairs. Martha had spent a good part of her early life attempting just to stay alive. Later, in the hands of evil people, who had no respect for life, she had been forced to make the most devastating betrayal and Martha had done that because *she* was *not* evil. Martha had seen and suffered, first hand, monstrosities of human nature that destroyed the soul and challenged the mind. Therefore, if Mister Darrington had decided to leave his wife after forty years and set up home with his mistress, Mrs Lovatt's home was so filthy, cockroaches ran freely on the floor, or two young people of the same sex happened to fall in love, this seemed of such insignificance to Martha and a wonderment that it could be of such incredible interest to others. Such dreadful things were happening in the world, she sometimes wondered if people had any sense of priority at all.

Martha was not shocked by anything and neither did she appraise a person by their background, sexual orientation or colour. To Martha, there were two types of people in life: good people and bad people and it was that simple to her. Nothing else mattered.

Liz was smiling at her, her mouth covered in doughnut sugar.

'Some people tend to live in a bubble all their life,' Martha observed, 'and they really shouldn't you know...because someone will always come along and burst it!'

Liz laughed.

'I wonder, Miss Kemp,' said Liz, 'if you have time, would you like to see my flat?'

'I would love to!' said Martha.

Liz appeared pleased as she drank her coffee and finished her doughnut. Martha knew Liz still had something to tell her but she had no clue as to what it could possibly be.

Liz slowed the car down as they came alongside a small block of bland looking flats. The place was reasonably quiet. Further along the road a white Ford Capri was parked halfway on the pavement. Behind them, a grey Vauxhall Cavalier slid smoothly alongside the kerb and came to a stop about twenty yards away. Liz swung the car into a parking space beneath the flats, jumped out and opened the door for Martha. Outside, gulls swung and dipped above them and Martha remarked it must be a rough day at sea for them to be inland.

Martha followed Liz up a flight of iron steps and along a balcony. Liz opened the door to the flat and Martha stepped inside. It was pleasant and compact, if a little untidy, with a faint smell of stale tobacco and the previous night's curry.

'Would you like a cup of tea?' Liz asked her.

'Yes, Lizzie. I would love a cup of tea. What a nice flat and how nicely you've done it up.'

'Have I? I thought it was a bit of a tip,' Liz replied honestly as she went around putting papers away and straightening cushions.

'Is it a comfortable tip?' Martha enquired.

'Yes, it is,' laughed Liz.

'Then it's a nice flat, isn't it?'

'You haven't changed, Miss Kemp,' Liz observed.

'Please call me Martha. Miss Kemp makes me sound like a geography teacher,' she admonished kindly.

'I remember what you said to me once when we were talking about my parents' accident.'

'What was that?' Martha enquired.

'You said, it isn't important what life throws at you, it's what you throw back at it that counts.'

'I don't remember that,' Martha told her.

'I do,' said Liz, making for the kitchen. 'I was only twelve, but it gave me courage somehow. It made me feel stronger that I could answer life back – challenge it even.'

'I'm glad I was of help,' Martha called out to her.

Martha amused herself reading book titles on a bookshelf while Liz made the tea. Wandering over to a coffee table, Martha saw a photograph album. Martha opened the pages one by one. There were photographs of Liz with her parents and some of Uncle Sam, fixing Martha's fence if she wasn't mistaken, a lop-sided grin on his face and a cigarette hanging from the corner of his mouth, hammer in hand. There was one of Liz dated 1976, kissing a blonde-haired girl about her own age and one of an attractive woman who looked about twenty years older than Liz with brown hair done up in a French roll, dancing with a drink in her hand. Martha turned another page to see Liz still as a teenager with her arm around a boy, their cheeks pressed together, laughing. Underneath was a written comment: "Me and Rich – Two lost souls". Martha studied the comment for some time. For some reason, it left a profound impression on her. Opposite was a photo of the same lad, older now in army uniform, but Martha's eyes went back to the photograph of Liz and the young lad together and the handwritten observation. There was something incredibly sad and perhaps oddly prophetic in that written line that deeply moved her. It was then that Martha realized why and she examined more closely the photograph opposite of the young man in uniform. Martha noted the fair hair and the broad forehead.

A chill enveloped her. How often had this happened, she asked herself: A chance meeting, a strange coincidence or a peculiar twist of fate? These had happened lots of times when she was helping the French Resistance. Undercover, away from home in a strange country, in a time of war, she played a game of chance and again and again fate had played a role, usually landing the dice in her favour. It was as if some invisible force had always been at her side arranging things and now…

Liz came in with the tray of tea and Martha closed the album and sat down.

'Help yourself to sugar,' Liz told her. 'Did you see the photo of Rene dancing? She's a bit of a card. Not as much as her brother, Danny, though, he's always the life and soul of the party.'

'I'm glad someone's been very good to you, Lizzie. The young man – Richard, is it?'

'Oh, yes. We've been friends since we were young. Rich was in the children's home.'

'Wetherhurst?'

'Yes, that's the one. We met on the seafront when the children came for an outing.'

Something in the atmosphere had changed and Martha noticed Liz take a deep breath.

'Actually, Miss…Martha,' Liz corrected herself, 'I was hoping you may be able to give me some advice.'

Ah, thought Martha, so here it was at last. Martha placed her cup and saucer back on the tray and moved round to face Liz who was seated next to her.

'Of course, what is it?' she asked, her eyes searching the anxious expression.

'It's...well, Uncle Sam once said that you worked for the Ministry during the war.'

'Oh, did he? Well, a branch of it. I was employed to do a little bit of organizing,' Martha responded modestly.

'But you dealt with confidential matters so you know, perhaps, how the army might go about things?'

'Is it something to do with your friend, Richard?' Martha asked her.

Liz nodded and began to explain. Martha listened carefully. When Liz had finished, moments ticked away as Liz's eyes, eager and hopeful, searched Martha's. Martha weighed up various options in her head, reassembling the cards, shuffling them and dealing them again.

Martha knew what she should do and that was to tell Liz there was absolutely nothing she could do about Richard's situation, whatever that may be, and advise her to concentrate on her own life while fate sorted things out, but there was something in the girl's demeanour. A young, enthusiastic energy emanated from Liz like an elastic band stretched taut. Martha could feel it like an electric current and it affected her judgement.

'I imagine this Richard means an awful lot to you?' said Martha.

'He's my best mate,' Liz replied.

'Then, I suppose, if it came to it, you would not be averse to sticking your neck out for this friend. You would be willing even, perhaps, to put your own life in danger if it could help him?'

'Yes.'

It was a definitive answer. Liz had not even had to think about it. Martha recalled the daring little girl she had known and she saw that same little girl before her now, older, wiser but essentially unchanged. Liz was capable of throwing back at the world: she *wanted* to throw back at it. Something in this young woman reminded her so much of herself at that age: eager and curious. Liz was a gambler. Martha made her decision.

'I'm afraid I can't help you,' Martha told her, 'but I know someone who may be able to. Have you a pen and something I can write on?'

Liz jumped up and fetched a pen and paper from the kitchen. Martha took them and began to write.

'My advice is that you do not contact this man by phone but approach him direct and tell him what you have told me. Importantly, tell him that the disappearance of your friend could well link up with his experience in Tibet.'

'Do you know something, Martha?' Liz asked eagerly. 'Have you an idea what's happened to Rich?'

'Oh Lizzie, I'm afraid not, it's just a hunch that this business with Richard could somehow tie up with something I've heard...'

Martha's voice trailed off then abruptly she said, 'Lizzie, I am old. I have no concerns, therefore, for myself, but I want you to promise me that once you have seen this man you will leave this well alone and let him deal with it. Don't become further involved. If he finds something out I am sure he will tell you'.

Liz was in silent thought for a moment then she nodded, took the paper and thanked Martha. Martha held up a hand.

'Don't thank me, Lizzie. I may have done you a great misdeed.'

Liz looked nonplussed by this but said nothing.

When they had finished tea, Liz offered to drive Martha back home, but she insisted on Liz dropping her off in the village saying there was something she had forgotten to buy.

As soon as Liz returned to the flat she picked up the piece of paper and read it:

Mr Nathan King
'The Old Forge'
Winton Fosters
Nr Petworth
Sussex.

Liz was now sure that Martha had been more than a mere administrator at the Ministry and had a strong suspicion that she knew more than what she was letting on.

CHAPTER SIXTEEN

THE DISCOVERY

Martha and Bertram sat facing one another in the same coffee house they had sat in previously. The same Italian waiter served them, still with a piece of his shirt hanging out but today it annoyed Martha to the point where she felt like leaping out of her chair and tucking it in. Bertram, in a grey coat, light grey suit, white shirt and navy tie, ordered for them and then glanced out of the window. Martha read the sign. It was not good news. Bertram did not want to look her in the eyes.

'You have informed them you have seen me, of course,' she guessed.

'I had little choice in that, Martha,' he said, his attention on her at last.

'Yes, I thought so.'

'You've rattled the big cheese; he is rather worried about your interest.'

'You reassured him on that matter, naturally,' she said.

'Oh, naturally,' he smiled.

'Am I being watched?' she enquired.

'You drew their attention,' he replied. 'Word of the incident you witnessed had already got back to them.'

'What of my soldier?' she enquired, watching him carefully.

'I'm assured it was just an injury and I think the CO will soon be drawing his pension.'

'Where is he, Bertram?'

'It's classified.'

'Will my soldier continue to be safe?' Martha asked.

Bertram breathed in deeply and let out a heavy sigh.

'Now Martha, you know I can make no guarantee on that score. There are no guarantees in life.'

'I see.'

The voice was terse.

'Sparrow...' said Bertram in a tone of disappointment.

'And the photographer?' she asked with acerbity of tone.

'Mister King is being closely monitored. Apparently, he returned to the square mile. I wonder if, somehow, he's found something out about Price.'

'But how could he have done?' Martha mocked. 'Even *they* don't know what happened to Price.'

'They seem certain Price went there,' Bertram replied.

'But it's ridiculous to suggest that King could know. Whatever he's doing, he's doing it blind,' Martha remonstrated.

'An innocent bystander caught up in something way beyond his comprehension?'

'Yes,' said Martha. 'I should say so.'

'Possibly,' muttered Bertram, uncertain.

The Italian waiter brought their coffee and cakes. To both, they had a slightly bitter taste.

Their walk along the Embankment was slow and pensive. As they parted company Martha looked Bertram long in the eyes.

'Goodbye, Bertram. Thank you for making enquiries.'

'For you, anything. Will we meet again do you think?' he asked with a sad smile.

'Oh, I hope not for, if we do, it will be for the worst possible reason, won't it?'

Bertram placed a hand on her shoulder and kissed her cheek.

'Dearest Sparrow,' he uttered and with the next breeze she had turned, her petite but sure-footed figure strolling away, her back facing him, her head held proudly.

Bertram held the image for as long as he possibly could, embracing it in his mind as something precious to treasure as, for all he knew, it was possibly the last time he would ever see her.

After lunch, Edwina Robertson went to the window and peered from behind the net curtain at Sidney Roche as he ambled down the road and disappeared around the corner. Edwina waited some minutes to make sure he did not come back and then she took a deep breath and went downstairs to the basement room. Stealthily, she opened the door and crept in. Glancing around at the small, unassuming room, she felt an impostor in her own house. This was after all, she thought, Mister Roche's room and she really had no right to be there. The shrill ringing of the doorbell made her jump and with a thumping heart she quickly left the room and went back upstairs to answer the door. Thelma was standing there in a blue skirt, top and jacket with her hair immaculate as usual.

'Well? Have you looked yet?' she asked in a purring voice.

'I haven't had the chance. He's only just gone,' Edwina replied in an agitated tone, while checking up the road again to make sure Mister Roche was nowhere in sight.

'Now I'm here, I can help you,' Thelma told her.

'You be careful what you touch!' Edwina came back at her. 'We mustn't leave any evidence that we have been in his room.'

'Of course not. I will be the soul of discretion,' Thelma promised her.

Edwina led the way down the stairs and once more found herself in Mister Roche's room, this time accompanied by Thelma.

The room was very tidy and had one single bed, a bedside table with a lamp, a single wardrobe, a chest of drawers and a worn armchair.

'Where do we start?' Edwina asked her friend.

'I'll check the drawers. You check the wardrobe.'

They found only clothes in both and very little of those.

'He doesn't have much, does he?' commented Thelma with a disdainful twitch of the nose.

'I don't feel right doing this,' Edwina told her.

'You want to put your mind at rest, don't you?' asked Thelma.

'Yes, but even so...'

'What about under the bed?'

Thelma bent down and pulled out a small brown suitcase.

'Now, this may be of interest,' she mused.

Thelma tried the lock.

'It's locked. Look for the key.'

Edwina looked around for the key and checked the jacket and coat in the wardrobe but found nothing.

'It isn't here, he must have it on him,' she told Thelma.

'Now, why would that be, I wonder,' said Thelma suspiciously. 'Never mind...'

Removing a long hairgrip from the side of her head, she placed the end in the lock of the suitcase.

'What are you doing?' Edwina hissed.

'What does it look like I'm doing?' Thelma replied as she wiggled the hairgrip back and forth in the lock.

'No, no I won't allow this. He will know we've broken into his case,' Edwina admonished.

Suddenly, the lock sprang open. Thelma and Edwina looked at each other but said nothing. Thelma lifted the case up onto the bed and opened it up. As she lifted a knitted jersey she retracted with a gasp.

'What's the matter?' Edwina demanded. 'What is it?'

'Look for yourself,' Thelma told her.

Edwina leaned forward and cautiously pulled the jersey aside to reveal a gun. The cold metal, incongruous against the soft wool, seemed threatening even though it was without life.

'I told you there was something wrong about that man!' Thelma reproved her. 'Now do you believe me?'

Edwina could not answer, her eyes still fixed on the ruthless metal object, her brain desperately trying but failing to associate this deadly weapon with the nice, amiable Mister Roche.

'Edwina!'

Edwina looked across at her friend.

'What?'

'You have to call the police,' Thelma told her.

'The police! I'll get Mister Roche into trouble.'

'Edwina! The man could be dangerous.'

'But Mister Roche is so polite and…I can't believe he's a danger to anyone.'

'He is a criminal on the run, mark my words. You could be in danger, woman. A man with a gun is living under your roof and you know nothing about him. You told me yourself he would not sign with the doctor and did not want you to know his sister's number. This isn't right, Edwina. There's something fishy about him and now this!' she exclaimed, pointing to the gun.

'Is it real? It might be a replica or a novel lighter or something,' Edwina suggested.

Thelma looked at her coldly then slid her hand underneath the gun and felt the heaviness of the metal.

'Edwina, I don't know much about guns but that looks and feels real enough to me. Now, if you don't call the police, I will!'

Edwina stared at Thelma, her mind in turmoil, but as the seconds passed the implications of the situation began to hit home. Edwina nodded.

'Yes, I'll do it,' she said.

Stanley decided to return earlier than normal to 14 Lime Place, Kensal Rise. It had started to rain, recent events had caused him loss of sleep and he had felt tired that afternoon as he spent his time walking along the Grand Union Canal and wandering around Kensal Green Cemetery. Now, as he turned the corner, looking forward to a cup of tea with Mrs Robertson followed by a quiet lie down, he was confronted with a scene that immediately sent a cold blade through his heart. A police car was outside the house. Stanley suddenly wondered if Mrs Robertson was all right but he saw her appear on the doorstep accompanied by a policeman carrying his suitcase. Stanley turned back round the corner and walked as fast as he dare, without drawing undue attention, towards the underground station.

By the time Stanley arrived at Veldman's Victoriana it was closed. Cursing, he hurried to the back door but that too was locked. Stanley knew Joseph could not have been gone long as it had just turned 5.00p.m. Joseph was either on his way to Ealing Broadway station or already there. Stanley tried to hurry without drawing attention to himself by taking longer strides than usual. Aware that Joseph lived in West Acton, when he got to the station he purchased a ticket and made straight for the platform for the Central Line. As he stepped onto the platform there was the familiar waft of carbon and a faint rumbling sound could be heard in the distance. Stanley spotted Joseph almost immediately standing close to the tunnel at the far end of the platform. Just behind him was a tall, ginger-haired man dressed in a black suit and black coat. A group of women stood talking, a couple of girls giggled over some private joke, a young man in jeans leaned against the wall reading a newspaper, businessmen in suits, shoppers, students and day trippers all mingled.

As Stanley considered Joseph he recalled their lives in the Merchant Navy. It had been, for both of them, a difficult life to give up. They were young and adventurous, eager to see the world, to learn things, to experience new countries, discover new places, try different food and meet foreign people with backgrounds totally alien to their own. It was Joseph who had decided to give it up first, partly because of his engagement and partly due to the fact that he had been approached by an aeronautics company for their engineering science department. Joseph had talked them into offering Stanley a job and by that time Stanley felt he should perhaps settle down. They had been there just over a year when they were approached by a man from TIDI.

It was the money that had attracted them. They had been seduced by it. Money! What use was it now to either of them? One good night's sleep would be worth more than anything money could buy.

As he slowly made his way towards Joseph through the rush-hour crowd, he suddenly envied, with a passion, those ordinary people in their ordinary clothes with their very ordinary lives.

A gush of air came through the tunnel and the vibration and rumbling of the oncoming train now grew louder, echoing around the archways like the roar of a wakened beast. As Stanley pushed his way through the waiting passengers he saw Joseph just yards away. The crowd began to make their way to the edge of the platform. The rumble had now become a raucous reverberation as the train face grew larger and came hurtling through the tunnel bringing with it a blast of air that smelt like ancient dust and carbon. The next few seconds seemed to pass in slow motion as Stanley witnessed the tall, black figure behind Joseph Veldman swoop forward like an eagle and surreptitiously push Joseph off the edge of the platform. A loud yell of protest in Stanley's head remained in its embryonic stage not leaving his lips. Joseph's anguished scream, however, was audible enough.

Joseph Veldman had seen the curved, metal face of the advancing train and the driver's fixed gaze through the window just before he felt the violent nudge in his back. The last image he saw was the rail before he hit it. The last sound he heard was his own agonized scream and the last split second things he felt were the enormous thud of the train as it hit his body and the intense pain of the crushing of his bones.

Stanley stood momentarily frozen. The loud screeching of the train's brakes burst upon his eardrums like the haunting wail of a dinosaur being slaughtered. The grating, ear-piercing squeal joined the shocked screams and shouts of the awaiting passengers. One woman continued screaming but the sound became lost, drowned by the sound of the squealing wheels. All eyes of the onlookers were on the train and the place where the body had been crushed but Stanley was watching the man in black.

As the man turned away and began walking towards him, Stanley moved behind a tall man and blended with the rest of the passengers. Every fibre of his body was taut as the dark figure came closer. Even when the man passed him by, his stomach remained tight and his heart continued to beat wildly in his chest.

They could not have put two and two together so quickly from the police visit to 14 Lime Place, he reasoned. If the police had the suitcase, they had the gun, his personal details and the notes and cuttings he had kept over the years, but the connection would take some time, possibly through MI5, for even the police were not aware that TIDI existed. TIDI had either witnessed his initial visit to Joseph Veldman or Veldman had simply served his purpose and was now considered excess baggage. TIDI did not like to leave loose ends.

A very uneasy feeling began to creep up on Stanley as he began to suspect the former. How long, he wondered, had they known he was alive? Veldman must have been watched. Stanley tried hard to cast his mind back to that first visit to Veldman's Victoriana: A man crossing the road, a woman with a child in a pushchair, a tabby cat, passing traffic, a grey Vauxhall Cavalier that should not have been parked there! The road had double yellow lines. Stanley silently cursed himself as an idiot.

Stanley surmised his visit to Joseph had been witnessed and had led to his old colleague's elimination.

Stanley swiftly took gold-rimmed glasses from his pocket and slipped them on, turned his mackintosh inside out to reveal a dark tartan pattern of velour and quickly ruffled his thinning hair. The whole process took less than fifteen seconds. Taking a brief, final look at what had once been Joseph Veldman sticking out from beneath the train – a severed foot and some sanguineous, mangled remains, like fishes' entrails, sprawled along the line – Stanley nudged his way through the crowd and left the dramatic scene on the platform to make his way out of the station. The tall, ginger-haired man in black was waiting by the exit as Stanley approached.

'Excuse me,' Stanley muttered coolly to the hovering shape in the black coat as he side-stepped him and walked leisurely out through the exit of the station.

The man in black gave him a cursory glance and although his trained eyes, with speed and accuracy, skimmed the crowds that were now streaming out of the station, the man in beige mackintosh who had been approaching Veldman was not amongst them. Meanwhile, the tousle-haired man in tartan coat and gold-rimmed glasses had mingled inconspicuously with the human conflux on Ealing Broadway.

CHAPTER SEVENTEEN

JOURNEY TO CAMP

Richard gave a jolt and opened his eyes. Above him was the inside roof of an aircraft. A faint humming sound filled his ears. The monotonous and subtle vibration from the plane soothed his breathing which was sharp and shallow. Screwing up his eyes and blinking, Richard slowly sat up. There was the smell of metal and canvas and opposite him sat a slightly built man in an American army uniform with a pinched face and piercing, bright chestnut eyes.

'Hi!' said the voice, which was a little high-pitched.

'Hello,' said Richard.

'You OK? You've been dreaming a lot. Having some kind of a nightmare, huh?' asked the American.

'Don't remember,' said Richard. 'What am I doing here? Where are we going?'

'I've no idea.'

The American held out his hand.

'I'm Toony. Bruce Toony. Nobody calls me Bruce. You can call me Loony if you like. That's what the guys call me. Loony Toony. Get it?'

'I'll just call you Toony if that's OK?'

Toony grinned.

'Sure, that's fine by me.'

'I'm Richard.'

'Nice to meet you, Rich. Is that OK, if I call you Rich?'

'Yeah, that's fine,' Richard agreed.

'You've been sleeping for over an hour,' Toony informed him.

'I don't remember getting on this plane,' Richard told him.

'No, I think they'd given you something for the pain. They said you were getting over some sort of an injury. What was it?'

'I got stabbed in the shoulder,' Richard told him.

'Boy! Bet that hurt. I busted a couple of ribs and damaged my calcaneofibular ligament. How about that for a mouthful, huh?'

Richard looked blank.

'It's er, a ligament in the ankle,' Toony explained. 'American football. That's what you get for being the smallest guy in the team!'

'What are we doing here?' asked Richard.

'I'm joining the rest of my squad. I guess you are too.'

Richard moved towards a window.

'You can't see much,' Toony told him, 'just sea.'

Toony was right. Richard looked down through a mist onto water. Nothing else, besides pale-grey clouds, was in sight.

'How long have we been in the air?' asked Richard.

Toony checked his watch. 'Eighty minutes.'

'An hour and twenty minutes,' murmured Richard.

'Do you want one of these?' Toony asked him, offering him some sort of a pill from a small box.

'What are they?' Richard enquired.

'Helps calm the queasiness. I get the air sickness.'

'No, I'm fine,' Richard told him.

'How about a gum?' he asked, producing a packet from his trouser pocket.

'Thanks,' said Richard, taking one.

'So, you got any family back home, Rich?' Toony asked him.

'No. How about you?'

'Na! I had a sister but she topped herself when she was seventeen.'

'I'm sorry,' said Richard with sympathy.

'Yeah, me too,' said Toony. 'She had depression, you know? It was bad.'

'What about your parents?' Richard asked.

'They drowned in a boating accident when I was eleven. We would have ended up in a home if it hadn't been for our neighbours taking us in, but they've both gone now. What about you, Rich?'

'I was placed in a home when I was young. My mother abandoned me and I've no idea who my father was or what happened to my mother.'

'Wouldn't you like to find out?'

'No. They didn't want me so what would be the point?'

'Hey! You know what they say. You can choose your friends but you can't choose your family, right?'

126

Richard smiled. Toony was relaxing company and easy to talk to.

'Does anyone in your squad have a family?' Richard tested.

'Sure.'

'Really?' said Richard. 'They haven't told us anything about this posting. What about you?'

'Nothing.'

'Though, I noticed that all the men picked to go on this mission haven't got any close relatives.'

'Is that right?'

'Don't you think that's a little strange?' Richard asked him.

Toony thought about it.

'Just coincidence I guess,' he remarked.

'I suppose it must be, if you say your chaps have families.'

'Well, I'm not sure about the ones they've chosen for this posting. I heard they were choosing guys from another squad as well as ours. I don't know what guys they chose because I was in hospital at the base, you know.'

Richard fell silent. Just for a moment, his hopes had lifted and now they had fallen again.

'Could I ask you a favour?' queried Richard.

'Sure,' smiled Toony.

'I have a friend...'

Richard took a piece of paper from his pocket and offered it to Toony. Somehow, Richard felt he could trust him.

'If anything happens to me, would you make sure she gets the message?'

'She'll find out soon enough, pal,' Toony smiled.

'No, I mean, I still want you to contact her if you possibly can. Please. Will you promise me you'll do that?'

There was something so desperate in Richard's tone, such a pleading in his eyes that conveyed to Toony how important this was to him. Toony leaned forward, took the paper and placed it in his pocket.

'You got it, buddy,' he told him. 'I'll keep it safe,' he added, tapping the pocket with his hand. 'I promise.'

'Thanks,' said Richard.

'Say, mind if I get some shut-eye?' asked Toony. 'I was up real early this morning.'

'No, that's fine,' Richard told him.

Toony spat out his gum, stuck it on the side of the aircraft and snuggled down. Richard gazed out of the window. They were flying through low cloud and everything outside was nebulous, like the posting. In fact like his whole future, Richard thought.

'How the hell would you know that?' demanded Glen Witchell.

Geoff Hains glanced up like a schoolteacher who had just encountered an unruly child he could not be bothered to deal with. Hains was stretched out on his bed, shoulders and head resting on the wall, his tall body and broad shoulders in strange contrast to his youthful countenance.

'I know,' he said in his slow and precise way, 'by the stars, the wind...'

'The wind! What's the wind got to do with anything?' demanded Witchell.

'...and the time of sunrise and sunset in relation to the time of year,' finished Hains, nonchalantly.

'Well, aren't you the damn know-all!' spat Witchell.

The cold and the waiting had now got to all of the men, making them irritable and short-tempered. In addition, they had lost a football match to the Americans that morning, mainly down to Hains who, although having attained the nickname Brains due to his scholarly disposition, was a very clumsy sportsman. Swimming was the only exercise Hains excelled in.

'Shut up Witchell,' said Jason. 'Let him speak.'

'I just have,' Hains reminded him.

'Do you really know where we are, Brains?' asked Foster, busy polishing his boots.

'Taking into account all four factors, by my calculus we are definitely in Lapland, though the snow's come early.'

'I could have guessed that from the temperature!' exclaimed Witchell.

'Guessed yes, but not *known*,' Hains told him. 'Equally you could have guessed we were in northern Canada, Alaska, Iceland, Greenland or the North Pole...if you are going by temperature.'

Witchell walked away. Hains was really beginning to needle him.

'What else do you know, Brains?' asked Foster.

'What do you mean?' Hains asked him, looking up from beneath long lashes, his blue eyes searching Foster's face.

'About what we're doing here?'

'We're doing our duty, aren't we?' remarked Hains.

'You know what he means,' said Jason.

'You were good mates with Wilson, weren't you?' asked Foster. 'Do you think he was posted here?'

The clattering sound of helicopter blades interrupted any further conversation. Time spent in the camp was monotonous so that any distraction was welcome. They all rushed to the window and looked out. A CH-46 Sea Knight was landing just outside the perimeter fence, sending snow scattering in all directions. The Americans were already outside so they joined them. The helicopter landed and minutes later the door opened. Snowflakes whirled all around the Sea Knight making visibility difficult but a slight figure emerged in American uniform and one of the American soldiers shouted, 'Hey, it's Loony!'

'Loony! Over here!' shouted another American.

Toony glanced up and saw his comrades. Pointing to his ankle he then stuck his thumb in the air. The Americans cheered and slapped each other's hands and shoulders. Toony came down from the helicopter. Close behind, another figure, swathed in a milky mist from the sweeping flakes, joined him on the ground. They were both met by a US major.

'It's Rich!' observed Foster.

Jason screwed up his eyes and as the figures walked slowly towards the perimeter fence he recognized the unmistakable figure of Richard Paulton.

'Rich!' shouted Jason.

Richard looked all about him, taking in the bleak, glacial landscape and noting the cage-like enclosure of the fence.

'Rich!' Jason yelled again.

Richard and Bruce Toony entered the enclosure escorted by the major. The waiting soldiers hurried forward to greet their newly arrived colleagues.

'Rich! How are you?' asked Jason as he clapped him on the shoulder.

Richard looked at him and gave him a glancing blow to the jaw with his right fist. Jason fell backwards into the other men who caught him before he hit the ground. The major immediately stepped in.

'Hey, cut that out!' then addressing Richard he said, 'You're lucky I'm not going to report this or you'd be on a charge. From what I hear, soldier, you're in enough trouble already.'

The eyes, hard and piercing from beneath crossed brows shot a warning glance that hit Richard harder than he had hit Jason. Richard swallowed hard and gave Jason a look of disgust. Jason, hauled up onto his feet by the other men, stood rubbing his jaw. The English had fallen silent but the Americans failed to notice, lifting Toony onto their shoulders and carrying him around with cheery banter.

The major gave Richard one final passing shot with his eyes before leaving.

'A major...?' observed Richard to the men in a lowered tone.

'I know,' replied Witchell. 'There's a major and a lieutenant.'

'That's odd isn't it?' queried Richard.

'Yeah,' Witchell confirmed, 'there's only eighteen of us, including the Americans.'

'What happened to you, Rich? Where have you been?' asked Foster.

'In the Medical Centre.'

'What was wrong with you?' Witchell asked him.

'I got knifed for being in the wrong place at the wrong time,' said Richard, his tone acerbic.

The men exchanged glances.

'We thought you might have gone AWOL!' laughed Witchell.

'Yeah?' said Richard, then giving Jason a look of contempt continued, 'I wonder what gave you that idea?'

'Any idea where we are Rich?' asked Foster. 'Did you see anything from up there?'

'Just sea and cloud from the plane and snow from the helicopter,' said Richard.

'Same as us,' said Foster. 'We stopped off on some tiny, obscure airfield then we were transferred straight onto the helicopter.'

'Brains reckons we're in Lapland,' said Witchell.

'Then Brains is probably right,' said Richard.

'Come on,' said Foster. 'We'll show you around…'

They headed for the barracks, Jason trailing behind, blood now oozing from his mouth.

The Sea Knight began to rise into the air, disturbing the snow beneath it and sending it swirling round and round. Jason thought of the boy in the dome again and watched, silent, as the helicopter rose higher and higher into the sky until it gradually became a small blob in the distance.

CHAPTER EIGHTEEN

THE YOUNG ALLY

Nathan sat in the armchair by a glowing fire, one foot resting on the coffee table and thought about the telegram that had arrived that morning. Immediately upon his return home from Kathmandu, he had arranged for an advertisement to go in all the prominent American newspapers. It had asked for any relatives of David Spontiak of the US Navy to please contact him urgently. The telegram had arrived four days later. It was from a woman living in Nova Scotia who claimed to be David Spontiak's wife. Nathan had rung her. A cousin, who still lived in the States, had alerted her about the advertisement. David had gone missing during active duty, presumed killed, in World War II. The woman had enquired about Nathan's interest and he had decided to tell her personally. The local travel agent had managed to find him a cancellation and booked his flight for the following morning.

Outside, the wind was whistling and rain battered against the window panes. A brandy with ice waited in a glass on the coffee table. Beside it, staring up at him, were the photographs taken at the monastery, a stark reminder that evil is never far from good. In his hand Nathan held the ID tag taken from the old monk. Turning it slowly over and over in his fingers he slipped into a doze. Events from the last few days wheeled around in his mind as the persistent rain pattered and blasted against the house.

The shrill ring of the doorbell brought him up sharp. Turning the photographs over and slipping the dog tag into his trouser pocket, he went to the front door. Leaving the catch on, he opened it and peered into the half-light. A young, epicene figure, wearing jacket and jeans, stood on his doorstep blinking away the persistent raindrops that splattered across an oval face. Nathan glanced up and down the lane. A red Mini was parked just outside the house. Further up the lane was a grey Vauxhall Cavalier. Apart from that, the lane was quiet and empty, the field opposite silent.

'Are you Nathan King?'

The voice was female.

'Yes,' Nathan confirmed.

'A friend sent me. She thought you may be able to help me with something.'

Nathan hesitated but the figure of slight build and hazel eyes looked at him with hope.

Nathan unhooked the catch.

'Come in,' he told her.

The young woman entered and vigorously wiped her shoes on the doormat. Nathan took her jacket and invited her into the living room to sit down.

'You're soaked. I'll get you a towel,' he told her. 'Would you like a drink?'

'Thanks.'

'Brandy? Tea? What?'

'Tea, please. Thanks.'

Nathan fetched a towel and the young woman wiped her face. It was youthful with flawless skin.

'What do I call you?' he asked.

'Oh, yeah, sorry. I'm Liz. Liz Stone.'

'OK, Liz Stone, make yourself at home and I'll get you some tea.'

Liz sat down on the settee. The room was modern and tasteful with cream and grey furnishings and dark grey carpet. There was a black, contemporary bookcase and framed photographs of landscapes and wild animals. The man seemed nice, she thought. Immediately, he had put her at ease. Liz wandered around and studied the photographs on the walls more closely before returning to the comfort of the settee.

Nathan came in with two mugs of tea and sugar on a tray.

'Help yourself to sugar,' he said.

Taking the towel from her, he threw it on the side of a chair.

'So Liz, how can I help you?' he asked.

Liz told him straight about Richard, his plans to go AWOL and her concerns at what had followed. When she finished, Nathan looked at her lost.

'I'm sorry but I don't see how I can help you. You said a friend sent you?'

'Yes, Martha Kemp.'

Nathan looked blank.

'Martha Kemp?' he queried. 'I don't know anyone of that name. Who is she?'

Liz looked at him puzzled.

'An elderly lady who lives in Masterton, Dorset,' she replied.

'Have you come from Dorset?' he enquired.

'Yes.'

Nathan racked his brains but could not think of any occasion when he had come into contact with a Martha Kemp.

'I'm really sorry,' he said, 'but I don't know the lady.'

'She knows you. She said you could help.'

The man had a pleasant face, thought Liz, with warm brown eyes and an honest way about him but her hope was fading fast. Had Martha gone a bit dotty in her old age, Liz wondered? To send her all this way on a wild goose chase...then she remembered something.

'Martha said whatever has happened to Rich might tie in with your experience in Tibet...'

Nathan tensed, every muscle in his body straining.

'...and she said I should not contact you by phone, but approach you direct,' continued Liz, sipping the hot tea.

Nathan gazed at her, allowing the words to sink in, thoughts whizzing around his head like a fairground ride, then a warning light switched on in his brain. Rushing to the telephone, he unscrewed the speaker and found a tiny metallic object, smaller than a hearing aid battery.

'What are you doing?' Liz asked him.

Nathan put a forefinger to his lips. Holding the object in the palm of his hand for her to see he then dropped it in his mug of tea. Liz looked astounded.

'I believe that's what they call a bug,' Nathan whispered. 'Someone's been listening in on my phone calls. How did your Martha Kemp know that, I wonder? Help me look for any more – they could be hidden anywhere – and be quiet,' he warned her.

Liz put her mug down and helped Nathan scan the room, checking behind picture frames, around the television and at the back of the bookcase. The search was detailed, orderly and very thorough, Nathan even turning the settee and chairs upside down before correcting them again. Satisfied, Nathan relaxed but kept to a low voice.

'Just a second, Liz,' he said, leaving the room to return with a large umbrella.

'Come outside,' Nathan whispered.

Liz followed Nathan into the back garden. The wind had died down but the rain persisted.

'Now, tell me everything you know about this Martha Kemp,' Nathan invited.

Liz stood and thought, nestled beneath the umbrella.

'There isn't much to tell, really,' she told him. 'I've known her since I was a kid. My uncle used to live near her. Sometimes he would help out at her place doing odd jobs.'

Liz paused.

'Is there anything else…?' asked Nathan.

'She used to work for the Ministry during the war. Only administration, she said, but my uncle always used to think there was more to it than that.'

The frown on Nathan's forehead cleared, his eyes widened and a smile crossed his face but he said nothing.

'Do you think you can find out what's happened to Richard?' Liz asked him.

'I don't know,' Nathan answered truthfully.

'What's this experience you had in Tibet?' Liz enquired. 'Why is your house bugged? Are you some kind of a spy or something?'

Nathan shook his head.

'No, I'm just an ordinary chap who happened to be in the wrong place at the wrong time and now I've got myself into something a little bit beyond my grasp.'

Liz warmed to this man. Like Richard, he was open and modest.

'There must be some kind of link to Richard otherwise Martha wouldn't have sent me,' Liz insisted. 'She must know about this business you've got yourself into. It's odd that she knew you were in Tibet if you don't even know her.'

'Tibet,' he answered mechanically, his brain now in a whirl with this new information. Who the hell was this Martha Kemp, he wondered? How did she know so much about him?

'How does she know about you if you don't know who she is?' Liz pressed.

Nathan thought carefully.

'Liz, I don't know and I have no idea what the link is, but I'm flying out to Canada tomorrow and by the time I come back I'm hoping to have some answers.'

'Do you think Richard may be in Canada?' she asked, suddenly hopeful.

'No. I haven't a clue where your friend could be,' he replied truthfully.

'Oh,' said Liz, casting her eyes down at the ground.

Nathan sensed her despondency and studied the young figure before him with the damp jeans, the cropped black hair and dejected expression. Suddenly he felt strongly protective towards her. Here was someone, like himself, who had wandered unknowingly into this web of intrigue and he wondered how well equipped she was to deal with it. Liz looked wet, tired and deflated, he thought.

'You must be hungry,' he guessed. 'I haven't eaten yet. Would you like to join me…?'

The worried countenance turned towards him and managed a weak smile.

'Say nothing about this when we get inside,' he warned her, 'just in case.'

They went into the kitchen and Nathan found some eggs and cheese for omelettes, all the time pondering on the mysterious Martha Kemp. Who was this woman? How did she know about him and perhaps, the most pressing question of all, if she knew the predicament he was in, what on earth had possessed her to send this young woman into what she knew must be a dangerous situation?

'It's a fair way back to Dorset. You're welcome to sleep on the settee if you like,' he offered, 'though I'll have to wake you really early in the morning because of my flight.'

'Thanks,' she smiled.

Nathan turned on a loud coffee percolator then whispered into Liz's ear.

'Liz, there's something I want you to do for me.'

Liz looked at him and waited.

'When you leave in the morning, would you hide a package under your jacket and pop it in a postbox for me on your way home? Check first no one is around.'

'Sure,' she said.

'It's important, Liz. It's just in case anyone is watching me and the house. I don't want them to see you leaving with it. Get rid of it as soon as you can.'

'I will,' she promised him and he believed her.

Nathan arose at 5.00a.m. Before waking Liz, he crept into his back garden with a torch and the photographs of the monks. The rain from the night before had left everything damp and fresh. Nathan went to the end of the garden and by the light of the torch pushed aside the thick overgrowth that concealed an old air-raid shelter. Nathan went down the steps, releasing himself from the straggling plants that coiled around him, unlocked the door and went inside. After placing the photographs inside a large, rectangular biscuit tin, he came back out, locked the door and crept back across the lawn. Someone may be accessing his house but they would not have a clue what was at the bottom of the garden. Nathan shone the torch back at the unkempt shrubbery that smothered the shelter making it totally invisible. Satisfied he had found a safe place for the photographs until his return, he stole back inside the house.

CHAPTER NINETEEN

THE DIRECTIVE

It had been the moment Bertram had half-expected: the call to summon him to TIDI Headquarters. The tiled floor echoed his footsteps with a cold harshness and it was with a heavy heart that he mounted the staircase. Today the stained window looked solemn with the reverence of a church and the buzzer sounded strident and alarming.

Alistair stood the other side of the huge desk looking subtly pleased with himself. The grinning skeleton, thought Bertram. As he took the cold, damp hand in his, he felt like crushing it, grinding the knuckles until the smug expression turned to one of anxiety and pain, but it was Bertram who felt the anxiousness today for he knew what was to come.

'Sit down, Bertram,' said Alistair in his cold, laconic manner. 'Coffee?'

'No thank you. I'm rather busy so best get on with it,' said Bertram.

Alistair sat down and held his gaze, confident and in charge. Today, the corpse held the cards.

'It's about your friend, Martha Kemp.'

'What of her?' Bertram asked crisply.

'You said she could be trusted.'

Bertram leaned forward in his chair and narrowed his eyes.

'I have never had any reason to doubt Martha,' he said.

'Then perhaps age has…loosened the tongue…withered the senses?'

'Explain,' Bertram demanded sharply.

'It appears she has been speaking to a young lady who is a friend of the young soldier you enquired about. It would also appear this young lady has been in touch with Nathan King, our worrisome photographer.'

'Perhaps it is solely the young lady's initiative. Martha may know this lady but it is no proof she has said anything.'

Alistair gazed at Bertram with the air of a very superior being. Raising his chin and staring at a point two inches above Bertram's head he commented, 'Bertram! We both know you are nowhere near that naive'.

Standing up and gazing out of the window he followed up simply with, 'This needs to be dealt with, Bertram. We can't have a loose cannon'.

Alistair had played his trump card and Bertram had nothing to match it.

'Very well,' Bertram replied.

'You must find out what she knows. Martha, after all, could turn out to be a blessing in disguise, if we all play our cards right.'

Bertram studied Alistair's back as he continued to stare out of the window and his countenance showed utter contempt.

'A spy in the camp you mean?' spat Bertram.

'Oh, let's not be so dramatic!' exclaimed Alistair. 'This isn't war you know. Martha would be doing what she does best – working for the good of her country.'

'Martha has strong values,' Bertram came back at him. 'Martha would have to be convinced it *was* for the good of the country.'

Alistair turned, his sharp, steel-like eyes piercing Bertram's own.

'Then convince her,' he said crisply.

'And if I can't convince her?' queried Bertram.

'You would be a fool to allow sentiment to get in the way. I trust if she does not play ball, you will have no further contact with the lady and leave our other branch to deal with her.'

'On the contrary…' murmured Bertram.

Alistair shot him a look of surprise and disdain.

'I made this mess,' said Bertram. 'If it comes to it, I should be the one to clear it up.'

'But that would be difficult for you, surely,' suggested Alistair.

'Oh! I see! You think old age has withered me too! Think again, Alistair. Like I said, it is my mess and I should be allowed to deal with it. It will be more pleasant that way – for her, I mean and it is she who I am thinking of. An old friend who will make sure it is quick and painless is the last gift that I can give her.'

'Our associates are quite capable...'

'Yes, like the way they dealt with the photographer. I have enormous respect for Martha and I will be the one to see her out of this world, not those monkeys!'

Alistair bristled, his thin lips tightening into an even thinner line.

'Very well,' he said when he had composed himself. 'If you wish to play executioner, Bertram, then you have my blessing. Just don't hash it up.'

'There was *never* a hash up in *my* organization when *I* was in charge!' Bertram bellowed. 'If it comes to it, it *will* be done and it will be done efficiently and, just for the record, I have to say I prefer the old ways when each branch was entirely separate and secluded. I think this newfangled idea of working together has caused things to get rather sloppy!'

Heaving himself up from the leather chair, Bertram marched his heavy frame out of the room, slamming the door behind him. Alistair felt the room vibrate in his wake. Pensively, he sank into the leather chair, placed his hands together and held them beneath his chin. A smile gradually evened itself across his face. The meeting had gone rather well, he thought.

CHAPTER TWENTY

THE CANADIAN CONNECTION

The plane touched down in Halifax and Nathan moved straight to the check out area having brought only one small holdall that he could take as hand luggage. The officials were friendly and welcomed him to Canada but his bag was thoroughly searched. They paid particular attention to the bottom of the bag, ensuring there was no hidden compartment. The Canadians were hot on drugs. Another traveller behind him, in a long black coat, had the same meticulous treatment. Having come through customs, Nathan arranged a car hire and was soon on the highway, stopping at a roadside café for a toasted bacon sandwich before continuing his journey to Mulgrave.

Nathan turned on the radio and the nasal tones of Gordon Lightfoot sang Me and Bobby McGee. It was the first time in ages Nathan had felt totally relaxed. The wide open highway in front of him, the acres of firs and the pale sky lifted his spirit and loaned him a sense of freedom so completely opposite to the world he had recently experienced. Through the open window the fresh cold air, with a subtle waft of pine, was like a disinfectant washing away the grime of recent events.

Mulgrave was what the English would call a village, facing Cape Breton Island which could be accessed across the Canso Causeway. Nathan slowly drove through, passing a wooden, white painted church with the Strait of Canso on his left. Mrs Spontiak lived in a house that looked like an upturned boat painted yellow and blue. Nathan stopped the car and climbed out. For a moment he stood and drank in the stillness and tranquillity before walking up the short track to Mrs Spontiak's porch and knocking on the blue door.

The woman who opened the door was tall and thin with a haggard expression and kindly blue eyes that looked out from large framed glasses. The grey hair was short and neat and she wore a beige jumper with brown trousers and beige casual shoes.

'Mrs Spontiak…?' enquired Nathan.

'Yep, that's me,' she said, in a distinct Canadian accent.

'I'm Nathan King who placed the advertisement about your husband.'

'Oh goodness!' she exclaimed. 'Have you come all the way from England?'

'Yes, I have. I'd like a talk with you if that's all right?'

'Goodness! Sure, come in,' she invited.

There was a strong waft of apples and pastry as Nathan entered the house. Rich, scarlet carpet covered the hallway and stairs and Nathan noticed framed oil paintings of a lighthouse and a rocky cove with lobster pots. Mrs Spontiak led him into a roomy living area where the wide window had a view over the porch and out onto the glistening water of the Strait of Canso.

'This is a charming place, Mrs Spontiak,' Nathan told her.

'Thank you. I've just baked an apple pie. Would you like some? I have ice cream to go with it.'

'That would be great. Thank you.'

Mrs Spontiak left the room and Nathan sat down on a large, green and lemon settee. There were quite a few antiques about the place, including a walnut writing bureau. There was a genuine wood floor and a 3' model of a boat on a sideboard. There were lots of photographs of children, young people and older people but one, in particular, caught Nathan's eye. It was an old, black and white photograph of a group of sailors standing in front of a ship. Nathan went to have a closer look. Five men in American naval uniform stood before a destroyer. The angle of the photograph meant the men had partly obliterated the name of the vessel but Nathan could make out USS R........lt.

Mrs Spontiak came into the room and placed a tray of tea and a piece of pie and ice-cream in a white and blue bowl onto the coffee table.

'Is your husband in this photograph, Mrs Spontiak?' Nathan asked.

'He's the one in the middle,' she told him.

Nathan studied the face carefully. It was a lean, slightly long face with nice eyes and a becoming smile.

'He was a handsome man,' Nathan told her.

'I always thought so,' she smiled.

A flashback of David Spontiak's skeletal body made him feel fraudulent.

'Do you know any of these other men here with your husband?' he enquired.

'I'm afraid not,' she replied. 'My husband only had one special friend and he was killed some time before David. I couldn't tell you who those men are except they might have served on the same ship as my husband.'

'What was the name of that ship in the photograph?' Nathan pressed.

'I really don't know. As far as I am aware, David only ever served on the USS Colyton.'

'The Colyton. What happened to that ship? Any idea? You say your husband was presumed killed? Missing in action?'

'The Colyton was torpedoed during the war. There were no survivors as far as anyone knew. Mister... Forgive me, your name has slipped my mind....' she apologized.

'King. Nathan King.'

'Mister King. You never actually told me what your interest was in my husband. I don't really understand.'

'I'm sorry,' said Nathan. 'I have something that belonged to your husband.'

From around his neck, Nathan lifted the dog tag and handed it to her. Mrs Spontiak took the tag, read it and gave a sharp intake of breath.

'Oh, good heavens!'

'It is your husband's?' he checked.

Mrs Spontiak's eyes were wide with disbelief as her thumb stroked the ID tenderly and thoughtfully. Tears welled up in her eyes.

'Where did you get this?' she enquired.

'That's the mysterious thing, Mrs Spontiak,' Nathan told her. 'I found it in Tibet.'

Mrs Spontiak looked at him strangely as if her mind could not quite take in what was being told to her.

'I don't understand,' she said. 'How could it have possibly got there?'

'That's what I don't know. Would he have been sent to Tibet for any reason?' asked Nathan.

Mrs Spontiak shook her head.

'No. There would be no reason for him to go there.'

Nathan did not want to give away too much, especially the fact that he knew where her husband's body was. The last thing he needed was for Mrs Spontiak to start making her own enquiries. For one thing, that would put her life in danger.

'Mrs Spontiak, I need to ask you a favour.'

The woman stared at him in a daze. This had started as an ordinary day and now here was this stranger from England in her lounge with a personal piece of her husband's property and some weird story about where it was found. It was all so surreal.

'Yes. What is it?' she asked him.

'I would like to keep the identity tag for a while. You see, there is some sort of a mystery here and I would deeply love to solve it.'

'I could ring the American Navy and…'

'No,' Nathan interrupted.

Mrs Spontiak looked at him puzzled.

'The fact is someone isn't too happy that I have found that tag.'

'Who?' she asked. 'Why would someone not be happy about it?'

'I believe something off the record must have happened to your husband and someone was responsible for that.'

'Who?' she implored.

'I don't know. That's what I'm trying to get to the bottom of. Please, could we keep this between ourselves for now? When I find any information I promise I will let you know,' he told her.

Mrs Spontiak studied the sincere and rather handsome face in front of her. The man had come a long way to show her the tag and he had been open with her. No one else had put themselves out this much for her husband. To the navy he was just another sailor who had died in the war. To this man, David was somebody significant as he still was to her.

'You can keep the tag,' she decided.

'There's something else,' he said.

'Yes?'

'That photograph. Would you mind if I get a copy made?'

'No, I don't mind. You'd have to go over to Cape Breton for that. I could take you tomorrow. Have you anywhere to stay this evening?'

'Not yet,' he admitted.

'Then you are welcome here,' she told him.

'That's very kind of you,' he said.

'You're welcome,' she replied. 'No one else has shown any interest in what happened to my husband and nobody ever talks about him. You're a breath of warm air on a cold, autumn day.'

Nathan smiled but there was sadness behind the gesture: a powerful regret that he could not tell this woman he had found her husband's body and an even deeper sadness that he could not bring it back to her.

Nathan did not sleep well that night. The cosy room with its comfortable chairs and New England quilt felt friendly and secure but the thoughts in his mind were far from easy. Images of a young soldier floated in and out of his restless repose like a butterfly flitting back and forth past his head. A young woman on his settee also disturbed him, her words drifting in and out of his memory, whilst in the background, like a distant figure in the shadows, the mysterious lady called Martha Kemp remained hidden but very vivid like a child who played hide and seek. Who was she? How did she know of him? How did she know he was on this quest and how much did she know? Why did she think this missing soldier was somehow tied in with this business and why had she sent the girl and not approached him herself?

'How the hell did she know my house was bugged?'

The words had come out loud into the quietness of the room. Nathan groaned. There was a dull ache in his head caused by jet lag and too many questions to which there seemed no feasible answers. This Martha Kemp had clearly done some investigating, but why on him?

'Who the hell was Price?' he muttered.

In the darkness the pages of the A4 book seemed to hover in front of him, the leaves turning: Geometrical lines and shapes, maps, chemical symbols, Latin, calculations and other strange drawings that seemed to make no sense at all. What the hell did it all mean?

Nathan twisted and turned beneath the sheets. Outside, the moon bestowed a lambent light upon the Strait of Canso, turning the shimmering water into a multitude of silvery worms that danced across its black surface. At the side of the road was parked a red Dodge car. Inside it a man in a black coat, resting but awake, watched Mrs Spontiak's house with diligent interest.

Nathan awoke with a start and called into the darkness, 'Chu?'

For a moment he was confused as to where he was, for he could have sworn he had heard the dog's growl, but slowly the shapes of the room came into focus and he recalled he was in Canada at Mrs Spontiak's house. For a few minutes he sat up in bed rubbing his eyes, allowing the shadowy images to form their proper outlines, but he could not settle down again. If it had been a dream he could not recall it but Chu's growl had awoken him. Stretching and rising from the bed he crossed to the window. Across the Strait of Canso twinkled the lights of Port Hawkesbury. A gentle, fresh breeze drifted in through the slightly open window and then, down below, Nathan spotted him. A tall man, in a long dark coat, stood smoking a cigarette as he leaned against a car. Nathan had a mental flashback of customs at Halifax Airport. The man who had stood behind him there had been very similar in stature and build. Another memory came vividly to mind: Chu's face, as Nathan was leaving Lhasa, projected brightly into the darkness. As he watched the sparkling lights across the water he thought of his canine ally and visioned him now, eyes alert, ears erect, somehow sensing across such a wide distance that Nathan was in danger and the image brought a heaviness to Nathan's heart for which he had no cure.

CHAPTER TWENTY-ONE

THE BET

Richard wandered across to the crowd outside the barracks. A number of both English and American soldiers had formed a horseshoe around Toony and another thickset American called Jim Brady. Toony and Brady had removed their socks and were sitting in front of two buckets of snow. Hal Davison, a tall, fair-haired American with acne, waited with a stopwatch. Another square-faced, good-looking American called Gav Hudson was hurriedly writing in a notebook as he took bets.

'What's going on?' Richard asked Hains.

'They're going to see how long they can keep their feet in the snow. The one who keeps his in longest is the winner. I've bet on Brady. Look at those stumpy legs. He's got more fat on him so, logically, he should win,' Hains reasoned.

Richard smiled and felt in his pocket for a ten-pound note.

'Here!' he called to Hudson. 'I'll have a tenner on the tough little guy!'

Toony stuck a thumb up at Richard.

'Right on, Rich! He knows a winner when he sees one!' Toony laughed.

'Hurry up, Gav!' shouted Brady. 'I'll have frostbite before we even start at this pace.'

'Getting cold already,' Toony teased him. 'You sure you're up to this, Brady?'

'My feet will do the talking, Loony, don't you worry about that,' Brady came back at him.

Hudson snatched Richard's money and called out like an auctioneer, 'Are we all done?'

There was a resounding roar from the spectators.

'Come on, Hal! Let it rip!' shouted Toony.

Hal Davison poised his thumb above the stopwatch.

'On your marks…' said Davison. 'Get set….'

Toony and Brady lifted their feet above the buckets of snow.

'Go!' shouted Davison.

There was a double squelch as the feet dropped into the buckets. Brady clamped his fists and gritted his teeth. Toony smiled and chewed hard on his gum. The soldiers shouted 'Go Brady' or 'Go Toony' to their respective bets. Brady leaned forward, his thick forearms tightening, his knuckles turning white as he tensed against the cold. Toony leaned back and laughed.

'Say, does anyone have a journal? I'm getting kinda bored sitting here!'

Toony's jest brought a roar of laughter from both the English and the Americans.

Brady's face turned purple as his whole body began to contort.

'Having problems, Brady?' teased Toony. 'Just relax and enjoy it.'

Brady clenched his teeth then let loose a string of expletives. Hal Davison kept a close eye on the stopwatch.

'One minute,' he announced solemnly.

Brady started banging his fists on his knees and grinding his teeth. More expletives filled the air.

'You can do it, Brady. Hang on in there, buddy,' shouted one of the American soldiers.

Toony grinned and continued to chew hard on his gum.

'Boy, it's just like being on vacation, huh?' smiled Toony.

Brady clasped his hands around his chest and began to clap the sides of his arms, shaking his head.

'Two minutes,' announced Davison.

'I can't feel my feet!' moaned Brady. 'Hell! I can't feel them. Are they still there?'

'They're still there,' Toony assured him, 'though I'm guessing they're going a real funny colour.'

Brady placed his hands over his mouth and made blowing noises.

'Say, what do you think you are? A whale?' laughed Toony.

'Zip it, Toony!' snarled Brady.

'Cold really getting to you now, huh?' gibed Toony.

'Three minutes,' announced Davison.

Stabbing pains started attacking Brady's legs like electric shocks and then cramp gripped his calves. It felt as if his muscles were in a vice. Brady's supporters, seeing his obvious discomfort, yelled louder for him to hang on.

'Four minutes,' announced Davison.

Brady leaned forward and let out a long, loud groan then he lifted his feet from the bucket to the disappointment of his backers and whoops of victory from Toony's supporters.

Toony leaned back and brought his forearms up, turning the palms of his hands outwards.

'Gee guys, I guess I may as well take my tootsies out of here now, huh?'

'Five minutes,' said Davison.

Brady was busy, briskly rubbing his feet dry with a towel as his teeth chattered away by themselves. Davison threw Toony a towel.

'You ain't normal, Loony!' said Brady, his jaw shivering and the words jerking out of his mouth.

'You're talking to someone who used to go skinny-dipping in December! Only a polar bear could stay in that kinda cold longer than me,' Toony informed him.

'That's an idea!' shouted Gav. 'Do you reckon there are any polar bears out there would take you on?'

'They'd sure have a fight on their paws if they did!' announced Toony.

The men formed a queue in front of Gav as he efficiently gave out their winnings.

'Hell! I think one of my toes is about to drop off,' complained Brady as two Americans helped him hobble away.

Richard walked over to Toony and shook his hand.

'Well done, Toony,' said Richard.

'Thanks for betting on me.'

'How do you manage to do that?' Richard asked him, intrigued.

'Easy. I imagine I'm in a hot tub. Real hot. Mind over matter. You see, it's not the size of your muscles or your nuts. What really matters is what's in here,' Toony told him, pointing to his head. 'Now Brady, he's got no imagination, so all he can feel is the freezing cold.'

Richard shook his head.

'That must take a lot of practise.'

'Oh yeah, but I've had plenty of time. Right from a kid.'

Richard was beginning to see why Toony was popular with the Americans. They liked his mettle.

'Is anyone up for a game?' called out Hudson, holding a baseball in the air.

'Yeah! Count me in!' replied Toony, pulling his socks back on. 'Is Brady gonna play?'

'Nah,' said Hudson. 'He's too busy tending to his frostbite.'

The Americans laughed.

Richard leaned against the cold wall of the barracks and watched the Americans playing baseball. Blowing a stream of smoke from his mouth he watched it curl upwards and dissipate into the air. The tall, ungainly figure of Geoff Hains appeared beside him. For a few moments they stood without speaking then Hains cut into the silence.

'It's like a prison, isn't it?'

Richard turned to look at him then turned away again.

'Yeah.'

'A prison from which there is no escape,' continued Hains, 'and yet, there is.'

Richard allowed the words to sink in before he asked, as casually as possible, 'What do you mean?'

'There's a blind spot behind the laundry area. It can't be seen from any other building. Those who must be obeyed have their daily meeting in the wooden hut behind the barracks between 2.00 and 3.00 every day. If someone climbed over that fence, they wouldn't be noticed missing for at least an hour, especially if there was some form of distraction from the men.'

'It's too risky,' said Richard sullenly.

'I disagree, especially if the focus of attention was elsewhere. On that little nutter, Toony, for instance. The Americans have been boasting what a good little boxer he is. I think Foster's up for it.'

Richard turned to look at Hains again.

'It just needs someone to arrange for those two wire ends to come together,' continued Hains, 'and...fzzzzz!' he smiled, making a quick firing gesture with his fingers pointing towards each other.

Richard blew smoke rings into the air and watched them leisurely twist, distort and evaporate.

'Are you thinking of going over that fence, Brains?' Richard enquired.

'Me? No. I'm too clumsy. I'd probably get snagged up at the top.'

There was a long pause.

'I believe there are trees out of sight a little way in that direction,' Hains informed him.

'What makes you think there are trees?'

'The birds,' Hains replied.

'Birds?'

'They always appear from that direction and they always return to that direction. There has to be trees.'

'You were wrong about Brady's feet,' Richard reminded him.

'True. I don't always get it right, but those birds are flying to and from that same place all the time and birds nest in trees.'

'We can't even be sure where we are,' Rich told him.

'I'm sure. I spotted a White-tailed Eagle the other day. Beautiful.'

From his pocket, Hains produced a compass. Nodding towards the fencing behind the laundry, he said, 'Over there, north, north west, that's the Norwegian Sea and over there,' he continued, casting his head to the right, 'north, north east, that's the Barents Sea'.

Richard thought long and hard, only shouts from the American baseball team interrupted the quietness of the moment.

'Why are you telling me this?' Richard asked him.

For the first time, Hains turned to look at him.

'Because I know you don't want to be here, Rich. You feel, as I do, that something very unpleasant is about to happen.'

The face was earnest, the eyes meaningful.

'What do you think is going to happen, Brains?' Richard asked him direct.

'They've got us lined up for something. I think it's something experimental.'

'Like what?'

'I'm not sure. Some sort of weapon. A new type of gas, maybe. Possibly a chemical weapon.'

'You don't think it's anything to do with UFOs do you?' queried Richard. 'One of the Americans…'

Hains pursed his lips and shook his head.

151

'No. I don't think it's anything like that. They've made something but they're not sure what effects it will have on us.'

'What do you think happened to those other men?' Richard asked him.

'I really don't know,' Hains answered with veracity.

'Do you think they're still alive?'

'Possibly. It could be that they're being monitored.'

Richard felt a certain sense of relief tempered by the knowledge that, if they were alive, they could be in a condition where they would be better off dead.

Richard finished his cigarette and dropped the butt onto the snowy ground.

'Are you sure you don't want to go over that fence, Brains?'

Hains gave a sad smile.

'No. You see, I don't think I'd be capable of making it, but if someone did and something happened, there would be someone on the outside still sane enough to ask questions.'

'Someone could get imprisoned for that. We've signed the Official Secrets Act. That's the bit that really scares you, isn't it?'

'True, but if someone had the nerve they could save lives.'

'What about tracks?' queried Richard.

'If it was snowing, it would quickly cover them up.'

'And you think Foster's up for a fight?'

'Definitely. If it's arranged at the right time on a day when it's snowing, all the chaps in the gym, focused on the fight...'

There was a prolonged silence until Hains spoke again.

'Do you think there might be someone ready to go over that fence?'

Richard glanced around the camp, studied his boots for a moment and then said, 'I've tried once and look what happened to me. Sorry, Brains. It's someone else's turn'.

CHAPTER TWENTY-TWO

THE ULTIMATUM

Martha wandered along the Embankment in a brown suit, brown shoes, knee-length brown coat and a pink scarf. As she approached the awkward looking figure with black trousers and long black coat she knew the news was not good. The colour he had chosen to wear and the preoccupied look across the Thames conveyed more to her than spoken words. Bertram had arranged this meeting because he had bad news.

'Bertram…?' she said, lightly touching his arm.

'Sparrow!' he smiled, presenting her with a bunch of pink roses.

Martha smelt the delicate odour. There was no breeze today. It was overcast with a still, cutting air that allowed the sweet smell to gently invade her nostrils.

'They have a very pleasant aroma, Bertram,' she said, 'but what you have to tell me is not so pleasant, is it?'

Bertram sighed and sat down on the seat behind him. Martha sat beside him, her slight body half-turned towards him, her face troubled.

'I read about Joseph Veldman,' she told him.

'Yes,' nodded Bertram.

'A tragic incident…or accident, perhaps…?'

The word, perhaps, lingered on her tongue giving it significance.

'They believe Stanley Hoffman may have contacted him,' Bertram told her by way of explanation.

'Hoffman! So, he is…after all this time…' she reflected.

'They can't be sure,' he told her.

'But they are almost sure, aren't they? Otherwise poor Joseph might have lived to see another day.'

'I often wondered…he was a very clever fellow,' Bertram confirmed.

'So, is the mouse in sight of the cheese?' she queried.

'No. He's gone to ground…if it was, indeed, him.'

Martha sat and thought about Hoffman: An innocuous individual with a sharp mind and a face much younger than his years. Martha remembered him as good company. They had often visited Sways, a Brighton casino, together during their time off. Seven red had been a private joke between them for Martha often bet on it and much to Stanley's amusement often won on it too. It had been some time before she realized Stanley was not from her branch but in a research initiative under the control of TIDI. An idea came to her.

Returning to the present she suddenly said, 'I was hoping not to see you again'.

'Yes, I know and here I am with, as you know, not good news. Why on earth did you involve the girl?' he asked.

A cold chill suddenly claimed Martha and she shuddered. Someone had just walked over her grave, she thought to herself.

'Ah! So they know about Lizzie. Yes, it was foolish of me, wasn't it?'

'You've never been a fool, Sparrow!' he corrected her. 'So why?'

'Because her dear friend turned out to be my soldier and my hands are tied, Bertram. I can't tell you how bloody frustrating that is!'

Bertram turned to look at her, carefully noting the silver-grey hair, the lined face and the wrinkled hands.

'We did our bit,' he reminded her. 'None of us stay young forever.'

'I know, but it's so unfair that one has to age. It's still there, Bertram: that need to *make a difference.* I miss it, you know. The adrenalin rush; living on the edge. It made me feel *alive!*'

'But there comes a time, dear Sparrow, when we must graciously give way. Go with the tide, so to speak.'

'Be acquiescent, you mean. I was never that, Bertram.'

Bertram gave a chuckle.

'No, you weren't,' he laughed.

The smile gradually left his face and the silence fell between them like the autumn leaves.

'I felt it was the only move I could make. It was a selfish move, perhaps, but I have a certain faith in the girl,' Martha explained.

'You ask too much of her,' Bertram said.

'Yes. Yes and yet...'

154

'She is *not* you,' Bertram pointed out. 'How will she cope? Has she any idea who she is dealing with?'

'None whatsoever. I could hardly tell her!'

'Ignorance is bliss? It's a philosophy I don't hold with. This young woman could not know the facts; therefore, you had no right to involve her.'

Martha became pensive and then slowly shook her head.

'You are right, of course. I did make a mistake with Lizzie. I should never have involved her, but it's done and I can't go back, but I believe Lizzie is too small a fish for them to fry. It's Mister King who is the present danger. It is he they will be tracking.'

'And if he discovers something, Sparrow? If he begins to dig beyond the boundary fence, have you thought of the consequences?'

'We are not at war now, Bertram. Soldiers should not be sacrificed unnecessarily, most certainly not our own.'

'We can only control what happens in our own backyard. You know that,' he emphasized.

'Well, you are here with one of two options. To silence me permanently, or strike some sort of a deal...involving the photographer, perhaps?'

'Ahead of me as usual,' he mused in a defeatist manner.

'I refuse to kill Mister King, if that is the proposition.'

'It is not.'

A tension slowly mounted in the air around them.

'Oh!' exclaimed Martha. 'So that's it, is it? Play both sides of the coin?'

'What did you expect?' Bertram sighed. 'It might, at least, buy you a little time.'

Martha became restive.

'What do they want?' she asked.

'I believe they would like to know exactly what Nathan King knows and how much of that he told the Chinese.'

'One can't have two gods, Bertram.'

'You understand what you are telling me, Martha...?'

'Yes, I do,' she said calmly. 'Let the game begin...'

Bertram sat silent and devastated for this was one game he definitely did not wish to play.

CHAPTER TWENTY-THREE

THE CONNECTION

Nathan sat at Mrs Spontiak's kitchen table drinking coffee. The door opened. With a waft of fresh air a tall, amiable man, wearing a thick brown jacket and brown corduroy trousers entered. The man removed a brown baseball cap from his head, shook it and hung it on a hook. The presence of Nathan seemed to take him by surprise.

'Hi there! And who might you be?' he asked.

Nathan went to stand up and introduce himself but Mrs Spontiak beat him to it.

'Willoughby, this is Nathan King from England.'

Willoughby MacIntyre stepped forward and shook Nathan's hand.

'Well, you're most welcome. Willoughby MacIntyre from MacIntyre's Motor Repairs.'

'Willoughby's a neighbour and comes in for his breakfast,' Mrs Spontiak kindly explained. 'Kathleen, his late wife, was my best friend.'

'There's nothing to beat Nancy's maple syrup and waffles during a cold fall,' Willoughby assured him.

'It's bacon omelette this morning, Willoughby. At Nathan's request,' Mrs Spontiak replied.

'Bacon omelette? Well, I guess if you made it, it must be good,' he acquiesced, sitting himself down next to Nathan.

'Are you a relation of Nancy's?' Willoughby asked Nathan as Mrs Spontiak served their omelettes and sat down to join them.

'No…' Nathan hesitated.

'He's come on a personal matter, Willoughby. Mister King is a writer and he's interested in the ship David served on in the Second World War.'

Nathan felt thankful and relieved for Mrs Spontiak's discretion.

'Is that right?' mused Willoughby. 'Then you know who you should be talking to…?'

Mrs Spontiak looked at her neighbour with renewed interest.

'Ransom Digden's daughter. Now Ransom was the same as David – an American who moved here after the war. He knew David,' Willoughby explained.

'He *knew* David! I didn't know that, Willoughby,' Mrs Spontiak admonished him.

'Not well, you understand. Ransom was great friends with John Weizberg who, in turn, was a great friend of David's.'

'John was David's good friend who was killed soon after the American's joined the war,' Mrs Spontiak commented.

'That's true,' confirmed Willoughby.

'There's a photo of David in the living room, Willoughby. Do you know the name of that ship?' Nathan asked him.

'I've seen that photo. I reckon it might be the USS Roosevelt, but that wasn't David's ship because David was on the USS Colyton.'

'That's what I told him,' Mrs Spontiak affirmed.

'John Weizberg was on the USS Roosevelt which was torpedoed and Ransom served on the USS Colarous. Now, something happened to the Colarous one day in March 1944 and it lost contact with its fellow ships but it was discovered later miles from its original position and with only a handful of survivors. Ransom Digden was one of them but he was wounded and was in a military hospital for over a year before he was discharged.'

'What had happened to the ship?' asked Nathan keenly.

'Ah, well that's a strange thing because no one ever really knew the answer to that. The survivors were so badly beaten up and it affected their minds pretty bad. Ransom was never the same man when he returned home, I know that. The family had a pretty bad time with him. The American sailors who found the ship said it looked as if there had been a fire. There were a lot of charred bodies. Ransom is badly scarred himself.'

'Did they ever explain how the ship came to be so far from its position?' asked Nathan.

'Nope! There were rumours the captain had got confused where he was, instruments were damaged or wrong decisions were made. Nobody ever really got to the truth of the matter. This omelette is good, Nancy.'

'So where is Ransom's daughter now?' enquired Mrs Spontiak.

'She's over at Antigonish still. I could find her address for you. I know I have it somewhere.'

'Do that, Willoughby. I can take Nathan over there.'

'That's kind of you,' Nathan told Mrs Spontiak, then addressing Willoughby he asked, 'Do you rent out cars?'

'Not really, though, strangely enough, there was another English guy dropped in yesterday to ask if he could hire one. Is he a friend of yours?'

'No,' said Nathan.

'That's odd. Two English people here at once. What are the chances of that, Nancy? A million to one?'

'Probably,' she laughed but the laugh was uneasy.

'Did you loan him one?' asked Nathan.

'No, but I drove him over to Cape Breton to hire one. He got a red Dodge. Seemed a nice guy. Gave me a generous tip.'

'Did he give a name or tell you anything about himself?' asked Nathan.

'No, but if you two guys want to get together I could make enquiries over at Cape Breton. We might be able to track him down.'

'No. I'm not really interested,' Nathan lied. 'I was just making conversation.'

'Perhaps you could just find that address for us and drop it by later,' said Mrs Spontiak.

'I'll do that, Nancy,' he said. 'I'll sure do that.'

Willoughby was as good as his word. Shortly after leaving, he returned with a name, address and telephone number on a scrap of paper.

'There you go. I couldn't remember the daughter's name. It's Lorraine. Lorraine Scott. I sure hope she's of some help to you.'

Mrs Spontiak thanked him and he went on his way. Nathan wandered outside while Mrs Spontiak rang the number. There was a frost on the ground, a crisp freshness in the clean air and a sharp breeze that drifted in from across the water. Nathan breathed in deeply, filling his lungs. For a few moments he stood thinking before wandering down to the road. There was no sign of the red Dodge but Nathan had a feeling it would be around somewhere.

'Good news,' said Mrs Spontiak as he re-entered the house. 'Lorraine has invited us over for lunch. In the meantime, we'll pop over to Port Hawkesbury to get a copy of that photograph.'

As they left the house, Nathan spotted the red Dodge. A few minutes into the journey, Nathan glanced behind and saw it following them at a distance.

Lorraine Scott lived in a rundown old farmhouse. Two shaggy dogs greeted them and a Quarter horse roamed in the field outside. Lorraine came out of the house, pushing long fair hair away from her face and rebuking the dogs for getting under her feet.

'Hi! Come on in,' she said. 'It's good to see you.'

They shook hands and were invited into a shabby but homely dining room.

'Make yourself comfortable. I've got burgers and home-made cookies. Do you want tea or coffee?'

They both said coffee and Mrs Spontiak sat down at the table. Nathan went to the window and looked out but could not see the red Dodge, though he was sure it would not be far away.

Lorraine brought in the coffee and they settled around the table for lunch.

'So, your husband knew my dad, huh?' said Lorraine.

'Yes. I never realized that until Willoughby told me,' said Mrs Spontiak.

'Dad knew a lot of folk. I don't recall the name though, I'm sorry. Fact is, when dad came back from the war he was really different. I mean his personality had changed. He'd always been outgoing and friendly and this guy who came back…I don't know, he just wasn't like my dad anymore. He was very short-tempered and yet he'd always been a very patient guy. Then there were his dark days, as mom would call them, when he'd just lock himself away in his room and wouldn't talk to anyone. He had nightmares too. We don't know what about. He never spoke to us about them but I would hear him calling out in his sleep.'

'Could you make out what he was saying?' asked Nathan.

'Sometimes. Most of the time it was just nonsense. "God help us", he would scream sometimes and "What's happening?" That's all I remember.'

'I believe there was some sort of incident on your father's ship. A fire?' queried Nathan.

'I don't really know what happened. The ship was charred, I know that. We asked dad what had gone on but he wouldn't say, he'd just shake his head and walk away from us. Whatever happened to him must have been terrifying because it changed him completely. I believe there was some kind of an explosion on the ship because most of the crew were killed and others, like dad, suffered burns, but like I said, he would never talk about it.'

'It must have been very difficult for you and your mother to cope with,' Nathan sympathised.

'It wasn't easy. When I got together with Eddie, my late husband, he took to trying to find out more about that incident. Boy! Did he rattle a few official cages! He believed dad should be entitled to some compensation for what happened. Eddie always believed it was an accident of negligence on the ship like faulty wiring or something. He did a lot of research. He even found out what happened to that ship after it was decommissioned.'

'What *did* happen to it?' asked Nathan, leaning forward eagerly.

'It was sold to the Greek navy. They changed the name to the HS Kakodaimon. It seems that comes from a Greek word meaning bad spirit, or something like that.'

'Did Eddie ever get to see the ship?' enquired Mrs Spontiak.

'Oh yeah! He gave the right guys a fistful of drachmas and got aboard. Eddie convinced them he was a naval historian. One of the crew told him when the ship was revamped the marine engineers found extra wiring that served no logical purpose. It just made no sense at all why it was there.'

'That's why Eddie thought faulty wiring had caused a fire?' suggested Nathan.

'That's right.'

'You said your *late* husband,' observed Nathan. 'What happened to Eddie?'

'He was killed in a road accident. In summer he was a lumberjack. In the winter he'd go to Alaska as a trucker. I guess you can imagine what the roads are like there in winter, but that's why the dollars were good. He could earn megabucks.'

'But he had an accident?' pressed Nathan.

'Yeah. It happens. Especially at night. He knew the risks. The truck ran off the road. It's easy to do with the ice. One misjudgement is all it takes. Then again, he might have swerved to avoid something. Some sort of animal may have surprised him. They said he bled to death before another trucker came across him.'

Mrs Spontiak made sympathetic noises but Nathan remained silent, visioning a trucker who had become a problem to the authorities driving on a lonely, icy road one dark night.

There was a lot more talk that afternoon but nothing that threw any further light on what had happened to David Spontiak. After a couple of hours they bid Lorraine farewell and went on their way. Although there had been no sign of the red Dodge, about a mile from Lorraine's, once again, Nathan noticed it following them from a distance.

As soon as they arrived back at Mrs Spontiak's, Nathan discreetly unscrewed the bottom part of the telephone receiver and replaced it again before making enquiries about his flight home. Directly after that he made another phone call to an old friend. The voice that answered sounded prim and a little tired.

'What's up, Joan? Have a bad night?' asked Nathan.

The tone immediately changed to a lighter and more cheerful note.

'Nathan! I thought you'd forgotten about me.'

'Never. Listen, I'm calling from Canada so could I have a quick word with Leo?'

'Yes. I'll get him for you. Hold on.'

'Nathan?' The voice was loud and brisk.

'Leo! It's good to hear your voice. Listen, there's some information I need you to get for me.'

'Shoot!'

'Two American navy vessels: The USS Colarous and the USS Colyton, both circa 1944. I need to know their history and exactly what happened to them.'

'What's this for, Nathan?' asked Leo.

'It's a long story. When I get home, we'll have dinner and I'll tell you about it. Hell, I need to talk this through with someone.'

'Well, my guess would be, if they survived the war, they've both been decommissioned. Probably gone for scrap.'

'I believe the Colarous was sold to Greece and became the HS Kakodaimon. It's very important, Leo. I need to know anything you can find out about them.'

'OK. You know me. Give a terrier a bone....'

'Yes, I know,' laughed Nathan.

'Do you want me to call you where you are? It might take a while to find the information.'

'No, don't call me at all. Wait until I call you. That's important too.'

'Nathan, you're not in any kind of trouble are you?'

There was just a moment's hesitation.

'Oh hell! You are. What is it this time?'

'I'll call you, Leo. Just try and get the information for me, would you?'

'I will...and Nathan...be careful.'

There was a click as the receiver went down the other end. Nathan remained pensive then he checked his watch.

CHAPTER TWENTY-FOUR

THE HIT

Rene stood halfway down the stairs that led from the nightclub to her private flat. The steady throbbing of the music accompanied the light globes that highlighted various members on the dance floor with ever-changing colours. Sipping a gin and tonic she pushed an untidy straggle of hair back into her French roll and watched Danny and Liz interacting. A smile crossed her lips as she saw them laughing, joking and teasing the punters. It was just like old times, except Danny's hair was getting a bit thinner on top and Liz, when away from the bar, had been distracted for the last couple of nights.

The strident ringing of the telephone disturbed the memories and she wandered back upstairs to answer it. The voice the other end was steady and subdued.

'Hello? Is Liz there, please?'

A man asking for Liz was unusual and Rene hesitated for a moment.

'Who is it calling?' she asked.

'Nathan King.'

'Hold the line,' she told him.

Walking back down the stairs she caught Danny's attention and pointed to Liz. Danny tapped Liz on the arm and pointed to Rene on the stairs holding her hand up to her ear as if she were holding a receiver. Liz nodded and said something to Danny then pushed her way through the throng to the stairs.

'It's someone called Nathan King,' said Rene.

'Oh! It might be about Rich,' said Liz.

Rene left Liz alone in the sitting room and went to make herself a coffee. Liz grabbed the receiver.

'Hello! Nathan?'

'How's it going, Liz? Any word from Rich yet?'

Liz's heart sank.

'No. I thought perhaps you'd got some news,' she said.

'No, sorry. I'm still in Canada, though I'll shortly be leaving for the airport. I think I'm making some progress but things aren't very clear just yet. Did you do the thing I asked you to do?'

'Yes, I did,' she replied.

'Thanks Liz. I'll be in contact when I get back and you can tell me exactly where this Martha Kemp lives. I really need to speak to her.'

'OK. Nathan, do you think whatever you've got yourself involved in does have something to do with Rich?'

'It's too early to say, but it's a possibility. Certainly, this Martha must have had a reason for thinking so. Liz, someone appears to be tailing me out here. Have you noticed anyone following you or hanging around your place?' he asked.

Liz thought but answered in the negative.

'Good, but keep an eye out for that, will you?'

'Why would anyone follow me?' she asked.

'They probably wouldn't. It's just that you've been in contact with me so...anyway, just stay alert.'

'OK. I could go and see Martha tomorrow and tell her you'd like to see her,' she told him.

'Thanks...and look after yourself, Liz Stone.'

Although she could not see him, she knew there was a smile on his face as he said those last words. The line went dead and as Liz replaced the receiver she turned and saw Rene standing in the doorway holding a cup of coffee.

'Is everything all right?' Rene asked her.

Liz sighed.

'I think so.'

'Liz, this man isn't bothering you, is he? Just say the word and I'll...'

'No. No, he's trying to help me with something.'

Rene entered the room, placed her coffee on a table and went and put her arms around Liz.

'If you've got a problem, you know me or Danny will sort it for you. You know that.'

Liz clung on to her, feeling the warmth of her body and the subtle odour of her perfume. Long ago, her mum had held her in the same protective way and for the first time, in a long while, she missed her acutely.

'Liz, you know I'm one to respect a person's privacy but I can see something's dragging you down and I want to help. Do you owe this man money?' Rene asked her, loosening her hold and carefully studying Liz's face.

'No. It's nothing like that. I think something may have happened to my mate, Rich.'

'The one in the army?'

'Yeah. He was posted somewhere but it was all hush-hush. He was scared and wanted out. He decided to go AWOL but he needed money so I left it in the graveyard for him but he never collected it.'

'Ah! That was the two-hundred pounds you asked me for?'

'Yeah,' nodded Liz. 'I'm sorry. I couldn't tell you at the time. Anyway, then the army said he had gone to Northern Ireland but if it was secret, why did they tell me? I know something's wrong. Rich would have contacted me. He wouldn't have just left the money there. I don't know, Rene. Something's just not right.'

'So who was this chap on the phone?'

'He's someone Martha Kemp told me to contact.'

'Martha Kemp! So, who is he? An army man? A private eye? What?'

'He's a photographer but he's looking into something he can't tell me about and Martha thinks it could have something to do with what's happened to Rich.'

'Liz, look at me,' said Rene.

Liz raised her eyes.

'Whatever's happened to Rich,' Rene told her, 'he's big enough to look after himself. As for this Nathan King, I'd keep well clear of him.'

'Nathan's all right, Rene, honest. He's walked into some sort of a situation and he's just trying to find out what. His telephone was bugged and now he says someone's following him.'

'Hell, Liz! You can't go getting involved with people like that. You don't know what you're getting into. Promise me you'll keep away from this Nathan King. He's bad news, trust me.'

'He isn't bad.'

165

'Maybe not, but he's somehow got himself involved with bad people and that's good enough for me. As for Martha Kemp, you know what they say about her...'

'What?' Liz snapped. 'What do they say about her?'

'She helped the French Resistance during the war. She's no innocent little spinster. She's taken a few people out in her time, believe me.'

'How do you know? What would you know about Martha?'

There was a short silence then Liz said, 'Oh, I forgot. Your old profession. Did you sleep with someone from the Ministry?'

Rene winced at the mention of her old profession. Liz pulled herself away and stood staring out of the window. Rene secretly cursed herself for being clumsy. Putting a hand on Liz's shoulder she said tenderly, 'Don't be mad with me, Liz. She would have been eighteen, you know, today.'

Liz turned round and saw the glint of tears in Rene's eyes.

'I'm sorry, Rene. I didn't realize.'

Rene stroked Liz's short fringe back from her forehead.

'I often wonder...you know...what she'd have looked like.'

Liz remained silent, feeling her pain.

'I sometimes wonder if it was a punishment for the lifestyle I led,' Rene confessed.

'No,' Liz admonished her. 'No Rene. You're a *good* person.'

'Am I?' she asked, 'or am I just a bitch playing at being good?'

The tone was acerbic. Liz kissed her on the cheek.

'You're a good person, Rene. Don't ever believe any different,' said Liz and with that final remark she made her way back downstairs to the bar.

Rene left the coffee, picked up the gin and tonic and let it slip down in one gulp then she took a deep breath and stood with her eyes closed.

'Rene?'

Rene opened her eyes and turned to face Danny standing in front of her in black trousers and open pink shirt with a dolphin medallion displayed on his chest.

'Are you OK?' he asked.

'Shouldn't you be at the bar?'

'Liz has relieved me for a while – she thought you might need some company.'

Stepping forward he clasped her in his arms and kissed her head.

'I know what day it is, you know. I hadn't forgotten.'

Releasing her he said, 'Shall I get you another one of those?'

Rene stared at the empty glass and itched to throw it against the wall, but instead she put it down on the table and shook her head.

'I'm worried about Liz. She's got herself into something.'

'Then we'll get her out of it,' he smiled, splaying his hands.

Rene wished she could share his eternal optimism. Danny had always been that way, right from young. Something would always turn up. Everything could be fixed.

'It's a bit more complicated than that.'

'Tell me. I'll sort it,' he said simply.

'It isn't my place. If she wants to tell you, she will. I'm fine. Best get back to the bar, it's a busy night.'

Danny gave a salute and marched out of the door, doing a funny little tap-dance on the way. Rene allowed herself a smile then went to retrieve the coffee but it was cold. Pulling a face, she went to the kitchen to throw it away.

At midnight Liz poked her head behind the sitting room door. Rene was stretched out on the settee in front of the television.

'I'm going home, Rene. Danny said he can manage on his own now.'

'Why don't you stay here tonight?' Rene invited.

'I need to go somewhere in the morning. I'll see you tomorrow.'

'All right, darling. Take care,' said Rene.

The door closed and Rene stretched and got up from the settee to wander across to the window. In the drizzle, beneath the street light, the slight figure of Liz appeared standing at the side of the road doing up the buttons of her jacket. Liz's red Mini was parked opposite. Rene watched her as she crossed the road. It came out of nowhere. One second the road was clear, the next the bonnet of the grey Vauxhall Cavalier hit Liz and sent her flying into the air like a rag doll doing a somersault. Rene gazed in horror as the slight figure bounced off the car roof and hit the tarmac. The car roared away into the night. A cold surge swept up Rene's body from her feet to her head as with trembling legs and shaking hands she somehow managed to run from the room and scream into the nightclub below.

'Danny! Danny!'

Danny looked up at the frantic image of his sister half-running, half-falling down the staircase. Danny dropped everything and ran after her out onto the street. A gush of cold, damp air hit him and he stopped suddenly as he saw Rene kneeling in the road. Horrified, he stepped forward, as if in a dream, barely able to take in the sight of the tragic, broken figure stretched out awkwardly on the shiny, wet tarmac. Then he saw it was Liz's head Rene was cradling in her hands.

'Oh, God help us!' he whispered.

Danny knelt down by Rene and saw the blood covering her hands. Staring into Liz's open eyes and ashen face he felt just under her jawbone for a pulse. There wasn't one. A number of people had now emerged from the club and stood staring on the pavement.

'Call an ambulance!' Danny shouted at them. 'For pity's sake, call an ambulance!'

Danny then took one of the limp hands into his own to feel for a pulse at the wrist. Gently he placed it back down. Placing a hand on his sister's shoulder his voice broke as he uttered the words, 'She's gone, Rene'.

Rene looked at him, gasping, choking back the tears that were threatening to emerge in a gush of grief and despair.

'It didn't stop, Danny,' she blurted out. 'It didn't stop!'

'What?'

'The car. It didn't...' but she could say no more. Liz's cheek felt ice cold against her palm. As Rene saw the pool of blood that was now seeping into the wet tarmac she felt as if something deep inside was sliding away from her, leaving a cold, dead hollow where warmth and life had once been. Losing Liz felt like another stillbirth.

Danny stood silent, gazing into the darkness outside the window. Rene sat shivering on the settee, a mug of cocoa and brandy clasped in her trembling hands. Noticing a spot of Liz's blood she had failed to wipe off on her wrist, she broke again, her whole body shaking, her chest aching with the emotional pain that was tearing through her. Danny knew what was happening but he could not turn round and comfort his sister for his own tears were running down his cheeks and it was all he could manage to hold it all together and not collapse with her.

After some moments, Rene managed to contain herself.

'She died on her birthday,' she announced.

'What?' he asked and his voice sounded distant and lonely.

'My daughter,' she whispered and the words sounded strange for it was the first time she had given the child her proper title. 'Liz died on Angela's birthday.'

Danny remained silent.

'Hell, Danny! What kind of evil, cold-hearted swine just drives off and…'

'What kind of trouble?'

'Sorry? What?' she asked.

'You said Liz had got herself into something. You wouldn't tell me. Well, she can't tell me now, can she? So you tell me.'

'It was something to do with her friend, Richard: the one in the army.'

'I know. What about him?'

'He'd planned to go AWOL or something and now he's missing, or Liz thought he was missing. The army said he was in Northern Ireland but Liz said he was supposed to be going on a confidential mission. Martha Kemp told her to contact this chap who rang tonight. Oh, what was his name…? King. Nathan King.'

'Do you think he could have been in that car?'

'No! She said he was trying to help her. She said this chap had accidentally got caught up in something and he was trying to find out what and Martha Kemp thought Richard's whereabouts might have something to do with what this chap was caught up in and I've got a bloody awful headache and she's dead, Danny! She's dead!'

Danny turned and rushed to his sister's side. Putting an arm around her, he whispered, 'We should have mentioned it to the police'.

'No! No, first, I need to see Martha Kemp to find out what it was all about.'

Danny held Rene close, realizing it was not just Liz she was grieving for but also the baby daughter she lost all those years ago.

CHAPTER TWENTY-FIVE

A DONE DEED

Martha saw the headline as she passed the Post Office in Masterton village. Immediately she entered and purchased a local newspaper. Sweeping her eyes along the print beneath the headline "WOMAN KILLED BY HIT AND RUN" the name Elizabeth Stone jumped out at her like a blade slicing her stomach. Martha calmly folded the paper and walked swiftly towards home. There was no time for sentiment – that would come later. Right now, there were plans to be made and she did not have much time.

Bertram stood staring at the bright pink roses he had purchased for Martha. It would be the last bunch he would ever present to her. The time limit was at its end and his mission could be delayed no longer. With a weary heart and a deep breath he got into his Rover and placed the flowers carefully on the passenger seat. In life, he thought to himself, one makes many journeys, some sad, some pleasurable. This would be the saddest journey he would ever make.

The kitchen clock ticked away each minute. It had just turned 6.00p.m. when the lambent light from The Foresters outlined a figure at the gate.

Bertram undid the latch of the gate and walked the path to Martha's door. A light was on in the kitchen. Through the red and white chequered curtains he could see a Welsh dresser and a cooker. Bertram rang the bell and waited. The cottage door opened and there she was, her eyes alight, her expression one of surprise.

'Bertram!'

'Hello, dear Sparrow! May I come in?'

'Yes, of course,' she said and as he went to hand her the roses she reached up and kissed his cheek.

Bertram retracted suddenly.

'Damn,' he uttered. 'The roses pricked me.'

'They're beautiful,' she told him. 'You never forget, do you?'

They entered the kitchen. Bertram stood awkwardly by the doorway. Martha looked at him questioningly.

'Won't you sit down, Bertram?' she proffered as she found a vase and half filled it with water.

'Yes, yes I suppose I should,' he muttered.

Removing a brown trilby hat, he placed it on the kitchen table but kept the cream raincoat on.

Martha undid the roses and placed them carefully in the vase, being careful of the thorns.

'I'd like to say this is a pleasant surprise,' she said.

Bertram pulled out a chair and sat down. There was a frown on his forehead and a haggard expression on his face. Martha sat opposite him and placed a hand on his.

'It's all right, Bertram. I know why you are here. It was kind of you to offer to be the one to dispatch me.'

Bertram leaned back in the chair, a look of pure anguish on his face. Martha laughed.

'Goodness, Bertram, don't look so peaked about it. Don't you think I knew the danger before I even contacted you?'

'Sparrow…I…' but he could not find the words.

Martha leaned forward and looked deeply into his eyes.

'Bertram, I'm ready to go. Growing old was never for me. Life is starting to become frustrating. I can't manage to do all the things I want to do. I can't make a difference any more. The younger generation must take up the cause. This body has been good to me but it's starting to falter now…to let me down.'

His eyes looked sadly into hers. Martha continued.

'Lying in some hospital bed amongst strangers with tubes stuck in every crevice. Is that what you would wish for me? No, Bertram. I was never meant to go that way. In your heart you know that. I was always meant to go out with a bang. Don't ever despise yourself for this duty for, truly, I believe it is the bravest thing you have ever done…and the kindest.'

'Sparrow…dear Sparrow…' he shook his head.

'Your mind is arguing with your heart, Bertram,' she told him, 'and that will never do. I never allowed my heart to get in the way. There is just one thing you could do for me.'

Bertram looked at her, his features contorted with the inner struggle that he was feeling.

'Anything,' he told her.

'It's a very long time since I went into a public house with a handsome man on my arm to enjoy a gin and tonic,' she smiled. 'One last drink together?'

Bertram smiled back, placed his trilby back on his head, stood up and offered his arm.

'I'll just get my coat and bag,' she told him.

'Where to?' he enquired when she was ready.

'We could go to The White Horse. It's just beyond the village. It's much quieter there. The village pubs get so crowded.'

'As you wish, Sparrow,' he said quietly.

Martha sat by the window in the far oak settle of The White Horse. It was a quaint, little, Dickensian type pub. The settles allowed privacy while some small round tables in the public area were already filled.

Bertram joined her moments later and placed a gin and tonic in front of her. Removing his raincoat, he eased himself into the settle opposite and sipped a whisky on ice. They talked of old times and old acquaintances, never mentioning the here and now that had no place in their intimacy. After thirty minutes had gone by, Bertram slipped his raincoat back on.

'Are we going so soon, Bertram?' enquired Martha.

'No, no, my dear. Just a bit cold that's all,' he assured her.

'Perhaps I have been selfish, Bertram, in requesting this outing. It would have been easier for you to get things over with quickly.'

Bertram smiled benignly at her.

'No. I'm happy that I have given you your wish,' he said reassuringly.

They continued to make conversation, though Bertram's voice had begun to slow and he could not somehow always find the words that he sought to speak. A little while later he began to look pale.

'I don't feel very well, Sparrow,' he said at last.

'No. I don't suppose you do, Bertram,' she replied.

172

Bertram sat looking at her, the slowness of his mind desperately trying to grasp what was happening and then his eyes widened with the dawn of understanding.

'Sparrow,' he smiled, 'you were always ahead of me. I should have known.'

Martha nodded slowly.

'But…it can't have been the drink. How…?'

Martha leaned forward and whispered.

'The prick was not a rose thorn.'

'Ah!' he uttered. 'A poison dart…curare perhaps or…ah, yes, of course' he slurred. 'Clever Sparrow. I taught you far too well.'

'You forgot the ultimate rule. Never let your guard down. It will have all the symptoms of a heart attack, Bertram. It will not be too painful. I'm so sorry, but you know, I always was a survivor. I will choose my time, not TIDI.'

Martha put on her coat, leaned across and kissed him tenderly on the forehead. While doing so she slid her hand into his inner breast pocket and removed the small, discreet gun that was standard issue.

'I have to go now, Bertram,' she said, concealing the gun inside her handbag. 'At least you will die with a drink in your hand. There are worse ways to go.'

Bertram watched as her trim figure turned and walked away from him for the last time. Once more, it seemed as if he were back on the Embankment with the Thames flowing past, a fine breeze stroking his face and the woman he had always loved walking away from him as if in a dream. Leaning backwards, with that last image in his mind, Bertram smiled his last smile.

The taxi was waiting for Martha as she left the pub. As always, her timing had been perfect. Tears glistening in the corner of her eyes, she took a deep breath and raised her chin before she climbed into it.

'I need to pop home and pick up some things,' she told the driver. 'It's just in the village. Then we'll be on our way.'

CHAPTER TWENTY-SIX

MEETINGS OLD AND NEW

Stanley Hoffman sat in his new lodgings in Ruislip and idly turned the pages of the newspaper. As usual he checked a particular column to see if he recognized any messages going back and forth amongst old acquaintances. Stanley's heart suddenly missed a beat. The words flashed out at him from the paper: Mt 1510. 7Red. Stanley sat staring for some time. It had to be her. Why though? It had to be a trap and yet...

For some hours Stanley turned things over in his mind until, at last, he left his lodgings to go for a walk to the local station. It was there he found information on trains to Brighton.

It had changed. It had all changed so much. The building still bore a faint resemblance, though it was now a fashionable restaurant, but the frontage had altered dramatically. Casting his mind back, he saw Martha as she used to be all those years ago when they would come to the casino to gamble away some of their earnings and have a laugh and a drink. Those social meetings had always proved to be a pleasant relief from the intensity of their daily work. As he stood gazing; remembering, there was a tap on his shoulder that made him start and turn fearfully, but there she was, dressed in a grey suit with a warm smile on her face.

'Stanley!' she gasped, offering her hand and he took it into his own and shook it warmly.

'Martha.'

'I often wondered if you were still alive. I believe they suspect that you are.'

'Yes,' he said. 'They killed Joseph Veldman.'

'I know. They dispatched a friend of mine too.'

'One of ours?' he asked.

'No. That was the despicable part of it. The straw that broke the camel's back, so to speak.'

'The old place has changed. No seven red today,' he smiled, 'always your favourite bet.'

'And it's closed. Let's go down to the front. No one's followed you, I take it?'

'No. I'm positive,' he replied.

'Yes, I was watching from a distance for some time. I believe we are safe. How about fish and chips on the pier?'

Martha slid her arm through his and they began to walk.

They sat on a pier bench, braving the nippy breeze and listening to the waves splashing beneath them.

'So, who are you now, Stanley?'

'Sidney Roche,' he told her.

'Shall we continue in that format?'

'No, please. Call me Stanley. It will sound good to have someone call me by my true name again. I've missed it,' he replied ruefully.

'You must have missed so many things,' she sighed.

In that one sentence she had summed up her complete understanding of his situation. There was nothing he need tell Martha about those "lost"' years. Martha *knew*. Their lives had been so totally different from other people's. Isolated, exceptional and secretive, they had been members of a very small and elite club.

'It's been resurrected,' he told her.

'Yes. I know. I'm afraid I've had to kill Bertram.'

The words were stated so coldly and factually, Stanley suddenly felt a sliver of ice run the length of his spine and he turned quickly to look at her.

'Bertram Tanner! But…'

'Oh, don't look at me like that, Stanley. I had to. They'd sent him to finish me. It had to be one of us, so it had to be him.'

'How did you get involved?' he enquired.

'I saw something I shouldn't have and began to ask questions. Stupidly, perhaps, I would not let it drop.'

'I see,' he pondered.

'I thought if you were alive you might not meet me,' she said.

'I was suspicious,' he admitted.

175

'You'd have been a fool not to have been, but I have no connection with them, Stanley. I refused to play their game. That's why they want to get rid of me.'

Stanley reflected. The younger Martha he knew had always played it straight down the line and he had no reason to believe she had changed.

'Why did you want to meet me?' he asked.

'Because I don't like what's going on and you are the only other person I can talk to about it.'

'I went to Joseph for the same reason,' he admitted.

'They are using our own,' Martha said with a hiss and the venom in her tone was not lost on Stanley.

'I see.'

An empathic silence sat between them for some time before Stanley asked, 'How did you find out about the project? Not now. I mean, all those years ago?'

'By chance. I picked up on a message I was not supposed to hear. A crossed line, so to speak. I became intrigued and gained access to TIDI information by devious means, I'm afraid. The knowledge was little and erratic but I began to piece things together, as one does.'

'To be honest, I thought you had slept with the Number One,' said Stanley matter-of-factly.

Martha laughed.

'I never had to get my information that way.'

'You were such a brilliant agent,' Stanley sighed. 'You were held in very high esteem. Most were in awe of you.'

'Really?' she said in genuine amazement. 'I never realized that,' she said quietly. 'There were so many of us…'

'You stood out,' he assured her. 'Your reputation was second to none, especially when…' he stopped short, realizing what he had been about to say and the emotions it might stir up.

Martha put a hand on his.

'It's all right, Stanley. No need to feel awkward about it. It was my duty and I went through with it. That is all.'

'And what now?' asked Stanley.

'I believe we should try to make contact with a Nathan King. Have you heard of him?'

'Yes, I have' said Stanley. 'Joseph Veldman mentioned him.'

'He's a professional photographer, but he visited the Tibetan square mile.'

'Yes. Do you think it could be something to do with Price?' he whispered excitedly. 'Do you think he found a lead on Price?'

'I'm not sure, but he found something, otherwise they wouldn't be so worked up about it. We have to know what that was; it could be very useful to us.'

'Joseph mentioned they suspected the monks knew something of Price. They could have been exterminated. King may have seen something, even photographed something.'

'I wonder ...?' she mused. 'They will kill him eventually, of course. We need to make contact with him first. As officially TIDI does not exist, we need proof of what we know and Nathan King might just have that proof, or at least a way to find it.'

'Then we need to contact him at once,' urged Stanley.

'It's difficult as he's being marked. The phone will be tapped for sure and his house will be watched. We can't risk a posted note either. If, as I suspect, they've placed a bug they will be accessing his property in his absence.'

'Does he have a workplace where we could contact him?'

'Too risky.'

'Then what?' he enquired.

Martha contemplated for some time.

'I fear direct action could be the only way.'

'What do you mean?' asked Stanley with some unease.

'Leave it to me,' said Martha. 'First, we have some shopping to do and we must see about hiring a car.'

'Martha…do you think there is some way we could end it?'

'All things come to an end, Stanley' she reminded him. 'It's just in this case we must be very careful how we do it. There is a thin line between morality and treachery and Britain must always come first.'

Stanley continued to eat his chips feeling a huge sense of relief he now had an ally he could share this awful existence with, stifled by the fact that the difficult road he had trodden for so long may, after all, reach an unpleasant end. Ahead was his destiny, a culmination of all that he had endured over the years, now waiting for him just around the corner. It was a fearful thought.

After a short drive, Stanley and Martha arrived at a cottage she had hired under a false name. Once inside, Martha put the kettle on while Stanley emptied the contents of a carrier bag onto the table. Martha poured the tea and set a cup down in front of Stanley. They sat in silence for a few moments, sipping the hot beverage, both lost in their own thoughts until Martha spoke.

'I don't know it all, Stanley,' she informed him, leaning forward keenly. 'I want you to fill in some gaps...'

Rene sat in front of the mirror attempting to apply eye shadow and wiping it off again. At the third attempt, she applied it successfully. Everything seemed too much trouble lately and her hands were still unsteady for she had not stopped trembling since the accident. Accident? Rene saw it in continual replay, during the day and in her dreams at night: The bonnet of a grey car and Liz, like a rag doll, flying through the air and crashing onto the hard, cold tarmac.

The door opened causing her to jump and throw her hand up to her chest.

'Are you all right?'

It was Danny, pale and thin in the face. Neither of them had eaten much since the night they had cradled Liz's body.

'Yes, I'm fine,' she lied.

'Are you sure you don't want me to come with you?' he asked.

'I'll be fine, Danny. I'm looking forward to having this out with Martha Kemp.'

There was an icy bitterness in her voice, so full of loathing and contempt that Danny hardly recognized it.

'OK,' he said, 'just take care.'

The door closed, Rene took a final look in the mirror, drew in a deep breath, blew it out slowly then went to get her coat.

Rene felt frustration and anger. There had been no response to her banging at the door of Martha Kemp's cottage so she went to the back of the cottage to peer in at the windows. It was tidy but seemed deserted. There was no sign of Martha Kemp. Going back to the front door, Rene bashed at it with her fists and kept banging until the tears began to flow down her cheeks and she slid down, crushed and exhausted, onto the doorstep.

The nightclub was already beginning to fill up. Rene was only vaguely aware of the thumping vibration coming from downstairs as she sat sipping a vodka and lime. Gazing motionless into the glass, her reverie was interrupted by a knock on the door and Tony entering. Rene glanced up at the thin frame with page-boy haircut and glasses.

'What is it?' she asked.

'There's a man downstairs asking for Liz. Says his name is Nathan King,' Tony announced.

Rene's stomach turned. Placing her drink down on the table she stood up, raised her chin and steeled herself.

'Send him up to me,' she said in an icy tone.

Tony nodded and disappeared. Rene walked slowly towards the door as she heard the footsteps on the stairs. The man appeared at the doorway and entered. Holding out his hand he smiled as he said, 'Hello, Rene? I'm Nathan King...'

The glancing blow she dealt him knocked him backwards against the wall. Nathan felt himself losing balance then going down with a stinging pain in his jaw. Momentarily dazed and confused he struggled to his feet, rubbing his throbbing jawbone.

'I know who you are, you swine!' she spat, her face set like a chiselled sculpture.

'Whoa lady! You sure pack a punch!' he stated, holding up a hand. 'Just em...calm down.'

'Don't you dare patronize me,' she warned him.

Nathan stepped further away from her, his back to the wall.

'Perhaps you could at least tell me what that was for...?' he suggested.

For a moment, Rene stood fuming, her nostrils dilating like a bull about to charge, then she shouted, 'Liz is dead!' and the sound seemed to reverberate all around the room and settle into an icy silence.

Nathan stood watching her, allowing the words to sink in.

'Liz? She's dead?'

'And it's all your damn fault!' she pointed an accusing finger at him. 'I told her not to get involved with you, but she confided in me too late. Why did you have to…why did you…?'

The words shuddered and crackled and she remained standing proud and defiant with tears running down her cheeks, leaving streams of black mascara.

'How?' Nathan asked her.

'A car.'

Nathan waited.

'It just…hit her and didn't stop,' sniffed Rene. 'I cradled her head in my hands. I felt her blood seeping away…'

The woman was fraught and Nathan found it hard not to be affected as his mind returned to the young woman on his doorstep.

'I'm so sorry,' he said sincerely.

'Huh!' she mocked. 'You're sorry. Oh well, that's all right then.'

'Did anyone see the car?' he enquired.

'*I* saw it,' she said.

'What sort of car was it?' he asked.

'A grey Vauxhall Cavalier.'

A memory flickered in the back of Nathan's mind and he forced it to come forward. Something about the expression on his face made Rene temporarily forget her anger.

'What is it?' she asked.

'There was a grey Cavalier in the lane the night Liz visited me. There was Liz's red car and further down, the grey Cavalier. It's unusual for there to be any cars there. It's a quiet lane. I didn't think anything of it at the time.'

'What did you get Liz into?' Rene demanded.

'I didn't. *Liz* approached *me*. She said a Martha Kemp had given her my name because she thought I might be able to help her find an army friend. I don't know this Martha Kemp and I don't know how she knew me, but she seemed to know my whereabouts and what had happened to me recently.'

'Martha Kemp has gone,' Rene smiled sardonically.

'Gone? Gone where?'

Rene shrugged.

'I went round there this morning and again this afternoon and Danny went round there tonight. The place is empty. Like a rat that's gone to ground, eh?'

'Damn!' cursed Nathan. 'I came to find her,' he said.

'Then you're too late. You're too late for Martha Kemp and you're certainly too late for Liz,' she added caustically.

Wandering back across the room, Rene picked up her vodka and lime and let the remaining liquid slip down her throat.

'Where could this Martha Kemp have gone?' muttered Nathan, more to himself than Rene.

'I don't care. I only hope the old witch is dead,' she said defiantly.

'My guess is that she is and I'm probably next on the list,' he replied.

'I don't understand any of this,' Rene said in a tone of defeat. 'I don't understand who you are or why Martha Kemp would send Liz to you or why Liz had to die.'

Rene slumped down in a chair. 'Hell! What a devil of a week!'

'She was a nice kid,' Nathan said quietly.

Rene looked at him.

'Yes, she was.'

There was a short silence and then Nathan spoke one word.

'Richard.'

'What about him?' Rene asked.

'Richard is the key to all this. I have to find Richard.'

'I don't care what you do,' said Rene.

Nathan looked at her long and hard.

'The people who want to kill me are the same people who killed Liz. That was no accident, but you already know that don't you?'

Rene raised her head and looked him straight in the eyes.

'What do you want from me?' she asked.

'There's nothing you can do,' he told her, 'but I'll give you a number. If Richard happens to get in touch, find out exactly where he is and let me know will you?'

Rene did not answer him.

'Or if you ever need to contact me…'

Nathan took a pen from his pocket and wrote the number on a magazine that was on the table.

'Is this your home number?' Rene asked suspiciously.

'No. I believe someone's been listening in on my calls. The number belongs to Leo, a friend of mine. If you ring him I'll be able to pick up the message. Just phrase your words carefully if you call and you'd be wise to make sure someone's in your flat at all times. Someone managed to get access to my phone when I was out.'

Nathan walked towards the door.

'You should never have involved her,' Rene called after him.

Nathan turned.

'It was Martha Kemp who involved her. By the time Liz came to me, it was already too late.'

Taking one final look at the broken woman in the chair, he quietly closed the door behind him.

CHAPTER TWENTY-SEVEN

A PROBLEM SHARED

A desk light shone in the dimness of the room. Bookcases appeared as set shadows in the gloom, frozen in sleep until the wakening light of morning. A lone figure sat crouched over the desktop gazing mesmerized at the open pages before him. Odd calculations, mysterious signs, Latin phrases, maps with figures and lines, dates that seemed to have no particular meaning and yet…

Leaning backwards and stretching his neck Professor Elling, once again, picked up the note that had accompanied the mysterious package:

> Jeremy,
>
> I am entrusting the enclosed to your safe keeping. Show it to no one. I have found myself caught in the middle of something both dangerous and unidentified.
>
> Please don't contact me. I will contact you when it is safe to do so.
>
> The contents mean nothing to me but by their very nature I believe they may make some sense to you. I'm relying on that infiltrating brain of yours to fathom it! It could be the key to everything.
>
> Take care. We'll meet soon.
>
> Nathan King

Professor Elling remained staring at the signature. By the nature of his job Nathan King was no stranger to dangerous situations, but there was something so terse in the tone of this message that Elling felt the unspoken urgency behind the written word.

Elling closed his eyes and attempted to clear his mind. If he studied them long enough the pages would open their secrets to him, of that he was sure. Time was enough. One could not rush the calculus of such configurations. To the casual observer this random display of words, drawings and figures would mean nothing at all, but to the educated, to the mind that leant itself to such matters, the scruffy A4 exercise book with its intriguing contents would first magnetize, then tease, then begin to reveal. To Elling, the enigma was a challenge and he would conquer it.

The clock in the study chimed midnight and the professor sighed. Closing the book, he switched off the lamp and retired to bed. A tired brain was of no use so he would take a fresh look at it in the morning.

'So what's the story?' asked Nathan as Leo pondered the lunch menu in the East of Bombay restaurant.

'Flaming hell! Have you seen the prices here?' asked Leo.

'It's my treat,' Nathan reminded him.

'Joan would have enjoyed this,' admonished Leo. 'I think it was mean of you not to invite her.'

'It was for her own good,' Nathan told him.

'If you say so. I think I'll have the chicken tikka.'

'Leo,' Nathan urgently whispered. 'The Colarous?'

'Hmm?' Leo mused, replacing the menu carefully on the table. 'We've got plenty of time, what's the rush?'

Nathan reacted with an expression that told Leo he was not in the mood for playing games. From his jacket pocket, Nathan took the photos of the dead monks in the Tibetan monastery and placed them on the table in front of Leo.

'What the hell are these?' enquired Leo, thumbing through them. 'Hell! They're gory. Did you take these?'

'I came upon this monastery in Tibet and that's what I found inside.'

Leo slowly raised his head and looked Nathan in the eyes.

'You just happened to come across…this…?'

'That's right. When I was taking photographs of the mountains. There was one old monk still alive and he had this…'

Nathan removed the dog tag from his neck and handed it to Leo.

'This is the ID tag of an American sailor from World War II,' said Nathan.

Producing the copy of the photograph he had seen at Mrs Spontiak's, he tapped the image of David Spontiak.

'This is the man, right here.'

Leo took a lingering look at the photograph.

'What's going on, Nathan?' he asked.

Nathan leaned forward and lowered his voice.

'I don't know. Since I found that, my camera's been stolen, the Chinese police have questioned me and there's been an attempt on my life.'

Leo frowned.

'Good grief, man! You don't do things by halves, do you?'

'Not only that, the telephone in my house was bugged. I also had a young woman come to my house, saying she had been sent by some old dear who used to work for the Ministry during the war. That same young woman has since been killed in a hit and run. Leo, it was no accident. The car that hit her was a grey Vauxhall Cavalier, the same make and colour of car that was parked down the lane when she came to my house. I've been followed too, even to Canada.'

Leo said nothing but just stared with his mouth ajar.

'Your thoughts would be appreciated,' Nathan smiled.

'You're not joking, are you?' Leo said at last.

'No, I'm not joking. I've stepped into something way too big for me and now I can't get out of it.'

'These ships you asked me to find out about…what have they got to do with this?'

Nathan tapped the dog tag.

'This chap served on the USS Colyton. I met someone in Canada whose father had known David Spontiak. That chap served on the USS Colarous. Something strange happened to it. Somehow it went off course and when it was found it looked as if there had been a fire or an explosion of some kind on board. Men were burnt to death and the ship was blackened.'

Leo clicked open the briefcase he was carrying and placed two files on the table.

'Not according to these,' he said.

'What are these?' asked Nathan picking them up.

'Copies of official war records containing the full logs of both ships.'

'Are you saying there's no official record of the Colarous going off course?'

'Correct. Neither is there mention of any fire. It's all there – see for yourself. According to these records the Colarous ended up in the Greek Navy after it was decommissioned in 1952 when it became the HS Kakodaimon. It was decommissioned from the Greek navy in 1969 and sent for scrap.'

'So it no longer exists,' sighed Nathan. 'What about the USS Colyton?'

'According to the official reports, it was sunk by a German torpedo.'

'This Lorraine Scott I visited in Canada told me her late husband had caused a bit of a stir, asking lots of questions and investigating.'

'And…?' queried Leo.

'He was a winter trucker in Alaska and one dark night he met with an accident.'

'That you don't think was an accident, right?'

'Something odd occurred regarding these ships. It's been kept off the record. That means…'

'We're dealing with authorities difficult to penetrate,' said Leo.

'I'd like to find this woman, Martha Kemp, who sent the young woman to me, but she's vanished. Upped and gone apparently, according to Rene, the employer of Liz, the young woman who was killed. By the way, I've told Rene to contact you if she hears anything. I don't know what the hell to do next, but I've sent Price's book to Jeremy Elling,' Nathan informed him.

'What is Price's book?'

'Ah, yes…perhaps I'd better start from the beginning…'

Nathan settled the bill then sat watching Leo. The fair hair, blue eyes and blue suit made him look like the perfect school prefect. Leo caught him staring.

186

'What?' he asked.

'I was just thinking you don't look much like a journalist.'

'Oh.'

'You've been very thoughtful but you haven't said much,' Nathan told him.

'That's because I don't quite know where to start,' admitted Leo.

'What do you think really happened aboard those ships?'

'I don't know. It could have been faulty equipment, human error, sabotage or…something more sinister. From what you've told me, especially about the wiring on the Colarous, I think these particular vessels could have been singled out for a test – something they wanted to use on the enemy.'

'I should find this Martha Kemp,' Nathan told him. 'I'm sure she knows something important. Come on, you're a journalist, you sniff out information. Where do I start?'

'I wouldn't. If I were you I'd just sit tight.'

'Leo, I can't just…'

'Martha Kemp sent the girl to you. She'll want to know the outcome. My guess is she disappeared the minute she discovered that Liz was dead. Perhaps she thinks she might be next. By now, either she's met the same fate or…'

'Or…?' asked Nathan anxiously.

'If not, *she* will come to *you*.'

'OK, let's forget Martha Kemp for the time being. How do I locate this Richard Paulton?'

Leo leaned back in his chair and ran his forefinger around the top of his empty coffee cup.

'That's going to be extremely difficult,' conceded Leo, mulling it over. 'There's this chap I know…' he began, but Nathan quickly interrupted.

'No. I'm in too precarious a situation to involve any other parties.'

'Just a second, hear me out. This chap is well known in journalism circles. He's the crème de la crème of his profession and *very* discreet. He's the chap we journalists go to when we can't get the information we want. Trust me, he's good.'

Nathan hesitated.

'I'm not sure, Leo.'

Leo leaned forward engaging eye contact across the table.

'Listen to me for once. You are in one hell of a situation and from what you've told me you'll be fortunate to get out of this in one piece. Your hands are tied. There are two ways to get impossible information. You have to have the contacts or you have to have the pull and forgive me, Nathan, but you have neither. Not for this.'

'Who is he?'

'Quentin Rogers. He's your only chance of finding Richard Paulton. That is all I can offer you, Nathan. Think about it.'

'All right. I've a feeling I may be running out of time. Go ahead. Can you deal with it?' Nathan asked.

'I think that would be best. That way you have no connection with him.'

'OK,' agreed Nathan.

'Do you know the fish and chip shop down the road from my office?'

'Yes.'

'The owner's a good friend of mine. I've been a regular customer for years. I'll leave any messages for you there. Here…'

Taking a pen and diary from his pocket, he wrote down the telephone number, ripped the page out and handed it to Nathan.

'If you'll take my advice, you'll do nothing until I have heard back from Quentin,' Leo advised.

Nathan slipped the ID back around his neck. Nodding towards the photographs, he asked 'Could you find a safe place for those?'

Leo scooped up the photographs then he and Nathan left the restaurant and split up.

As soon as he arrived home, Leo checked his telephone then made a call. The voice at the other end sounded as it usually did, slow and methodical.

'It's Leo Phillips, Quentin. Have you got much on at the moment?'

'I always have a lot on,' came the immodest reply.

'This is urgent. Extremely urgent. I need you to track someone down for me. The problem is, he's in the army.'

'Ah! That may be a problem for you but for Quentin Rogers nothing is impossible.'

'I knew you'd say that. I need him found as soon as possible.'

'Give me the details.'

Leo gave a satisfied smile. Rogers would not let him down.

Professor Elling wrote frenetically on a blackboard in the lecture room. With the A4 notebook open in one hand he jotted down figures, crossed them out, wrote more figures, shook his head, rubbed his chin and started the process over again. On the desk behind him was a globe of the world and books on advanced physics, mathematical expressions, geological tables and Latin.

Frustrated, he shook his head again, stood back from the board then rubbed it clean. For a few moments he studied the open page of the book then began to write the letters and numbers in a vertical list on the board. Once completed, he then attempted to copy the little drawings at the top of the page. When he had finished, he stood back, sat on the edge of the desk and studied the list pensively.

The door swung open and Enrich Leitner entered in his usual brusque way, his grey, tousled hair giving him a look of eccentricity.

'So this is where you have been hiding yourself! You realize we're twenty minutes late for dinner,' he reminded Elling as he checked his watch.

'Yes, sorry Enrich,' said Elling, placing another book over the notebook.

'What are you doing?'

Enrich approached the blackboard, placed his spectacles at the end of his nose and peered at the list.

'Oh, it's...em...a bet. A little enigma a colleague sent me,' shrugged Elling uncomfortably.

'What is the bet?' asked Enrich.

'That I can solve this before ten tomorrow. There's a lot of money at stake.'

Enrich smiled. Elling knew Leitner to be a brilliant mathematician and outside the box thinker. Already he could almost hear the cogs of his brain turning over.

'Have you come up with anything?' Enrich asked him.

'No. Not yet. It's very frustrating. Can you see it...?' enquired Elling tentatively.

Enrich pursed his lips and rubbed his nose.

'Something to do with the solar system possibly...could that be...no.'

'No, I couldn't fit them to any planets.'

'How fascinating,' muttered Enrich. 'What could that be, I wonder...?'

Both forgetting the time and dinner they stood together now, their eyes playing over the mysterious elements of the enigma.

'What are those?' asked Enrich. 'Those funny little drawings in the corner? Is that part of it?'

'Yes, a clue I think.'

'Ah! Good. It is always helpful to have a clue. Sometimes the clue itself can answer the question. If only I could make out...is that a mouse?'

'Cat, I believe.'

'And the other is a bird, is it not?'

'Yes. I think it's meant to be a bird.'

'And that clearly is a fish, I think.'

'Fish. Yes.'

'So, what do we have here? One cat, one fish and one bird. The letter w appears twice,' pointed out Enrich. 'Did you notice that?'

'Yes, I noticed that,' smiled Elling, 'though noticing it doesn't seem to have helped me much.'

'LW? RW? TF? Perhaps we are looking too deeply,' mused Enrich. It could be something as simple as people's initials.'

'Then, what are the figures after it?'

'Door number and...no, no. I don't think that is it. They can't be map references. One cat and one bird. What does one cat, one fish and one bird have? EUREKA! Yes, I have it!'

'You do?' said Elling, amazed.

'Oh, come on, you can see it now surely. A cat has one tail, a bird has two wings, LW, RW, left wing, right wing. A fish has a fin.'

A bright light suddenly came on in Professor Elling's brain.

'Two wings and a tail fin. It's a plane! It's the measurements of a plane!'

'Exactly! Oh, you owe me a bottle of champagne, my friend, when you pick up your winnings.'

'You'll have it, Enrich,' laughed Elling. 'You are a genius.'

Enrich Leitner shrugged and put his head to one side.

'It has been said,' he admitted, 'on more than one occasion.'

CHAPTER TWENTY-EIGHT

THE LIVING HELL

'Look sharp, soldier!' shouted the American lieutenant as Richard jogged sluggishly towards the helicopter. The Boeing CH-47 Chinook was parked in the darkness, glowing beneath searchlights like some primeval beast. The English and Americans, in camouflage outfits, had become one section and the men now ran up the ramp and into its belly. Richard seated himself next to Hains on the platform that ran along the inside and Foster immediately joined them, settling down the other side of Richard. Opposite Richard sat Toony. Checking his watch, Richard saw it was midnight – the haunting hour and he shivered. Hains seemed to feel it and gave him a fleeting glance.

'Hell's bells! What a time for an exercise,' muttered one of the Americans.

'Do you think this is it – the big one?' whispered Hains, but Richard could not answer, his mouth was so dry he could not spit, let alone speak.

'Are you talking about my privates again?' laughed Foster, but it was a nervous laugh and nobody joined him.

As the last of the soldiers entered the Chinook, the lieutenant closed the door. The clamp of cold steel was a chilling sound in the silence of the night as they were locked into the flying vessel and Richard felt like a mouse that had just entered a trap.

The lieutenant moved to the front to address the men.

'OK, listen up and listen good. This is a survival exercise…'

'Ah gee!' commented one of the Americans.

The lieutenant turned on him like a tiger who had just been taunted.

'If you don't like exercises, you shouldn't have joined the army, soldier. You should still be at home sucking your mother's bazoom!'

The men fell silent and attentive. There was a strain in the atmosphere that put Richard on edge. Now he felt sure that whatever

192

it was he had anticipated and dreaded all these weeks was coming to a conclusion right here, right now. As Hains had put it, this was the big one. The lieutenant continued.

'This is crucial to the future defence of our countries. Think of yourself as pioneers.'

Richard felt a nudge from Hains and he knew they had simultaneous thoughts. They were nothing more than guinea pigs.

'This helicopter will fly us out to a United States destroyer,' continued the lieutenant. 'Once you have embarked you will be under the command of US Commander Tom Grenham. You will follow his instructions without question and to the letter. The minute you are on the USS Augustine there will be no verbal communication except from your commander and your orders will be carried out in total silence. Are you clear?'

There was a resounding echo of 'Yes, sir'.

'Are there any questions?' asked the lieutenant.

'Why have our dog tags been taken from us, sir?' enquired Hains.

'A precaution. Two dumb suckers lost theirs on the last exercise. We know exactly who is here. Your tags will be handed back once you have completed the mission.'

Richard raised a hand. When he spoke, his voice sounded distant to his own ears and his throat felt restricted.

'Sir! The two dumb suckers. Did they get their tags back after the exercise and was that on their chests or their coffins?'

It was like an icy arrow had just shot right through the Chinook. All eyes, except Toony's, were now turned on the lieutenant. Only Toony stared at Richard. The intense silence felt like a bomb about to explode. The men all seemed to be holding their breath. Slowly, purposefully, the lieutenant came and stood directly in front of Richard. The lieutenant eyed him shrewdly and with distaste.

'That is none of your business, soldier. No exercise is without some danger. That's why you joined the army. Are you a soldier or not?'

The lieutenant's nose was an inch from Richard's face, his features twisted and ugly, distorted into those of a snarling pit bull. Richard swallowed hard and Hains stepped in to defuse the situation.

'Could you tell us what you hope to attain from the outcome of the exercise, sir?'

For a moment, it was as if the lieutenant had not heard him with his contorted face and blazing eyes still fixed on Richard. Slowly, the features returned to normal as he turned to look at Hains.

'To place you as close as possible to a real-life situation; to encourage co-ordination of response and interaction between sea and air units essential in a modern war situation and to make you better soldiers...' glancing across at Richard '...if that is possible. Now settle in and gear up; you're in for a tough night.'

'Sir...'

The voice belonged to Hal Davison. The lieutenant stared at him as he would an insect he was about to put his foot on.

'What is it, Davison?'

'I just wondered why we were boarding a decommissioned ship, sir?'

All eyes turned to Hal Davison then to the lieutenant. The underlying fear that Jason Turner had felt building up amongst the soldiers the last few days had now become tangible. The uncertainty was evident in their faces and wary eyes. For a few seconds the lieutenant looked uncertain. Davison had caught him off guard.

'It's just that I happen to know...' Davison continued.

The lieutenant leapt across to Davison and stared down at him, every muscle in his body tight, veins in his neck protruding.

'You know nothing, soldier! Now zip it and prepare for your exercise.'

The lieutenant moved to the back of the aircraft but his presence still had an impact. The soldiers sat in silence, lost in their own thoughts, listening to the increasing drone of the engine and the sound of the rotor blades above their heads as the Chinook gained height and took them forward to their destiny.

With a subtle bump, the Chinook landed on the deck of the USS Augustine and Richard was aware of a slow churning in his stomach.

Within minutes, the door was opened, lights illuminated the landing pad and wearily the soldiers got up and disembarked. A cold wind met them. As Richard went down the ramp, lights shone in his face, temporarily blinding him. As he followed the rest of the men lining up on deck he heard the rotor blades start up again and watched as the Chinook immediately took off. The sea could be

194

heard but not seen, lapping against the ship. Beyond the ship, total darkness engulfed them, only the lights from the Chinook visible as it rose like an eagle into the sky and gradually disappeared from sight. As Richard watched those lights vanish into the distance it was as if a lifeline had just slipped from his fingers.

The ocean sucked at the ship as if inviting it to join the depths of its icy fathoms. Richard had always loved the sea. Tonight he hated it for he felt it was nothing more than an icy tomb waiting to devour him.

An overweight, intimidating figure made an appearance on the deck and the men immediately stood to attention. Commander Grenham came across sharp and loud.

'At ease,' he commanded. 'Men, tonight you will go through an exercise to test your nerve and courage. You are to remain where you are, on deck. Keep your positions no matter what other sound or action is taking place until you receive further instructions. Is that clear?'

There was a resounding, 'Yes, sir'.

Commander Grenham left the deck. Within minutes the ship's lights were extinguished and they were left in total darkness. Richard was aware of a slight weakness at the back of his knees and a nausea in the pit of his stomach as he wondered what was about to happen. As his eyes became adjusted to the darkness he could just make out the figures of Hains to his left and Toony to his right. Moments later there was the sound of a small engine and churning of water that slowly grew fainter.

'They've left the ship,' whispered Hains to Richard, barely audible.

'Who?' breathed Richard.

'Commander Grenham and the lieutenant. We're on our own.'

'Hains! Did you manage to persuade anyone to go over that fence?' ventured Richard.

There was a short silence before Hains replied, 'No. All present and correct'.

Richard felt tight in the chest as a flame of hope went out. Minutes that seemed like hours ticked by and then, zooming towards them from the vast eternity of space overhead, came an oval light followed by two others.

'What the hell is that?' uttered Toony.

'Shush!' came a warning from the blackness.

'Don't worry. The big boys have abandoned ship,' came an American voice. 'What did you think that engine was? It's just us poor suckers now.'

Richard watched the strange, oval lights above them in the sky as they appeared to grow bigger and fluctuate.

'What are those lights?' asked Brady, nervously.

'Aircraft of some type,' one of the Americans suggested.

'I've never heard silent aircraft before,' Foster answered.

'Me neither,' came another American voice.

'They're too far away for us to hear them yet,' came another voice. It could have been Gav Hudson, Richard could not be sure.

The men fell silent. Terrified but fascinated, they watched the mysterious lights as the fluctuating shapes danced in the sky and began to coordinate into a perfect triangle. From out of the black obscurity someone began to pray.

Aboard a smaller naval vessel, two nautical miles away, Alistair Milestone stood on deck closely watching the oval lights and the USS Augustine through binoculars. One of the officers called out to him.

'Energy fields coordinated, sir.'

Milestone's face was impassive.

'Good. Let the operation proceed.'

Below deck the Radio Operator began transmitting: 'Energy fields begin countdown. Operation TR015 is now underway.'

Richard remained spellbound by the luminous, oval shapes now hovering and quietly humming way above the ship. Not since a child had he felt so totally vulnerable. For some time nothing happened. The weird lights at three points of a triangle remained above them as if waiting, as the men too were waiting. For them time had stopped. Richard was aware of his heart thumping within his chest as seconds ticked by.

They appeared very suddenly: a ray of light source emanating from each oval and meeting together at the centre of the triangle which was at a point exactly above midship. The fusion of the energy sources started to form a green mist that gradually began to engulf the whole ship.

Richard knew that overboard waited a merciless sea: a lethal, undulating serpent writhing with a crushing force. There was a choice to be made and Richard swiftly made it. Suddenly breaking from the ranks, he turned and walked towards the edge of the ship.

'Rich...?'

The voice was Toony's but Richard did not turn, did not reply. The green mist was spreading and the silence was broken by nervous whispers. Richard heaved himself over the side. The plunge through the air seemed to take minutes though, in truth, it was only seconds until he hit the sea and felt the impact send vibrations up the length of his spine as he was swallowed into the alien world beneath.

As he emerged above the waves the coldness took his breath away. For a few terrifying moments he frantically fought to breathe against the onslaught of the waves. The salt stung his eyes and his boots weighed him down. Gasping for breath, his teeth rattling with the intense cold, he witnessed the whole ship become entirely enshrouded in the mysterious green mist like a corpse being wrapped in a ceremonial robe. The mist crept and wafted like a predatory demon, its wispy fingers enclosing the ship and claiming it as its own. The oval lights, through the haze, lambently illuminated the whole ghastly scene: a ghost ship against a black backdrop. Suddenly, within the mist, Richard saw figures eerily show themselves and then disappear again into the green cloud. As he fought for breath, two, then three more transparent figures appeared before being swallowed up by the swirling fog until, once again, only the now blurred image of the USS Augustine remained.

Waves slashed at Richard's face like razor blades. Ice cold and sharp, they stung afresh with each whooshing sound as the sea filled the night air with its unleashed fury. Richard felt as if his chest was being crushed by the pressure of the tide then, to his horror, he began to witness the stern of the ship slowly begin to disappear like a mistake being erased by a rubber. Simultaneously, he saw nebulous figures of men on the ship levitate and walk on air, some of their limbs becoming invisible. Richard refused to trust what he was seeing, believing it to be an optical illusion caused by a drop in blood pressure and body temperature. As he stared mesmerised, three soldiers spontaneously combusted forming human fireballs and the crashing of the waves was temporarily muffled by the horrific screams of terror-stricken and agonized men.

All this Richard viewed through the mysterious mist that now began to spread from the ship to the sea beyond, like the breath of a dragon exhaling towards him. Richard gasped as its ghostly fingers began to spread out, stretching to reach him and take him within its grasp. Like a spider's web, it spun itself in fine, delicate strands, enveloping him as the waves lashed over his head and water filled his mouth.

The ship was now fully transparent with individual fires burning on deck. Desperate figures ran in all directions, their shouts and screams becoming a torturous crescendo. Some threw themselves overboard: human fireballs falling through the air to be swallowed up by the sea below. The tide was taking Richard further away from the ship but the green mist followed him incessantly. Howls and cries of torment filled the air, resounding on Richard's eardrums like a harrowing imprecation. Richard thought he recognized Foster close to the edge of the port side, stumbling and clutching at his head. Richard waved an arm and yelled at him to jump ship but his voice was lost amid the crashing of the waves and the screams of the men. Half the ship was now evanescent and the oval lights had become a blur, meeting together to form one huge light that shone down, illuminating the horror.

Richard was light-headed and realized he was in danger of passing out as he felt his body rushing through a long, black tunnel. Moments later, he came to, immediately aware of a sheer burning sensation that ripped at his nerve ends and brought him sharply back to consciousness. The sea was bubbling; the white wash churning and spitting frothy foam like the mouth of a rabid animal.

The ship was now barely visible, only the tip of the bow remaining. The horrific screams that ripped through the night had stopped, leaving only the sucking and lashing of the waves. Richard knew his only chance for survival was to get clear of the green fog that was consuming everything within its boundary.

Richard tried to pedal the water but he could not feel his legs and was unaware whether they were moving or not. Throwing his arms back, he attempted to swim backwards, away from the horror that confronted him, but something bumped him from behind and as he swung round he came face to face with a human corpse, the face partly melted away.

Richard cried out and tried to push it away from him. In cruel response the waves threw it back at him, casting the body almost on top of him. Richard screamed out in anguish, lashing out at the molten corpse until it was sucked under and swallowed by the sea.

Fear creating new energy, Richard began to swim again focusing on the outer boundary of the fog where it thinned out to a very fine mist. An evocative cry for help cut through the night and distracted him. Richard ignored it, focusing on the outer limits of the mist, but it came again: a heart-rending plea.

'Help me! Please! I'm blind!'

Richard looked all around him trying to locate the voice amid the wash of the waves. The merged lights, their energies still concentrated on the area where the ship had now completely vanished, threw a lambent glow, just enough for Richard to recognize Glen Witchell struggling in the sea just a few yards away from him. Torn between his own and another human being's desperate fight for survival, Richard followed his conscience, fighting against the tide to reach Witchell. Richard was only a few feet away when the frantic splashing stopped and the figure of Witchell became covered by the sea, his hand reaching out the last visible image to slip away before the sea consumed him completely. Richard made a strong attempt to lunge towards where the hand had disappeared but a powerful wave picked him up and threw him backwards, momentarily smothering him. When Richard emerged again there was no sign of Witchell.

Crying and shaking but unaware of either, Richard once more swam with the tide but his arms grew heavy and his consciousness vague until he was no longer sure whether his arms were moving or not. Exhaustion and cold overcame him and he felt as if he were slipping away beneath the waves into the icy tomb below.

'Rich!'

Richard was vaguely aware of a hand on his forehead pulling his head backwards. Salt water entered his mouth and he spluttered.

'OK, Rich. I got you, pal!'

Richard recognized the voice and attempted to say the name but his lips could not form the words.

'It's OK, buddy. Just hang on in there, pal.'

It was Toony. Again, Richard tried to answer him but his lips were numb with the cold and would not cooperate.

'Stay with me, Rich. OK, buddy? Stay with me.'

The words seemed to linger in Richard's mind, repeat themselves and grow fainter.

On the naval vessel, two nautical miles away, Alistair Milestone lowered his binoculars. Raucous cheers filled the deck. Hands were shaken and congratulations exchanged. Commander Grenham appeared at Milestone's side.

'Well, sir, if your calculations are correct, the USS Augustine will be in the zone in exactly...' Grenham checked his watch, 'six minutes.'

Alistair Milestone returned Grenham's euphoric smile with a cold stare.

'I do not expect our calculations to be wrong. This time, there will be no mistakes. We have had the best – the very best – working on this project.'

'I've no doubt about that, sir. No doubt at all,' smiled the commander.

Twenty minutes later a call came through to the captain. An officer delivered the message to the commander who relayed it to Alistair Milestone and the officials on board:

'Gentlemen! The USS Augustine has failed to appear in the designated area. Our tracker satellite is now trying to trace any signs of highly compacted electromagnetic energy.'

Alistair Milestone's features became like alabaster. Lips set, eyes like icy steel, he stood silently cursing.

Richard awoke and saw sequins on a huge black background. Eyes staring up, he had a sensation of floating. There was a sucking noise and something stroking his face.

A shout broke through the night. Richard closed his eyes and forced them open again. Sea lapped around him, streams running over his face and the sequins above were stars in a deep black sky.

Richard tried to speak but was too weak to make the effort, neither could he feel his limbs, in fact, he appeared to be totally devoid of any sensation at all.

'Hey! Over here!'

It was Toony shouting and Richard became aware of a new sound: a chugging noise accompanied by lights on the sea. It was a boat and it was coming towards them.

'Hey, hey, Richie boy! We're gonna be OK!'

Richard could not share Toony's rapture for he felt nothing: no elation, no emotion at all.

'Come here, my beauty! There's a sight, huh Rich!' Toony laughed into Richard's ear.

Within minutes the boat reached them and two Sami fishermen hauled Richard up over the side. Lifeless, he flopped onto the deck like a landed fish. The men hauled Toony up behind him.

The fishermen spoke in their native tongue but Toony realized from the urgency of their tones and the turning round of the boat that they were heading back to land. Toony came alongside Richard and slapped him round the face.

'Hey, Rich! Come on, bud! We're home safe and dry now. Come on, Rich. You've gotta stay with me here, buddy!'

One of the fishermen pushed Toony aside and wrapped a blanket around Richard then gave one to Toony. Minutes later, he brought a hot drink. Toony tried again to bring Richard round but without success. Feeling for a pulse, he felt a faint throb. The fisherman brought another blanket and wrapped it around Richard then nodded at Toony.

'Hey, you speak English?' enquired Toony of the fishermen.

One shook his head in the negative, the other made a sign with his finger and thumb that he spoke very little.

Richard opened his eyes and let out an incomprehensible sound from his mouth. Toony knelt over him.

'Rich? It's OK. Everything's OK now. We've been rescued,' Toony told him.

Toony put his arm around Richard's neck and pulled him upwards. With the other hand he placed the hot beverage to Richard's mouth but his lips were so frozen he could not part them.

'Damn!' muttered Toony.

One of the fishermen came to help him. Kneeling the other side of the weak, limp body, he rubbed Richard's face and mouth with his hands, attempting to bring some feeling back to them.

'Toony!' Richard uttered between closed teeth.

'Yeah, that's right, Rich. I'm here buddy. You're gonna be just fine. Try and drink this…'

Toony, once again, offered Richard the beverage to drink. As he did so, the blankets fell off exposing Richard's arm.

Suddenly, the fisherman yelped like a dog and sprang back. Toony looked up and saw the horror on the fisherman's face as he stared at Richard. Just behind him, his companion too, stared in undisguised fear.

Toony turned back to Richard and saw the reason for their shock. Richard's left arm was missing from the elbow down and yet there was no blood and no noticeable injury. It was as if a magic rubber had erased it.

Richard stared at his own arm in frozen terror and then he let out a blood-curdling howl that chilled Toony to the marrow.

'What the hell happened, Rich? What happened to your arm?' Toony demanded.

Richard continued to make a sickening, agonized sound. An urgent verbal exchange took place between the two fishermen. One of them stepped forward towards Toony. With his hand, the fisherman made a waving motion and simply said one word.

'Lights?'

Again he waved upwards towards the sky and asked, 'Lights?'

'Yeah,' said Toony. 'There were lights. What do you mean by that?' he enquired, imitating the wave.

The two fishermen, misunderstanding, exchanged petrified glances.

'The souls are claiming him,' said the fisherman in his native language to Toony. 'You should not have waved at the lights.'

The other fisherman suddenly rushed forward. Grabbing hold of Richard, knocking the drink flying, he attempted to pull him to the side of the boat. Toony quickly intervened.

'Hey! What the hell's going on! Back off!'

Toony tried to pull the man off Richard but the other fisherman grabbed hold of Toony and dragged him back. As Toony attempted to fight him off, he saw the other man haul Richard half over the side of the boat.

'No! What are you doing? Are you crazy!' Toony yelled.

The fisherman held Toony in a vice-like grip and Toony could only struggle frantically as he witnessed Richard's legs hauled up and his body tipped over the starboard side of the boat by the man's companion. There was a loud splash as Richard hit the water.

'No! You psycho! I'll kill you!' yelled Toony.

The man let Toony go and he immediately rushed to starboard but all he could see were the jade-black waves heaving and sucking at the hull of the boat.

'Give me a light! Give me a light, you low-down piece of...!' yelled Toony as he landed a punch on one fisherman's jaw.

'Let the souls have him,' the other man said in his native tongue, but Toony did not understand.

Toony jumped over the side and thrashed blindly in the water, diving beneath the waves, desperately feeling for Richard. Again and again he came up for air and went down again into the cold, unrelenting sea.

On the fishing boat the Sami conversed in their own language.

'That's incredible,' said the fisherman who had held Toony back. 'I don't know anyone who has actually witnessed it, but our ancient belief, handed down through generations, must be true.'

'My grandmother always swore her neighbour had been taken. One night he waved at the guovssahasah and the souls claimed him. Never was he seen again,' muttered the other.

'Poor man! Now, this stranger too...'

'We had to let the souls have him. They'd only seek revenge on us otherwise.'

'What shall we do about the other one?'

'I can't see him now. The souls have claimed them both.'

'Do you think anyone will believe us? Perhaps we should have taken him to the Elders.'

'Are you insane? They would believe we are cursed too. We allowed him onto our vessel. They would blame us for every bad thing that happened from now on: miscarriages, accidents, extreme weather would all be our fault for denying the souls. I think it is best that we say nothing.'

The other man looked out onto the sea where the two strangers were now no longer to be seen, swallowed up by the depths.

'Yes,' he agreed with his companion. 'Perhaps that is for the best.'

'They were dressed as soldiers. I wonder where they came from and what they were doing out here?'

'Who knows? Do you think they were really human? It looked as if the souls had already tried to take them. You saw his arm!'

'Shall we go out again?'

'No. I've had enough for tonight. Let's go home.'

One of the fishermen took over the helm from a comrade. The other picked up the upturned cup and blankets from the deck and took them below. None of them noticed the figure the sea had regurgitated who now hung grimly onto a net the starboard side of the boat as it chugged its way back to the shore.

Alistair was approached by Douglas Hawken, an imposing, grey-haired American official with thickset features and keen eyes sheltered below broad and heavy eyebrows.

'Damn it, Alistair. What happened?'

'I'll find out. Heads will roll,' replied Milestone. 'I was assured they had ironed out the problems.'

Hawken sidled up to Alistair and rasped in his ear.

'We're running out of time here. If the Japanese beat us to it…'

'I know the risks only too well,' Milestone replied.

'Then what the hell went wrong?' Hawken repeated between gritted teeth.

Alistair sighed.

'They must have been working to the wrong calculations. They'll have to start over again.'

'Oh for pity's sake!' shouted Hawken, shaking his head. 'Do you realize how much money we've sunk into this? We've halved our budget for the space programme to accommodate this work!'

'We've all sunk money in: us and the Germans.'

'Nowhere near as much as we have!' argued Hawken.

An officer appeared.

'Sir! They've located the site.'

Alistair followed the officer and disappeared from view. Hawken gripped the rail at the port side of the boat and swore into the night.

Moments later Alistair Milestone returned with a face like thunder. Hawken was on him like a vulture the second he appeared.

'Well? What happened? Where did it go?'

'Tibet. The Chinese Army are making their way there now.'

'Damn it!' bellowed Hawken. 'I've got to inform the President…'

'Wait!' said Milestone, catching him by the sleeve. 'In all previous experiments the reappearance has only been visible for less than five minutes. It appeared ten minutes ago. They won't get there on time.'

'We can't take that chance!' Hawken remonstrated, his eyes almost popping from their sockets.

'Sir!' the officer called to Milestone.

Milestone stared into the glaring face of Hawken and said calmly, 'Just wait.'

Hawken gritted his teeth and paced the deck. Minutes later, Alistair Milestone returned.

'It's vanished. No trace. The Chinese are still two miles away,' he informed the officials on deck.

Hawken visibly defused with relief.

Alistair Milestone went to go below deck.

'Just a second,' said Hawken, catching him by the arm. 'What about the rest of the story…?'

Milestone swallowed hard then raised his chin defiantly.

'It was only fifty per cent successful,' he informed him.

'Fifty per cent? Fifty per cent! You do realize there's a limit to how much the USA can keep putting into this project? Mess-ups like this are not going to reassure the right people,' Hawken warned him.

Milestone gave a lop-sided smile of confidence.

'The Japanese are close on our heels. The Chinese are sniffing around. I believe the President knows how much is at stake now. I don't foresee any financial restraints. Do you?'

Hawken refrained from punching him in the mouth and instead turned away with gritted teeth. As Milestone went to see the captain, Hawken looked across at Commander Grenham and announced, 'That smug piece of crap will bankrupt this project!'

Commander Grenham heard him but did not reply. Grenham was too busy giving instructions to the armed mop up team just leaving to circle the area in four, small speed boats.

Hawken was joined by German official, Gernot Voigt.

'I did not realize it would be like this,' said Voigt. 'Those men: It was ghastly.'

'I know. The price of progress,' Hawken replied with distaste.

Gernot Voigt thought long and hard. Some progress, he at last decided, was simply not worth the cost.

CHAPTER TWENTY-NINE

THE REVELATION

With dawn still hours away, but unable to sleep, Professor Elling sat down, once again, to work on the strange symbols and notes from the ragged A4 exercise book sent to him by Nathan King. Frustrated, he continually worked his way along scientific and mathematical alleyways that always led to the same inevitable brick wall. Sometimes, he felt he had almost got it, that the final calculations would add up, but always total disappointment followed. The enigma was laid out before him like a story without an ending. What was that vital calculation that enticed him, teased him and yet failed to provide?

The notebook was old and faded with an inexplicable slit right through it. In his mind, Elling pictured the writer as he imagined him to be: original and eager with a slightly disorganized mind that was, nevertheless, approaching genius. A loner, Elling felt, a man unafraid to maintain his own values against the wishes of others. Someone prepared to go his own way and break new ground. This man must have been valuable to someone, or something, once upon a time. Who was he? Was he still alive? What new ground had this man broken?

Elling picked up Nathan's letter and reread it. An unease that had been resting on him for some time became sharper and more focused. Nathan, he thought, had become involved in something very sinister and still there had been no word from him. Taking a deep breath, Elling picked up a pen and a fresh sheet of paper, turned another page of the book and began to make notes. It was four hours later when a sharp tingle of excitement shot through his stomach and filled his head with a fountain of light.

'Yes…' he muttered. 'Yes…'

Dropping the pen, he leapt from his chair and rushed to one of his many bookcases. Running his finger along the various spines, he grabbed a brown book and opened it to the index. Flipping through the pages, he found what he was looking for and returned to his seat without lifting his eyes from the page.

'Now we may be getting somewhere,' he uttered.

Price had been clever. Price had used a code to represent the most essential elements of his calculations. Four pages of this book were in code and Elling would not have the full story until he had managed to decipher that code. The coded parts were the most crucial.

Elling continued to read. Taking up his pen and meticulously making notes, he continued to write for the next five hours until the words, numbers and symbols began to run into one another. At last, when he was just about to stop, something leapt from the page at him and he took his pen up again and began to write. Elling stopped. A knot tightened in his stomach as he realized he was on to something. Frantically, he jotted more notes.

'Yes,' he muttered. 'That is it!'

Elling dropped the pen and leaned back, closing his eyes, feeling the exhaustion and exhilaration coming over him in waves. Like someone who had just completed an exam, he felt overwhelming relief that another test was successfully completed and encouragement for the sessions yet to come.

Toony opened his eyes and stared through a crack at a clear blue sky. The first sensation he became aware of was the sheer cold. Painfully pulling himself up to a sitting position, he rubbed his legs until he began to feel them. The night had been spent in a small shack at the back of an isolated wooden house on stilts. The shack housed a snowmobile, skis, a small upturned boat and sheets of canvas that Toony had wrapped around himself to combat the cold. Toony stood up and ventured outside. A small way off there was a metal framework from which dried fish hung in the open air. Toony helped himself to some and ate them ravenously before making his way up to the house. Toony bashed on the door but there was no reply and he discovered the door was unlocked. Walking in, he found himself inside an untidy but homely wooden cabin. There was nobody at home so he helped himself to clean clothes. After changing into them, he found an empty knapsack in which he placed his camouflage outfit, food and some coins he found in the bedroom.

Outside he collected more dried fish. As he placed it in the knapsack, he surveyed his surroundings. There was forest on three sides and sea just ahead. In the early hours of the morning, when the fishermen had docked their boat and gone on their way, he had eased himself out of the water and staggered for about a mile along the coast. Now he continued in the same direction figuring he must, at some point, find a road where he may be able to hitch a lift to a port and make for Britain.

Leo responded to the trill of the telephone.
'Hello! Leo…'
There was the sound of pips followed by the leisurely voice of Quentin Rogers.
'Leo. The matter you asked me to look into…'
'Yes?' Leo butted in.
'I cannot help you.'
Leo hesitated for a moment, confused. These were words he never expected to hear from Quentin Rogers.
'I don't believe that,' Leo replied.
'It appears you have touched upon the edge of a national security precipice and I would advise you to stop before you go over the edge.'
There was a clear warning in those words that frightened Leo and simultaneously annoyed him.
'Before I'm *pushed* over the edge. Is that what you mean?'
'I mean you would be strongly advised to forget the matter,' Quentin came back at him.
'Is that what happened to Richard Paulton, Quentin? Was *he* pushed?'
'As I said. I cannot help you there.'
'Have you been threatened, Quentin?'
'How mildly you put it.'
Leo could detect a cynical smile at the other end of the receiver.
'Where was his last whereabouts? Can you tell me that?'
There was a slight hesitation.
'Sadly, as mentioned, I…'
Leo waited but Quentin did not complete the sentence.
'Is he alive Quentin?'

'I do not know.'

'Quentin, who has warned you off?'

'You do not need to know. I have kept your name out. Be thankful and take my advice. Think it over carefully.'

'Thanks anyway,' said Leo, despondently.

'You have nothing to thank me for and we have not had this conversation.'

There was a click the other end and the line went dead. Leo thoughtfully stared at the receiver before slowly placing it back down. For a long time he continued to stare at the telephone. Quentin had left a sentence unfinished. Quentin would never do that and there had been a slight pause followed by emphasis on those words: Sadly, as mentioned I....

Quentin had also put a stress on the words: Think it over carefully.

Leo studied the initial letters of each word of the stressed, unfinished sentence. SAMI. Leo grinned. Cleverly, Quentin had given him a clue to Richard's location.

Nathan entered the fish and chip shop and ordered rock and chips then he addressed the cheerful, ruddy-faced man behind the fryer.

'Excuse me! Are you the owner of this place?'

'That's right,' he smiled. 'Do you have a complaint?'

'No. I'm Nathan King. I believe you know a friend of mine. Leo.'

The man lifted his head in a sign of acknowledgement.

'I'll serve this gentleman, Shelly,' he informed his young assistant. 'Perhaps you could serve this lady...'

While Shelly busied herself with a large order for a very harassed looking young mum with two annoying children in tow, the owner came to the counter.

'Do you want salt and vinegar on it?' he asked.

'Yes. Thanks,' said Nathan.

'As the owner handed over the order he said, 'Leo said The Witch's Hat at seven this evening.'

'Thanks,' smiled Nathan and left.

Rene carefully folded Liz's clothes and placed them into large plastic bags. Each item was studied and felt fondly with fingertips that ached for their owner's return. With no other living relatives, it seemed it was down to Rene to clear the flat and arrange the funeral. Danny had offered to help but someone had to run the club and this was a job she preferred to do alone. It was too personal to share. Rene had decided to remain at the flat for the next few days. Here she felt closer to Liz and she needed a break from the club. Danny readily agreed, seeing that it would be the most practical thing to do but told her to call if she needed anything. Right now all she needed was Liz, but Liz was not there and never would be again.

There was a heavy weight in Rene's heart that suddenly felt too much to bear and she left the clothes and went to the kitchen to make herself a cup of tea. In the sink were a teaspoon and a mug with a dark, sticky substance in the bottom. Rene suddenly gripped the edge of the sink and fought back the pain that seared through her very being.

Good grief, she thought, was this all a young life had come to? A used mug and a dirty spoon in an otherwise empty sink. Why was that so poignant to her? There was something terribly sad and desolate about that spoon and mug. It stood for the last drink that Liz had taken in her own home. Rene pictured her drinking it then placing it in the sink. If she had known that would be the last time she would ever perform that act in that particular place. How strange life was. In a way, death made more sense than life. Death was definite; final. Life was never like that. Life was a perverse swine, twisting and turning, being kind then creeping up on you from behind with a vicious blow. Yes, death was more straightforward and honest somehow.

The shrill and alarming ring of the telephone suddenly caused Rene to jump and shiver. It was a rude, intrusive sound interrupting her private thoughts and her precious time with Liz's memory.

Irritated, Rene left the kitchen and picked up the receiver. At first, the voice was not clear. It was a man's voice but she did not understand what he said. Rene's thoughts were still pixilated. Perhaps she was not really here, she thought, perhaps she was still drifting in from the kitchen…

'Liz? Is that Liz?'

The voice was clearer now.

'Liz isn't here, I'm afraid,' Rene told him and she was surprised at the calmness of her own voice. It was a fake voice because inside she was trembling and her stomach felt full of cold water freezing her insides.

'Who is that?' asked the man with a twang to his voice.

Now Rene sensed the urgency in the tone and something else...wariness?

'I'm a friend: A close friend. I'm sorry, but Liz died recently,' she explained.

The next words caught her by surprise. No apology, no empathic words, no sense of shock or surprise.

'Was she killed?' asked the voice.

Rene stood holding the receiver in her hand and she was shaking all over now. Shaking and silently screaming.

'Was she killed?' came the voice again, more urgent and demanding.

'Yes...'

The word trickled out of her, quietly like an apology.

'Who is...?' but she didn't manage to finish the sentence before the line went dead.

Nathan edged his way into the tiny public house where broomsticks adorned the walls and a distasteful, stuffed black cat grinned at him from the bar. A hand came on his shoulder and he turned to see Leo.

'I've already got them in,' Leo told him. 'We're over here.'

Nathan followed him to a settle near a blazing fire. The pub was noisy and full which made it easy to converse.

'Well?' enquired Nathan.

'It's worse than we thought. Apparently we've touched on a matter of national security. Quentin was warned off.'

'Who by?' asked Nathan.

'He wouldn't say, but he did manage to give me a discreet message. Richard is in Lapland but Quentin didn't know whether he was alive or dead.'

'Lapland?'

'Yes. Odd isn't it?'

'It's more than odd.'

'I really think you should drop it, Nathan. This is way beyond anything we can deal with.'

'I can't drop it,' Nathan told him. 'Anyway, I'm in this so deeply, I may as well go the whole hog.'

'And get killed?'

Nathan sighed and shook his head.

'I wish I'd never seen that monastery,' he rued.

'Drop it, Nathan. Where the hell are you going to go with this anyway?' Leo reasoned.

'I don't know,' Nathan admitted.

'Your life is already in danger. They must be aware that you only know so much but not enough. They're keeping tabs on you. If you drop it now, they'll have no reason to dispose of you. If you don't…'

'I know.'

There was an uneasy silence during which Leo considered his friend carefully. At last he said, 'You're not going to drop it, are you?'

'I have to contact Jeremy. If he's got to the bottom of this enigma then at least I'll have a clearer idea of exactly what I'm dealing with.'

'You don't think…'

'What?'

'Whoever's warned Quentin off knows Jeremy's got something of value?'

'No. I wouldn't have thought so.'

'I really think you should consider this carefully, Nathan. You're really messing around with the big boys. Why don't you take a holiday and give yourself time to clear your head,' Leo suggested.

Nathan sat rubbing his chin with his hand.

'No,' said Nathan. 'I have to see this through.'

Leo heaved a sigh.

'OK,' Leo sighed. We'll go to Lapland!'

Nathan ran a hand through his hair and studied his friend.

'I can't ask that of you, Leo. I need you to stay on the outside. The less you see of me the better.'

'It's what's in your head though, isn't it? You wouldn't know where to start. I'm a journalist, I can sniff out information. That's what I do.'

'No,' said Nathan firmly. 'If you come with me, asking questions, they'll know you're involved. It's best I go alone.'

'I don't like this, Nathan. I don't like it at all,' Leo warned him.

They finished their pints in silence.

CHAPTER THIRTY

THE RUSE

The watcher sat in his car in the dark, silent lane and yawned. King's house was in darkness. Checking his watch, he pressed the receiver in his ear and spoke into a microphone attached to the inside lapel of his coat.

'A one four checking in. King is still absent.'

A crackling reply came back through the receiver.

'Message received A one four. OAO.'

Lights sweeping past him suddenly disturbed the tranquillity of the lane and a small green car pulled up just ahead. The driver switched off the engine and the watcher remained still as two old people emerged from the car. The old, white-haired chap wore a smart suit. Placing something on top of the car roof his moustached, bespectacled face was suddenly illuminated by a torch and the watcher saw it was a map he was attempting to unfurl. The old lady with him, in a dress and jacket, had corn-coloured hair cut into a bob and she shakily attempted to help her companion spread out the map.

'Oh for pity's sake,' muttered the watcher.

The couple appeared to be having some kind of dispute and the watcher lowered his window a couple of inches to catch what they were saying.

'I said we should have taken that road, Rupert,' came the old dear's voice.

'I can't understand it. I think you're wrong. We've just come too far down this one, I think. Hold it still, I can't see properly.'

'I said we should have left earlier, we're going to be late,' the old dear admonished.

They spoke with a posh accent and the watcher hissed to himself.

'No, no, that's wrong. We're not in the right place at all. I haven't a clue where we are now,' muttered the old chap.

The watcher rolled his eyes and groaned to himself as he saw the old lady peer towards his car and strain her neck to look. A finger

215

pointed towards the car as she said something to her companion and then she came towards the watcher with the map. As she approached the window, the watcher wound it down. The sooner he sorted this old couple out and got them on their way the better.

'I wonder if you can help us...?' the old lady began, but the old chap came up behind her and nudged her aside to push the map under the watcher's nose.

'Let me explain, Moira,' he said to the old lady then, addressing the watcher, he said, 'We're trying to find our way...'

The sound was subtle, not at all what Stanley had expected. Just a quick 'phut' noise and then the man's head slumped forward and Stanley saw the blood running down the side of the man's face and neck. Martha checked for a pulse, slid the gun fitted with a silencer back inside her pocket then turned to Stanley and said, 'Mission accomplished'.

Nathan found a telephone box and rang Jeremy Elling's number. The sound of his voice at the other end of the line was a relief.

'Jeremy, it's Nathan.'

'Nathan! Where are you?'

'On my way home. Have you studied the book I sent you?'

'Yes, I have. It's fascinating. Where did you get it?'

'Jeremy, do you understand any of it?'

'Yes, I think I've made some sense of it but I fear the implications. I'm still working on it. I've only just touched the tip of the iceberg. There is so much more...'

'Jeremy, I'll come and see you but I'll have to make sure it's safe first. I'll be in contact.'

'OK, Nathan. Take care.'

'I will...and you too,' Nathan replied.

There was a click the other end and Nathan replaced the receiver. Stepping out of the telephone box, he looked around him. All seemed well. The only thing he needed now was a good night's sleep.

Nathan arrived home just after 8.00p.m. Perturbed, he noticed the grey, Vauxhall Cavalier in the tenebrous lane. Another small, green car in front of it barely registered. After leaving his motorbike at the

216

side of the house, he angrily marched over to the Cavalier impulsively deciding that, as he was a marked man, if they were going to finish him off they may as well do it now. Nathan was half-expecting the car to suddenly come alight and speed off. Instead, an elderly man stepped out of the car in front. Nathan ignored him and continued to march up to the Cavalier, noticing the driver was looking down with the driver's window open. As Nathan approached, the old man walked up behind him and spoke.

'Don't worry about him. He won't be tailing you any more.'

Nathan turned to see an elderly gentleman with spectacles and a moustache. Joining him, as he spoke, was an elderly lady. They both looked as if they were dressed for a visit to a theatre or concert.

'Who are you?' Nathan demanded.

It was the woman who spoke.

'Mister King, my name is Martha Kemp. I believe you have heard of me.'

Nathan stared, struck numb by this sudden appearance. Turning, he took a closer look at the man slumped in the car and now noticed the blood. Turning again, he gazed at the two elderly people who looked so innocent and yet so disturbing. Things were beginning to feel very surreal.

'Who is he?' Nathan managed to ask, pointing to the body in the car.

'He worked for an organization called TIDI,' Martha informed him. 'We had to dispatch him I'm afraid.'

'You...dispatched him?' said Nathan, astounded. 'You *killed* this man?'

'I assure you, Mister King, he would have had no qualms about killing you...or us. We are on the same side you and I.'

'Are we? I'm not so sure about that,' he said and she saw his expression was one of disapprobation. 'That young woman you sent to me. Liz. She's been killed.'

'Yes, I know,' Martha replied calmly. 'This was probably the man responsible,' she informed him, pointing to the body in the Cavalier.

'We can't talk here, we could all be in danger,' the elderly man informed him. 'Would you care to come with us?'

'Where to?' Nathan queried.

'I've hired a cottage here in Sussex,' Martha told him. 'They won't find us there, not for some time anyway. They will assume we will get as far away from here as possible.'

Noticing Nathan's hesitation she told him, 'When he doesn't report in, they will come to check out what's happened. I don't think it would be wise for any of us to be here when they do'.

'I'll follow you on the bike,' Nathan told her.

'Not a good idea. They will have your registration number and would probably use the police to track you, on a false pretence of course. Probably, they would make sure you were a suspect for a murder.'

'A murder!' exclaimed Nathan.

'This man is dead outside your house,' she pointed out.

Nathan stared in disbelief then walked with them to the green car, opened the back door and got in. The woman got in the driver's seat while the man took the passenger seat. As the car moved away, the man glanced back and offered Nathan his hand.

'I'm Stanley Hoffman,' he introduced himself. 'I, at one time, worked for TIDI.'

'What is TIDI? What does it stand for?' asked Nathan.

'The Transference and Invisibility Development Initiative,' replied Hoffman.

'That sounds like science fiction,' said Nathan.

'No. It's science but definitely not fiction.'

'Are you talking about a degausser?'

'Not quite,' replied Hoffman. 'That only makes an object invisible to radar but the object still remains where it is.'

'What are you saying? This organization is working on making things disappear and re-form, like in Star Trek?'

'No, I mean invisible transporting,' replied Hoffman.

'Oh hell! That's what happened to the ships in World War Two. That's what Price was working on.'

It was as if he had sent a bolt of electricity through the car. Both of them turned in surprise.

'You know about Price?' declared Hoffman.

'Price is dead. I saw his body in Tibet.'

218

Martha and Stanley exchanged glances then Martha commented, 'No wonder they are watching you so carefully, Mister King. I'm surprised you're still alive. Where was the body?' she enquired.

'In a cave, below ground,' Nathan told her. 'Only the monks know about it. Look, I need to know what's going on here.'

'We will explain everything, Mister King,' Martha told him, 'but we need to know exactly what you found in Tibet.'

'First I need to know why you sent that girl to me?' he demanded.

'In 1952, Price discovered TIDI were using members of our own armed forces in experiments,' Stanley explained. 'I worked with Price and he was a brilliant scientist, but just after we discovered what was happening he disappeared. Price took important documents with him when he left. TIDI was thrown into complete disarray and there's no doubt they put a hefty price on his head but no one ever found him.'

'He was disillusioned with his own Government,' mused Nathan.

'Assuming the Government knew, of course. It is not unusual for certain top secret organizations to go their own way. Price was appalled. For the first time, I believe the consequences of his discoveries really hit home. Price felt personally responsible for the death of those men because he was the head of the development team. He believed that his work on the project had led to him becoming an unknowing accomplice in the murder of those men. To say he felt bitter is an understatement. One problem he had was that none of us were sure how much the Government actually knew about TIDI. Who could he trust? Once Price disappeared, I knew I had to go too. I couldn't continue working on the project knowing how it was being used and also, having worked so closely with Price, I felt that the powers that be may suspect my misgivings also. I knew enough to realize that my own life could be in danger. That evening I left work and left my life. I never went back. The project was shut down. They couldn't find anyone to replace Price, plus there were other concerns and funding was routed elsewhere. It seemed our associates, the Americans, also discontinued, probably to fund the space programme. Recently, I realized the project had come to life again.'

'That's where Liz comes in,' said Martha. 'I happened to bump into her and she confided to me her concern for a friend of hers.'

'Richard Paulton,' sighed Nathan.

'That's right. On reflection I was wrong to involve Liz but I thought she would be insignificant to TIDI. I made a serious misjudgement.'

'So you think Richard may have been used in one of these experiments?' Nathan asked.

'Yes. A certain incident alerted my suspicions,' said Martha.

'He's in Lapland apparently,' Nathan informed them. 'A friend of a friend came up with the information.'

'Lapland?' queried Martha. 'Why would he be there?'

'The Norwegian Sea...' began Stanley but Martha interjected.

'Exactly how many people have you involved in this, Mister King?' she enquired urgently.

'Well, when I called to see Liz I saw Rene, who runs the nightclub. It was Rene who told me Liz was dead but she knows nothing significant. However, I did confide in a journalist friend and another friend of mine who is a Professor at the Oxford Institute of Flexible Science.'

'They'll be in danger,' Martha informed him.

'No!' insisted Nathan. 'I've been very careful.'

'I fear you don't know this set-up well enough,' Martha told him.

Nathan's silence conveyed to Martha more clearly than words.

'What is it, Mister King?' she asked.

'Jeremy. Professor Jeremy Elling. I sent him Price's notebook.'

'Price's notebook!' exclaimed Stanley.

Martha suddenly stopped the car and cut the engine.

'What are you doing?' Stanley asked her nervously.

'We have to get to Professor Elling. Does he live in Oxford?'

'Yes, he has an apartment at the institute,' Nathan told them.

'I could go,' suggested Stanley.

'Mister King, did you find any other documents that belonged to Price?' Martha enquired.

'No,' he said emphatically. 'That is...I didn't actually find anything. A monk led me to the body and gave me the notebook.'

'Why?' asked Stanley.

'I came upon a monastery cut into a mountain while I was taking photographs of the landscape. Curiosity led me to go and take a look at it. I wish I hadn't. At first, I thought it was deserted but then I came across the hall where the monks took their meals. The monks were all dead. They'd been massacred.'

Nathan hesitated to await some kind of reaction but the two people in the car with him listened as if he were reciting something he had watched on television the previous night.

'I took photographs and left,' Nathan continued. 'I felt sick by that time. Then I heard a sound and discovered an old monk in a well. He'd been thrown down but survived because there was a ledge halfway down. The old boy was close to death but he called me The Sign of the Light, as if he thought some divine providence had sent me to him. I was too late to help him and he died shortly after I found him. When he was lying dead, I noticed a metal tag around his neck. It was an ID from the Second World War. It belonged to an American sailor. I have it on me.'

'Ah!' said Martha. 'That's interesting.'

'When I returned to the monastery the bodies had gone. It was as if the massacre had never happened.'

'Ours or the Chinese?' Stanley queried with Martha.

'Martha shook her head and requested Nathan to continue.

'Suddenly, this young monk appeared from nowhere,' Nathan continued, 'and asked me what I wanted. When I told him what the old monk had said to me, he claimed he'd been expecting me and led me underground to two bodies. One was David Spontiak, the owner of the ID. The other was Price. That was when the monk gave me the book.'

'How would he have known about the book?' Stanley asked Martha.

'They are a deeply religious people. The old monk would have been revered. Price clearly sought sanctuary at the monastery and they earned each other's trust. It sounds as if Price left instructions that were passed down. Possibly they saw Mister King as a sign.'

'Could I ask you, Mister King,' said Stanley, 'what state the bodies were in?'

'Skeletal. Hair still attached and some remnants of clothing.'

'Did you notice anything odd about them?' Stanley enquired.

'No, I don't think so. Oh yes,' said Nathan, suddenly remembering. 'The shinbones on Spontiak's skeleton were a yellowish-green. When I commented on it, the monk said the man had come in a fog from the skies.'

'Good grief!' uttered Stanley. 'So there could have been witnesses!'

'I wish you'd explain to me...' began Nathan but Martha cut him short.

'There will be time for that later,' she told him.

'I need to ring Jeremy and Leo, my journalist friend,' insisted Nathan.

'No,' said Martha firmly. 'We have to prioritize. Leo will only know as much as you but if Professor Elling has a book they are desperate to get their hands on...'

'It was posted to Jeremy. Liz popped it in the box after her visit. How will they know?' Nathan asked.

'They would have done extensive research on you, Mister King,' Martha informed him. 'There's no telling for sure if they know about the book but they will know everyone you are in contact with. They would have bugged your telephone I should imagine.'

'Yes. I found that during Liz's visit,' he recalled with rancour.

'Yes, well that means your friends' telephones could be bugged as well..'

'There was someone else...' Nathan suddenly remembered. 'Because of the nature of the information I wanted, it was beyond Leo's means but he hired a Quentin Rogers. That was the friend of a friend who indicated Richard was in Lapland.'

'Quentin!' exclaimed Martha. 'Good heavens, is he still going?'

'The thorn in the side of bureaucracy,' laughed Stanley. 'That's what they used to call him.'

'Well, the thorn's lost his edge because he backed out and warned Leo to do the same,' Nathan informed them.

'MI5?' queried Stanley, looking at Martha.

'I should think so,' she replied. 'Can you do this Stanley?' she enquired, her tone taking on a doubtful note.

'I'm sure. It's best you protect Mister King.'

'Stanley, you realize if there is danger to your life or Professor Elling's, you must not hesitate?'

There was a short silence before Stanley heaved a sigh and nodded.

'Is there security at the institute?' Stanley enquired.

'They have a security man on in the evening. Visitors always report to the main gate,' said Nathan.

'Excellent,' said Stanley.

'It won't be a problem Stanley getting in,' said Martha. 'It's getting your friend out.'

'There will be a way,' said Stanley.

'Oh yes. There's always a way,' smiled Martha.

'Trains from Paddington go to Oxford,' said Stanley. 'I'll go to Victoria and pick up a train from there. Where do you want to meet?'

Martha thought for a moment then checked her watch. It was 8.26p.m.

'You won't make it back in time tonight unless you get a cab part of the way,' Martha told Stanley.

Martha and Nathan both gave Stanley money. As Stanley placed the notes in his pocket, Martha opened the dashboard compartment and took out a small gun.

'You might need that, Stanley,' she said, aware that killing was anathema to Stanley but knowing the need for survival was as inherent in him as it was in herself.

For a moment Stanley and Martha looked at one another. No words were spoken and yet Nathan felt a silent message pass between them. Martha started the car engine.

'I'll drop you at the nearest station, take Mister King to the cottage then return later to wait for you,' she told Stanley.

'I will need you to give me a description of your friend, Elling,' Stanley told Nathan.

Toony had been fortunate. Exhausted and still shocked by his horrific experience and Richard's death, he was currently unaware of how benign fate had been to him. After walking for about an hour, he had come upon a road which had led him to a wider road which he had walked along with his thumb in the air. A trucker, with a decent command of English, had stopped and picked him up. The trucker was on his way to Bergen and advised Toony of the overnight ferry from Bergen to Newcastle. Toony did not have a clue where Newcastle was or how far it would be from Liz's address in Dorset, but anywhere in England was fine by him.

The trucker had stopped at a cafe on the way and after conversing with other truckers and cafe staff, had managed to obtain the international code for Britain and helped Toony to make a call. The news that Liz had been killed had come as a huge blow to Toony for he had hoped she would pick him up from his landing point in England. Although the news had come as a major disappointment it had not come as a surprise. Toony had read the note from Richard to Liz and memorized the address. It had been clear from the note that Richard had voiced serious concerns to Liz about his posting. Seated in the cafe, Toony had felt the now worn and delicate piece of paper in his pocket. Only a few words were now legible but for some reason he had not been able to bring himself to throw it away.

At Bergen he had asked around about the overnight ferry to Britain and had found a helpful Australian who had pointed it out to him. Toony then discreetly hung around the dock trying to think of a way onto the ferry. The kroners he had taken from the cabin had paid for the telephone call and a cup of coffee at the cafe. Suddenly, he had spotted some supplies being taken aboard. One man had just taken a box up the ramp, when someone had called away the other two men who were with him. Toony did not waste any time. Swiftly dashing forward and grabbing a box, he had quickly made his way up the ramp and along the deck when a crew member appeared, looked at the box and waved him in the right direction. Toony had made his way down some stairs where another crew member waved him along a small corridor. Here, Toony left the box and checked out a couple of doors near the galley. One was a tiny store room, the other a cupboard holding cleaning equipment. Toony sneaked into the cleaning cupboard.

Now the ferry had set sail for England and Toony sat with his knees under his chin, shivering, not with cold but with memories. Toony remembered the previous night: moving lights, an eerie fog and the splash as Richard had jumped ship. It was then he had instantly made his decision. The drop into darkness had been a strange sensation, for he had known the sea was there but could not see it until it had met him like concrete. For one awful moment, he thought his arm had broken but it obeyed his silent command to move and he had begun to fight the waves, racing the weird, green mist until the sky had lit up with an orange light and he had turned to see the instantaneous combustion. Strange shapes, like aliens, moved about the deck and it had been a few seconds before he had recognized them as his comrades on fire. The screams and shouts of the tortured as their souls were ripped from their bodies had chilled his blood. Swimming in the blackness, the sharp sting of the waves slapping his face, the momentum of the sea pulling his body first one way then another, he had fought to keep his head above water, to escape the transient wafts of green that breathed on his shoulder and then he had spotted Richard about ten feet away. At first, he believed him to be dead but had grabbed him anyway and called his name.

The door opened. Toony jumped. A ruddy-faced member of the crew stood looking at him. Toony stared back, numb, knowing his fate was in this man's hands.

CHAPTER THIRTY-ONE

THE EXECUTIONER

Stanley spotted it immediately: A dark car in the hazy, outer glow of a street lamp, shapes within moving so slightly it was difficult to tell whether they were shadows or people. Stanley had been at this game for so long he had learned to actually smell the enemy by the fine sensors of the body hair which his brain then translated to an odour. It was a stale, sharp redolence. Once, when he was a small child, Stanley had lost his mother in a busy high street. As the realization dawned on him, lost within a maze of rushing strangers, he became aware of it: danger. The danger had a smell and it was a smell he had never forgotten.

Glancing across the road, towards the imposing building of rectangles and towers, he wondered if Professor Jeremy Elling was aware of that smell. Then again, how could he be? For Jeremy Elling there would have been no urgency of survival to invite it to his senses.

Stanley stood in the shadows for some time, watching the car and the building, unsure of what to do and then he spotted it just a little way along the gutter. On the murky edge of the light cast by the street lamp was an empty beer bottle and it was easily within reach. Cautiously, Stanley squatted down and eased his hand towards it until he felt the cold, glass neck at the tip of his fingers. Intrusive lights unexpectedly lifted the night and Stanley had to dodge back into the shadows of a gateway in the wall. The car passed by and Stanley took his chance. As the lights reared up in the front window of the parked car, Stanley leaned forward and grabbed the bottle. Ruffling up his hair he suddenly staggered out, tripping over the kerb before wandering into the middle of the road.

A growl, from a motorcycle suddenly illuminating the tarmac, was followed by a gruff shout as the biker was forced to swerve before rebalancing himself. As the motorbike roared off into the night, Stanley spun around on the spot and yelled a curse. Left in the middle of the road, Stanley stood still, swaying slightly. A window of the parked car slid down and a man's voice shouted, 'Get out of the road!'

Stanley looked skywards.

'Is that you, God?' he demanded.

'No, it's me, you silly old duffer. Get out of the road. Go on, be off with you!' came the authoritative voice.

Stanley peered into the darkness at the shadows within the parked car.

'Is this the road to Tipperary?' he called.

'Just get out of the road. You'll get yourself killed!' came the reply.

Inwardly smiling, but outwardly serious, Stanley flung out an arm and waved the bottle in the air. Staggering across to the other side of the road, he walked like a crab between the archway pillars of the Oxford Institute of Flexible Science. Stanley leaned on one of the pillars for a second and then tumbled inside out of view.

Stanley quickly straightened up and found himself in a large courtyard. Further along he could see a small light in what looked like a reception area. Placing the bottle carefully beneath a hedge, he tidied his hair and keeping to the screened wall, out of sight of the archway, he approached the uniformed man on reception who was engrossed in a crossword. The man, in his fifties with a moustache, pulled the window open as Stanley stood waiting politely.

'I am here to see Professor Elling. I've run terribly late. Would you direct me, please?' asked Stanley in his best Oxfordshire accent.

'Certainly, sir. Through there, turn left and he's in the third apartment along,' obliged the security man.

'Thank you,' nodded Stanley then, turning, he asked, 'Has there been any other visitors for Professor Elling this evening?'

'Not to my knowledge, sir. I came on at nine.'

'Thank you,' said Stanley again then he followed the directions to a square archway behind which was a large garden. Turning left, he found the third apartment along and rang the bell. Seconds later, a tall, rather handsome man with dark hair opened the door and stood looking confused.

'Professor Elling?' asked Stanley.

227

There was a slight hesitation. 'Yes...?'

'I am here on behalf of Nathan King.'

'Nathan! Is he well? I've been waiting to hear from him.'

It was then that Stanley noticed the shoe and ankle lying sideways on the floor, behind and to the right of the man in the doorway.

'You must come with me at once and bring the notebook,' said Stanley, controlling his tone to sound urgent but unruffled.

Once again there was hesitation.

'Ah! Right. I'll just get it...wait here...'

As the man turned, careful to half-close the door, he went to take something from his inside pocket. Stanley swiftly followed him in, pulled out the pistol and shot him in the head. The man made a gurgling noise and fell to the floor. Stanley closed the door behind him and rushed to the other prostrate figure lying still with his head touching the wooden feet of the antique oak desk.

'Professor Elling, are you all right?' enquired Stanley.

There was a faint groan.

'Professor Elling!' he said more urgently.

The eyelids flickered and then a hand moved slowly to feel the place on his head where he had been coshed.

'What happened?' he asked.

'Listen. Listen carefully,' said Stanley. 'I know you are injured but I must get you out of here. Your life is in danger. Do you understand?'

'Yes,' he said slowly. 'I understand.'

'Nathan King sent me. You have a notebook that he sent you. Where is it?'

The injured figure eyed Stanley suspiciously.

'Who are you?' he asked.

'Professor Elling, you have to trust me. This is the man who coshed you...'

The suspicious eyes left Stanley and moved across to see the body of a man with blood running from his head, the sanguineous liquid spreading into the carpet and forming a shape that looked strangely like a pig's head.

'His colleagues are in a car outside waiting for him,' Stanley explained. 'We have to get out of here. Nathan is waiting for us to join him but you must bring the notebook.'

'It's on the desk,' he replied.

Stanley noticed the open drawers. Grabbing the dog-eared A4 exercise book from the desk, he ignored his shaking hands, knowing he had to support Professor Elling and guide him to safety.

'Is there some way we can get out of here without passing through the main archway at the front?' Stanley asked him.

'There is a back way through the garden that leads onto a side road.'

'No. I am not happy with that. Is there a low wall somewhere in the grounds? An unofficial exit?'

Stanley waited for him to think. Clearly his head was aching, making thinking very difficult.

'There's a hole in the wall, but it's covered in brambles. It leads onto a playing field.'

'Then that's the route we must take,' said Stanley, helping him onto his feet.

Martha waited as Stanley walked towards her with a tall dark-haired man by his side.

'Professor Elling,' Stanley introduced him to Martha.

They shook hands and then got into the car, Martha surreptitiously reclaiming the gun from Stanley's pocket. They made their way back to the main road.

'This isn't the right way,' said Stanley as he observed Martha going in the opposite direction.

'No, we moved to another place. I felt it would be safer. They could already be onto us,' she remarked.

Further along, Martha slowed the car and took a turning down a small country lane where she pulled the car into the side and switched off the engine. Producing a torch, she killed the car lights and stepped out of the car.

'We can walk from here. I have to give Nathan the signal,' she remarked.

Stanley and his colleague emerged from the car. It was dark but the moon was bright. As Stanley walked ahead, Martha turned and smiled at the newcomer then produced the gun and swiftly shot him through the head.

The shot made a cracking sound and in the moonlight Stanley turned to see the man slumped on the ground, blood running from the wound in his head.

Stanley staggered forward, feeling his empty pocket.

'Martha! Why?' he asked, shocked.

'Because that isn't Elling,' she told him. 'Nathan remembered he had a recent photo of himself and Elling, attending an institute dinner, in his wallet and I assure you, that was not him.'

'Oh good grief!' uttered Stanley.

'What went wrong, Stanley?' she asked.

'Oh no! I must have killed him,' gasped Stanley. 'Martha! I've killed him!'

'Explain,' said Martha crisply.

'Men from TIDI were waiting outside the institute in a car. I fooled them and got inside the grounds of the institute. The security man said Elling had no visitors. When the door opened, the man said he was Elling but I spotted a shoe lying sideways on the floor. I could just see the ankle and realized someone was lying behind the door. I assumed it was Elling and the man was an imposter and had attacked Elling, so...I shot him. God forgive me! I shot him.'

Martha took a deep breath.

'Very well. What's done is done.'

Stanley glared at her. Something about her coldness, her matter of fact manner, shocked and yet composed him at the same time.

'But...I've killed an innocent man,' he repented.

'Yes,' she said, 'and there's nothing we can do about it. It was an understandable error. You had to think on your feet.'

'Error? It's not an error. It's murder! How can you...?'

'Get a grip, Stanley,' she told him forcefully and the look in her eyes turned him to stone.

'I'm just a scientist,' he said. 'This isn't my field. I'm not used to this as you are. Running and hiding, yes, but killing....'

'Neither was I, Stanley. Neither was I used to it, but it was necessary, you see? I had to do it, just as you had to do it. It's unfortunate but it was just that: an error. If you see it any other way, your brain will overload and you will go mad. Do you understand?'

Stanley looked straight ahead of him and fell silent.

'There's a ditch up ahead. It's deep and overgrown. It will be months before he's found. You'll have to help me,' she told him.

Martha went towards the dead body and slid her hands beneath one of the arms.

'Help me, Stanley!' she commanded.

Stanley felt a waft of cold air and shivered. Stanley's legs seemed to move of their own accord and he walked slowly towards Martha, but all he could see was Professor Elling lying in a pool of oddly shaped blood resembling a pig's head.

'God forgive me! What have I done?' he beseeched.

Martha stood waiting.

'Hurry, Stanley,' she instructed him.

Grabbing an arm each, they dragged the dead body and disposed of it in the ditch, being careful to pull the undergrowth back over to conceal it. They got back in the car. Martha drove back out of the lane and they went the rest of the way in silence.

The three of them sat around the dining table of the cottage. Nathan faced the window. Martha was to the left of him, Stanley to the right. In front of each of them was a glass of brandy.

Nathan studied Stanley with a look of disbelief. How hard they took death, these ordinary people, Martha pondered. Death had once been such a part of her life, she no longer considered it a stranger or taboo as others did and she thought of Bertram Tanner and his obituary in The Daily Telegraph where he was described as a retired civil servant. That had made Martha smile. It was so understated. Only the British could do it so well.

Martha's mind came back to the present and she studied Nathan and Stanley carefully. They had to stay strong these two men. The hardest days were yet to come and she had to be able to rely on them.

Nathan took a swig of the brandy and banged the glass down on the table. Stanley looked up and with difficulty he met Nathan's gaze but did not like what he saw there. It reflected Stanley's own pain and torture.

'I'm sorry about your friend,' Stanley reiterated.

'So you said,' replied Nathan caustically.

'You should get some sleep, Stanley. We should all get some sleep,' Martha said.

Stanley and Martha finished their drinks and got up from the table but Nathan remained and he was still sitting there two hours later, vivid images rushing through his head: The mauve and black tongue hanging from a dead monk's mouth, Liz Stone seated on his settee, Nancy Spontiak clinging to her husband's ID tag, Rene's fist coming towards his face and Jeremy Elling on the rugby field at university, young, alive and full of promise. Feeling suddenly weak in the knees, Nathan stood up unsteadily, made his way to the toilet and vomited up all the disgust that he felt inside.

CHAPTER THIRTY-TWO

TORMENT

Hains felt very strange, as if he were floating. Lights flickered on and off in his semi-consciousness. For a while he believed he was flying high above white clouds before falling through the air on a stomach-churning spiral, heading for the ground.

It would be weeks before Hains would vividly recall a fierce shock through his battered body, followed by a powerful sucking sensation pulling him into the nullification of invisibility shortly before Chinese soldiers arrived on the scene.

Hains opened his eyes and looked at the horizon. It was sideways with mountains and sky. Hard ground pressed against his face. Groaning, he became aware of a burning sensation that seemed to travel upwards from his legs to his upper body. Stretching out a hand he saw the raw, red, blistered skin that covered it. Above his wrist he could see nothing but a black and red mass that he found difficult to recognize as his own arm. The flesh smelt. It was an acrid, unpleasant smell. Turning slowly and painfully onto his back he stared at the light-blue sky.

Once again, his eyes opened. Had he lost consciousness again? Hains could not be sure. Moaning with the pain that tore at his whole body he struggled to get up and then he saw the space below his knees where his lower legs and feet should have been. Hains screamed. Panic flew around the inside of his head until he felt dizzy and sick and then he became aware of an eerie sound. The sky above him distorted with what looked like waves of pale green gas dancing and contorting. Gradually it took the shape of a ship's hull. Hains heard a violent, lingering scream and he suddenly realized the sound was coming from his own mouth. Moments later, his world darkened into insentience.

Hains came to again. The sky was blue overhead and the misty mountains oscillated slightly. Hains groaned with the pain that racked his body but the groan was barely audible as his throat felt on fire. Images flickered in his mind and he struggled to look down at his feet. They were in molten black boots. Had he been dreaming? Was this a dream? No, he considered. No dream was this painful.

Sounds now alerted him. Turning his head slowly, he saw green trucks in the distance. There was a whole line of them, their engines producing a combined roar as they rushed towards him, forming clouds of dust. Suddenly Hains was inside a Chinook. Screams came into his head then lights and the splashing of ocean waves. The images were disjointed but they came fast and furious until he cried out for them to stop and he remained that way, on the ground in the Tibetan square mile, trapped in his own private nightmare, unaware of the Chinese troops that now surrounded him.

It rained the morning of the funeral. A few of Liz's friends turned up. The girl from the café was there, though the owner did not bother to show his face. There were two gay lads who surreptitiously held hands by the graveside, a couple of old school friends, some familiar faces from the nightclub and Tom and Ellen McCarthy. One of Liz's old school friends, a skinny girl with short dark hair, sobbed on her boyfriend's shoulder all through the service. For some reason, Rene felt like hitting her. Standing apart from the huddle of friends stood another man, unknown to her, who kept gazing around the churchyard and shifting uncomfortably. Rene wondered why he'd bothered to turn up as he seemed more interested in the scenery than the coffin.

Danny stood next to Rene at the graveside, holding a large black umbrella over her. Tears ran down her face and onto the black and silver scarf around her neck as the vicar went through the ritual. The congregation then retired in the long black cars back to The Black Bull public house where Rene had hired a private room upstairs. The room was too big, the guests too few but the landlord had come up trumps with the food. People whispered as if they were in church but as the drink began to flow the conversations became a little louder. Rene could not do the round of introductions and thanks for attendance. Danny stood in for her and Rene thought what a comfort he was and how fortunate it was that she had him to rely on. A voice at her shoulder caused her to jump.

'I'm sorry, I didn't mean to startle you.'

Rene looked up at the owner of the voice: a man with fair hair and blue eyes who resembled a middle-aged public schoolboy.

'I noticed you at the funeral,' she said, 'but I don't know who you are.'

'I'm Leo,' he told her, 'a friend of Nathan King's.'

Rene indicated the chair next to her and he sat down, the blue eyes searching her face.

'So, where is your friend and does he know why Liz was killed?' she asked him.

'Rene, you have to be careful. What Nathan's got himself into involves some very powerful people. Your phone could be bugged.'

'I've made certain no one has had access to my flat without my knowledge,' Rene argued, 'but talking of phones, I was at Liz's flat when there was a call. It was a man with a twang to his voice. It could have been a Canadian or American accent. The man asked for Liz and when I told him she'd died...it was odd, there was no message of sympathy, he just asked straight out if she'd been killed.'

'Did you get a name?' Leo asked urgently.

'No. I did ask but before I could finish the sentence, he hung up.'

'Rene, is there somewhere you could disappear for a while? You could be in some danger.'

The woman eyed him coolly.

'I've no intention of going anywhere,' she replied stubbornly.

'I'd strongly advise...'

'I'm not interested in your advice,' she cut him short. 'Whatever your friend's got himself involved in, that's his problem. I'm staying out of it. Liz should have done the same, but she didn't.'

'I know you don't think you're involved, but *they* do.'

'Who are *they*?' she queried. 'Exactly what is going on here?'

'Nathan is trying to find out. Please, for your own safety, just make sure you are never alone.'

'Is everything all right?'

It was Danny standing next to her.

'Get this man a brandy, would you? A large one,' Rene instructed.

Danny made for the bar and Rene grabbed Leo's arm.

'You tell me who I'm in danger from and where Nathan King is now,' she demanded.

'Wherever Nathan is, he's in a precarious situation.'

'Then so are you,' she reminded him. 'After all, you're involved now aren't you?'

Danny came back with the brandy and placed it on the table. Leo downed it in one, thanked them and left.

Nathan opened his eyes. As he raised his head he groaned.

'You drank too much last night,' Martha scolded him.

Nathan glanced at his watch and saw it was almost twelve noon.

'I'm going to bed for a couple of hours,' he told them.

Nathan emerged two and a half hours later.

'I don't like the thought of Jeremy's body just lying there in his apartment,' Nathan announced.

'We daren't go back. Someone will find him,' said Martha soothingly.

A rat-a-tat-tat sound made itself evident as Henry ran inside his plastic wheel. Stanley turned to study him intently.

'Is he annoying you, Stanley?' smiled Martha.

'No,' he replied. 'I was just thinking of wheels. The wheels of life. The circle of life. How it begins and it ends. How every beginning has an end and every end a beginning. How the beginning and the end meet. That's all.'

Outside, the wind threw rain against the window panes. Nathan too, was thinking of wheels: prayer wheels in a Tibetan monastery and the lost brown eyes of a sandy-coloured dog.

'Why a hamster...?' asked Nathan suddenly.

'Henry is nocturnal, as indeed am I. Hamsters have to live alone. They are independent creatures, not pack animals. Henry is a lone wolf, like me. See how he tucks food into his pouch to save for later? Hamsters are well organized, so you see we have a lot in common. I find him a comfort, safe in his own little world. Henry's world is one of repetition which, psychologically, I find calming. Also, he is good, amusing company and easily transportable,' explained Martha.

Nathan drifted into a reverie.

'I'm making cheese and pickle sandwiches,' said Martha, interrupting his thoughts.

Nathan stared at her, busying herself. This elderly lady looked so normal, going to and fro from the living room to the kitchen, stopping to offer some small, caged rodent a piece of apple. The whole situation seemed ridiculous to him and then he remembered that Jeremy was dead and it changed from surreal to very dark and foreboding. Nathan joined Martha in the kitchen to make himself a coffee. On purpose, he made it bitter and black.

'I know it isn't much consolation,' Martha said to him, 'but your friend would have died anyway. Trust me. They had already tracked him down. Stanley made a fatal error, but at least he did it quickly. Do you understand?'

Nathan slowly nodded. Of course he understood, but it did not make him feel any better.

'So what's the plan?' Nathan asked her. 'We've got to alert someone about this. We've got to go somewhere.'

'Always the action man eh, Mister King?' responded Martha. 'Go where and say what exactly?'

'We have to tell the authorities what is happening. Someone somewhere has to know.'

'You are forgetting that old fashioned thing called "proof". We have to be armed with it before we do anything. We have to justify what we have done.'

'Don't you mean what *you* have done. I don't recall killing anyone,' Nathan reminded her.

'You don't go into enemy territory without being fully conversant with the area in which you are operating and the means and know-how to respond to enemy attack. Plan not just for the expected but the unexpected, Nathan. That way you may just survive. The problem we have at the moment is that it is difficult to know who to trust.'

Nathan wandered across to the window and stared out. The rain had stopped. The day looked fresh, clean and untouched. Nathan was so lost in his own thoughts that he was barely aware of the faint brush against his arm as Martha came to stand at his side.

'Who was she…?' she asked.

Nathan turned.

'Who?'

'The one you carry in here,' she smiled, touching her heart. 'I sense that deep sorrow within you.'

Nathan turned back to stare out of the window and slowly shook his head.

'She was the one,' he said simply.

Martha did not reply but waited.

'She got killed, helping others,' he added.

'Fate likes to throw missiles at us,' she sighed and he felt her sense of loss also.

'How do you deal with it?' he enquired.

There was a short silence before she replied, 'The only way you *can* deal with it. Take the pain.'

Martha took the sandwiches through and placed them on the table, then put a mug of tea in front of Stanley. An appreciative look passed between them.

'How are you getting on, Stanley?' she enquired, nodding at Price's notebook open in front of him.

'Elling's notes were helpful,' he said, almost apologetically.

'I'm glad his life was worthwhile,' retorted Nathan as he joined them.

Stanley winced but continued, 'However, there doesn't appear to be anything that new here.'

Martha sat down and Nathan joined them at the table.

'When I was working on the experiment with Price, the experiment was usually partly successful. It had worked with some matter within the laboratory but outside there were two main stumbling blocks. Firstly, we had great difficulty controlling the routing which was, of course, crucial. Secondly, there was the amount of energy we needed to generate to carry the experiment over long distances. This is what we were working on when Price discovered our own soldiers were being used as guinea pigs. Price believed it was wrong to use anything live for our experiments until the process had been perfected. Price refused to use animals, believing that to be morally wrong and scientifically inaccurate. Once the experiment had been perfected with material objects, the agreement was to use dead bodies and then volunteers from Death Row. These men were going to die very unpleasantly. This way, they stood a chance to survive.'

'So what more have the notes told you?' Martha asked him.

'It appears that Price may have found a reason for the routing problem. From his notes, it would appear he believes it was ley lines emitting and attracting energy. As they absorb the energy they charge it along to the next ley hot spot. It's basically natural electrical interference. Just like when a storm interferes with your television reception. In fact, if Price is correct then I should imagine weather conditions at the time of the experiments would play a major part in the outcome.'

'I don't quite understand,' said Nathan.

'All right. Think of the underground railway system. Now, if you get on a train at Ealing Broadway, that train won't take you direct to Russell Square. Why not?'

'Because Ealing Broadway is on the Central line and Russell Square is on the Piccadilly line. You'd have to change at Holborn,' replied Nathan.

'Exactly. There is a diversion and the Ealing Broadway train wouldn't take you there. The electromagnetic energy is being affected by natural energy interference from ley lines that attract it and shoot it off in directions that we can't control, which is why a ship in the Atlantic ended up reappearing in Tibet,' explained Stanley.

'Is there more?' asked Martha.

'Not really. There appears to be a missing link in the notes here. If you look carefully, it seems there have been some pages torn out.'

'Were the pages torn out when you recovered the book from the underground cavern?' Martha asked Nathan.

'I'm not sure. I didn't look that closely. The contents didn't mean anything to me.'

'Of course, it's a possibility that Professor Elling pulled them out,' suggested Stanley.

'Why? Why would Jeremy do that?' Nathan challenged him.

'We may never know,' Martha gave them a stark reminder.

'What proof do we need?' Nathan appealed.

'It would help if we could find Richard Paulton, that's if he's still alive,' said Martha.

'Listen, I have to contact Leo. There's a possibility he may have heard something from the woman who employed Liz. I'll call a mutual contact from a public phone box.'

Stanley glanced at Martha. For a moment or two she contemplated then she agreed but warned, 'Mention nothing of what we have discussed here today'.

'No, of course not,' Nathan affirmed.

Hains had not understood a word that was said to him. There had been concrete walls around him and a dirty, stained ceiling. A plastic bag with clear fluid had hung from a metal pole with a tube attached to his arm. Every now and again a Chinese man in a white overall had studied his face carefully and smiled at him like a wolf about to devour his prey. Hains had been too weak and helpless to do anything as he saw his own arm lifted and the liquid in the syringe plunged into his vein.

Was it minutes or hours later that he woke up? Perhaps it was days. Hains was uncertain. The heaviness in his head was swirling around. By the light of some kerosene lamps, Hains saw a Chinese man in a uniform sat at a desk in front of him. Apart from that the room was bare. Throwing his head back, Hains stared at the ceiling but there was no stain. Now he was in a different room to the one before or had there been a previous room? Had he dreamed about the man in the overall and the injections?

'How are you feeling?' the Chinese man asked him in English.

Hains became aware he was seated in a chair. As his head slumped forward he saw the bandaging to his arms, hands, legs and feet.

'We saved your life,' the Chinese man said pontifically and smiled at him, but it was a derisive smile. 'Your Government and your military have deserted you. They believe your life is worthless.'

Hains tried to speak but his mouth felt dry and his lips were numb.

'You appeared to be in shock. We had to give you very strong medication,' the Chinese man justified himself. 'Your arms and legs were badly burned.'

Hains said nothing.

'You must be thirsty.'

The Chinese official went to the door and barked out an order.

'Would you like a cigarette?' he offered when he returned to lean on the front of his desk.

Hains shook his head in the negative.

'I know you are very tired. You will feel better after a long rest. First, I need to ask you some questions. If I am satisfied with your answers I can make you very comfortable.'

The door opened and a younger Chinese man, also in uniform, entered with a white mug.

The elder man indicated to him to give it to Hains. The young man stepped forward and held the mug to Hains's lips. The lips peeled apart, painfully, like a fastened envelope and he had to let the liquid slide down his throat gently as he could barely swallow.

'Tea with milk and sugar as you westerners like it,' smiled the elder official condescendingly.

Hains put his lips to the mug again and eased the liquid down his parched throat. It tasted strange and he realized it must be the milk. Hains wondered if it was goat's milk. The young Chinese man placed the cup carefully in Hains's bandaged hands and then stood back against the wall. The elder official waited patiently as Hains drank the tea until the cup was drained.

'Where am I?' Hains managed to form the words with difficulty and his voice sounded weak and crackly when he spoke.

'You are in an official Chinese Government building in Lhasa.'

'Tibet!'

'You seem surprised,' said the Chinese official. 'Where did you think you were?'

Hains could not answer.

'Where did you expect to be?' the official repeated.

'At home. I must have been dreaming,' Hains replied.

'Where is home?' asked the official.

'England,' Hains said with an ache in his voice.

'We had reports of an airship,' said the official.

For a fleeting and uncomfortable moment, Hains was suddenly back on the deck of that ship with the darkness bearing down on him and the terrible sense of foreboding strangling him like a black, shrouded ghoul. Involuntarily he shivered. So, they thought it was an airship. That's what he would go along with.

'You spoke, under sedation, of a fire. Where were you going on this airship?'

Hains felt disorientated but his brain was still functioning. If he lied through his teeth and did it convincingly, he just might survive for now. Beyond that…he would deal with it when the time arrived. For now, the present was all he had to worry about: to live for the moment and to stay alive.

'Can you protect me from my own people?' his cracked voice begged and he was surprised at the authenticity of his tone.

The official smiled warmly.

'Yes. We can protect you. We look after our people. We respect our soldiers. We will find a way to help your family too,' he assured him.

'I have no family,' croaked Hains. 'None of the men chosen for this mission had families.'

'Ah! So they never expected you to return?' proclaimed the official, pensively.

'Obviously not,' muttered Hains with genuine bitterness.

This time when the official offered him a cigarette and held it to his lips, Hains took a puff as he realized this was going to be a long and exhausting session.

Nathan was pleased to get some air. There was a small village store, pub, postbox and telephone booth within half a mile of the cottage. The trees were damp and tinged with late autumn hues of red, brown, gold and yellow and the air was brisk and fresh. The walk gave him time to think and blow some cobwebs away. When he entered the telephone box he dialled the number of the fish and chip shop. The owner answered and Nathan asked him if he could get an urgent message to Leo by just telling him his order was ready for collection. Nathan said he would ring back in five minutes. When he did it was Leo who answered the phone.

'Where the hell have you been?' Leo enquired.

'Leo, listen. Have you found out any more? Anything at all?'

'Oh yes. There's been some developments here. I attended Liz's funeral this morning. I've only just got back. I met her employer, Rene, who told me she had been at Liz's flat when there was a phone call and she said it was strange. It was a man. Not English. American or Canadian she thought. The man asked for Liz. When she told him

Liz had died she felt his response was odd because he asked outright if she'd been killed. Before she could get a name he hung up.'

'Rene could be in danger,' Nathan sighed.

'I did try to warn her. I suggested she keep her head low but she's a strong-minded woman.'

'I know and she packs quite a punch too. It was good of you to attend the funeral and smart thinking too. Thanks, Leo.'

The dejection in his tone caught Leo's attention.

'Are you OK? Is everything all right?' he asked Nathan.

'Jeremy Elling is dead,' Nathan told him.

'Don't be ridiculous,' laughed Leo.

Nathan was taken aback by his flippancy.

'Leo, he's dead and it wasn't natural causes.'

'Nathan, Elling is with me. That was the other development.'

'What!'

'Elling is with me. Well, not actually with me right now, right here. He's staying at the holiday flat. I couldn't let him stay at the house. Veronica would have…'

'Just a minute!' interrupted Nathan. 'Are you sure it's Elling?'

'Of course I'm sure. I've met him before haven't I? What made you think he was dead?'

'Someone got killed at his apartment at the institute.'

'Ah, well, according to Elling he had a visitor who enquired about you. Elling wasn't sure about him and asked him to leave. Apparently, he then attacked Elling but Elling got the better of him, smashed him over the head with a vase and got out pronto. I went back to his apartment really early this morning but the chap had gone. I noticed the floor had been washed and there was a strong smell of bleach. Elling said you'd sent him Price's book but that was missing. It's not all bad news though. Bearing in mind the importance you'd placed on it, Elling made a copy and removed some essential pages from the original. Elling has those with him.'

There was a short silence then Leo asked, 'You've not been coerced to make this phone call have you? Just say "I'll be in touch" if there's someone with you'.

'No. I'm on my own and I'm safe. I'm with friends. Make sure Elling is safe and tell him I have the book. I'll call tomorrow.'

'You have the book!' Leo gasped. 'How?'

'I'll explain when I see you. Take care,' Nathan told him.

'You too,' came the reply and with that the receiver went down.

'Then…the man I killed…?' muttered Stanley.

'Must have been someone from TIDI,' said Martha. 'The first man must have gone in. It was too long before he re-emerged so a colleague went to investigate. That must have been the man who opened the door to you, Stanley. The man who you first thought was Elling.'

'Then…the two in the car outside the institute…?'

'Either back-up or just ordinary chaps waiting there for a different reason.'

'I felt sure they were from TIDI,' murmured Stanley.

'Then your instincts were probably correct,' Martha told him.

'I don't understand how…I mean, there must have been blood…' said Nathan.

'Oh these people are very quick and very efficient, Nathan. Professionals would have been sent in immediately to clean up the mess.'

'Yes, just like the monastery,' recalled Nathan.

'I don't think we can ever be sure who was responsible for that mess,' said Martha.

'So Elling has the missing pages,' mused Stanley.

'I believe we should no longer remain here. We have to get to Elling. We'll leave now and you can call your mutual contact to get an urgent message to Leo,' said Martha and the two men, unquestioningly, followed her lead.

'Do you think the call to Liz's flat could have been someone from TIDI?' Nathan asked Stanley when they were in the car.

Martha answered for him.

'No. They would have known for sure that Liz had been killed. They wouldn't have needed to make the call. It's possible there's a joint mission happening. I think it was a soldier and a scared soldier. It's possible he's gone AWOL. Whoever he is, he knows too much.'

'He also must know Richard,' remarked Nathan. 'Richard must have given him a message to give to Liz.'

'Which probably means that something has happened to Richard,' Martha concluded.

'Can't we try and get to this soldier?' asked Nathan.

'We don't know where he is and clearly he won't want to be found so how could we trace him?'

'I could go to Lapland. I could try and get a lead somehow,' Nathan offered.

'No you can't. It would be too dangerous and you are far too important. You are a witness to what happened to Price.'

'I agree with Martha,' conceded Stanley.

'Besides,' said Martha, 'this man is clearly aware there is a situation that could endanger his life, otherwise he would not have assumed that Liz had been killed. I believe this soldier, if he is, indeed, a soldier, knows what he is dealing with. Sooner or later he will have to contact someone. Let's have faith in him.'

'Like you had faith in Liz,' Nathan remarked unkindly.

'That was uncalled for, but understandable,' Martha coolly replied.

Nathan could not help but feel a grudging regard for Martha. There was something frighteningly cold about the woman, but she was a wise sage and he admired the direct and meticulous efficiency of how she operated. Nothing seemed to catch her off guard. There was a calm, ever-present, self-assurance that radiated from her. When Stanley had told him of her background, Nathan had not been entirely surprised. What a formidable agent she must have been in her time, he considered. Nathan could imagine her young, vibrant, filled with a tenacious passion to serve her country and outdo the enemy. The young woman on his sofa, however, haunted him and Nathan closed his eyes and shook his head as if by doing so he would shake away the pictures and memories that so disturbed him. When he opened them, he saw Martha's keen eyes watching him through the driver's mirror.

As if reading his thoughts, Martha advised, 'You need to focus on the here and now, Nathan. It is essential for your survival that you do so'.

CHAPTER THIRTY-THREE

THE FAREWELL

At his holiday flat on the outskirts of Littlehampton, Leo opened the door to Nathan, Martha and Stanley and hustled them in. From an armchair in the corner of the living room, Jeremy Elling stood up. For a moment he and Nathan gazed at one another then Nathan's mouth eased into a broad smile and he stepped forward, tightly clasping his friend's arms. Nathan stood back and looked him up and down.

'I thought you were dead,' Nathan told him.

'I heard,' smiled Elling.

Stanley stepped forward and introduced himself.

'I'm very relieved that you're alive,' said Stanley.

Elling shook his hand and took in the keen eyes and childish face that looked incredibly pale.

'So am I,' Elling told him.

'Shall we all sit round the table,' suggested Leo. 'I've got sandwiches and coffee and I'm sure we've all got a lot to talk about.'

Nathan introduced Martha and then explained who she and Stanley were and about the Transference and Invisibility Development Initiative Stanley had worked for. Martha took the lead and suggested Nathan explain in detail exactly what he had discovered in Tibet and what he had done subsequently. Stanley then briefly told of his work at TIDI, of Price's sudden departure and of his own life since. Martha noticed Nathan's tension as Stanley told of the incident at Ealing Station. Elling too, she observed, was growing increasingly uneasy, but it was to be expected she reasoned. They were not used to it. Neither was Stanley really though he had stepped up to the plate remarkably well, she thought. Research and deduction was Stanley's niche, not the kill or run world she had been part of. For the first time, she noted the shaking of his hands and the greyness of his face and she wondered if he had slept at all for the past few nights.

When Stanley had concluded, Martha leaned towards Professor Elling and said, 'What we need now are your deductions of the notebook. We know you removed certain pages and some of your written observations, I imagine, contained a few red herrings?'

'I took sensible precautions,' confirmed Elling, 'after reading Nathan's note.'

'Jeremy,' interrupted Nathan, 'Stanley has gone some way in working out the notes. Stanley…?'

'Invisible transference. It is what Price and I were working on before he left TIDI, but I believe Price may have discovered the reason for the routing problems. I believe he found that the diversional problems we had encountered could be explained by ley lines and could somehow be rectified. Did he discover the rectification?' Stanley asked eagerly.

'This has echoes of The Philadelphia Experiment, Stanley,' Elling said earnestly. 'I believe you started off using Einstein's Unified Field Theory as a basis for your work but Price decided instead of scanning an object, transmitting the information and constructing a replica from atoms of the same kind in the same pattern, he decided to transfer the original.'

'I just don't see how any of this is possible,' said Nathan.

'Don't personalize,' suggested Elling. 'If you stick with basics, we, like everything else on the planet, are made of matter. A complicated matter, but matter nevertheless. It is the difference between Plan A: Taking a house apart brick by brick, travelling with the material and plans then rebuilding it in a different location and Plan B: Taking the house as it is and transporting it to a different location.'

Leaving the table he went to a drawer and took out the lacunas from the notebook along with calculations of his own. Once seated, he displayed them in front of Stanley who eyed them with great interest.

'You see here,' said Elling, pointing at some calculation that the others could not clearly see. 'The experiment partly used electromagnetic radiation to transfer the object elsewhere. As a matter of pure coincidence, I was on a plane recently from London to Montreal, via Reykjavik, when we saw some unidentified lights appear in the sky. I couldn't understand what they were. They just seemed to hover before disappearing and reappearing in front of the plane. I'd never seen anything like it. The captain told me there had been a lot of unexplained sightings for some time though sightings of these particular lights were more recent.'

'What were they?' asked Nathan.

'I now believe they were something to do with this. This organization – TIDI – I believe use specially designed aircraft, virtually invisible to radar and with an anti-stalling device. These aircraft are generators used, perhaps three or four at a time, to project rays of energy. TIDI has a magnet for this energy. We will call this the target. When the energy is produced, the magnetization causes it to home in on the target area. The target in question would probably be a ship or an aircraft. It has to be something they can get isolated. The target vessel is equipped and wired up in such a way as to be able to deflect the energy around it whilst still attracting the energy required for invisible transference.'

'Like deflecting a punch,' suggested Nathan using a karate block and twist to demonstrate.

'Yes, exactly. The blow coming towards you would be powerful but you, the target, would deflect the energy as it made contact, just as you have demonstrated. Am I correct so far, Stanley?'

'Yes. Absolutely,' he replied.

'Now, Stanley,' continued Elling, 'you were aware that a changing magnetic field that produces a more powerful electrical current could be used to transport the object…'

'Yes,' said Stanley, 'but the target vessel was always fully or partly destroyed in the process because the power was never strong enough.'

'Right. That would be like walking over burning coals. If you run over them fast, you don't burn your feet. If you walk over them slowly, you get badly blistered. You see, to make the target invisible it had to move faster than the speed of light.'

'Plus we had problems controlling the routeing of the target vessel,' Stanley told him.

'This is where it all started to go wrong for Price so he decided to change tack and theorize on a nuance of what you had already been working on. Price refers to ERRM. Basically he's referring to electromagnetic replication.'

Elling flicked over some of the pages he had removed from the notebook. Beside one page he placed another page of careful calculations he had constructed from Price's notes.

For some moments, Stanley scanned the calculations and then lifted his head.

'But this is…good grief!' uttered Stanley.

'Multi-copying,' smiled Elling. 'Here's his calculation right here. Instead of transferring the invisible matter some distance away, Price had to concede that even overcoming the power problem, the transference would be far too complex and unreliable, due to interference from earth's energy lines as well as other naturally or artificially occurring magnetic and electrical forces, so he decided to use the object in situ which would allow much more control.'

'For what purpose?' Martha asked Professor Elling.

'To allow the object to become a duplicating machine. Electromagnetic, refractive, reflection multi-copying: ERRM. Ships or aircraft, duplicated many times to make a navy or air force appear much larger than it is, to dupe the enemy into firing at the ghost ships or planes instead of the real ones. Think of a person walking through a hall of mirrors. Which is the real image? How can you differentiate between the real one and all the reflected images that you see?'

'Goodness!' declared Stanley. 'You can see the advantages, Martha?'

'Oh yes,' she mused.

'These ghost vessels would intimidate as well as confuse,' said Elling. 'The enemy would waste an enormous amount of time and energy, as well as using up weaponry resources and ninety per cent of the time to no avail.'

'Where and how could you produce the amount of energy to compress and radiate onto the target? You'd need the equivalent of a nuclear power station,' Nathan pointed out.

'Exactly,' said Elling. 'A power station in the sky.'

'But how is that possible?' asked Nathan.

'Oh,' said Stanley, who looked haunted, as if he were suddenly coming out of a dream, 'where Professor Elling saw the lights should give you a clue.'

'The aurora borealis!' exclaimed Martha.

'But how would anything survive that?' Nathan protested. 'The northern lights! That would be like being hit with multiple bolts of lightning. Nothing could survive that.'

'You would need a very advanced type of deflector,' replied Stanley.

'Yes,' agreed Elling, 'and in this case the energy would be simultaneously deflected and reflected, spreading the power. Imagine a row of mirrors each reflecting the next.'

'The simultaneous deflection and reflection would make it safer for the object of the experiment as the force would impact over a wider area,' said Stanley excitedly. 'It's like the difference between your foot being trodden on by a stiletto heel or a flat shoe!'

Martha sat back in her chair and went silent. The others too, became quiet, taking in the information and its implications.

'Price has calculated it all, though he mentions they would have to find a way to contain the amount of energy produced to use when and where necessary, otherwise it would only work in areas of the sphere where the aurora borealis is present,' explained Elling. 'It seems he was playing with the idea of attracting then storing power surges from the aurora borealis in moveable containers. Basically he is talking about what amounts to giant batteries, possibly in the form of container ships, aircraft or satellite. You know, it's possible that TIDI is already onto a similar idea and that is why this soldier, Richard Paulton, is in Lapland.'

'Not necessarily,' said Stanley. 'The Norwegian Sea was one of the areas TIDI used for the experiments because of our good relationship with that country, though, of course, it would have been referred to as a naval exercise only.'

'How far do you think they've got with this, Stanley?' asked Elling.

'It's my guess they are still attempting invisible transference not very successfully,' Stanley replied.

'Well, whatever experiments are taking place, I'm not surprised that TIDI are so desperate to get their hands on any knowledge Price had,' said Elling.

'You know what this means...' Martha remarked.

The faces around the table all turned their attention to the petite but charismatic figure that was Martha Kemp.

'We can't possibly make this information public. We can't afford to let a hostile country know about this.'

But the soldiers…Liz…?' began Nathan.

'Yes, we must bring it to public attention when we can and we must oust TIDI as it currently stands. Someone has to take the ultimate responsibility. People must be aware that our own soldiers have been used in experiments and that a young woman died when she attempted to find out what had happened to one of those soldiers. However, the actual nature of the experiment must never become public knowledge. As far as the media are concerned it must be a form of degauss to make vessels completely invisible to radar and that is all. As far as TIDI are concerned, Nathan, you are ignorant of the facts. You may have discovered that some sort of experiment was carried out in 1944 but certainly you cannot prove anything or you would have already done so. The same applies to you, Leo, if TIDI are aware of your involvement with Nathan, which is more than likely. However, as well as the threat that Stanley and I pose, I feel sure TIDI will believe there are two people who possibly hold all the cards. Price, who is safe because he is already dead though they are unaware of that yet and…'

An uncomfortable silence filled the room and then Jeremy Elling spoke.

'It's me isn't it? TIDI know I'm involved and I know too much.'

'They may assume so,' sighed Martha. 'It is very unfortunate, but I fear they will realize you are a walking time bomb because of the knowledge that you may carry. They would not be prepared to take risks,' Martha told him.

'Jeremy,' said Nathan with a pained expression. 'I'm so sorry.'

'Then what are we going to do?' queried Stanley.

Martha saw the grave expression on Stanley's drawn face, noticed again the shaking of the hands and she knew what was going through his mind.

'It's all right, Stanley. We must expose TIDI before they reach the professor or us.'

Elling got up and walked up and down the length of the room, rubbing his fingers through his hair, deep in thought.

'I suppose leaving the country isn't an option?' he enquired.

'Even if by some miracle you got out, they would track you down. You heard how Stanley has lived these past years. Is that the life you want...?'

Martha stopped, her attention caught by Stanley who had turned an ashen-grey colour and was now visibly perspiring.

'Are you feeling ill, Stanley?' she enquired urgently.

'I...feel a bit dizzy...' he said, before his head suddenly crashed forward onto the table and his hands dropped to his side.

Nathan immediately dragged him from the chair onto the floor.

'I can't feel a pulse,' Nathan told them.

Martha had already reached for the telephone to call an ambulance. As Nathan and Jeremy attempted resuscitation, Martha calmly gave instructions.

'I must give a false name for Stanley and myself. I will say I'm his sister and his only living relative. I'll say he paid me a surprise visit from South Africa and that way we can say there is no known address. Leo, you are an old friend and we were here for a social evening with you. I will go with Stanley to the hospital. I'll take this telephone number so I can call and let you know what's happening.'

In between giving mouth to mouth, Nathan was filled with awe but simultaneously vexed, not only by Martha's calmness but her ability to think so swiftly and logically at a time of crisis and he realized why this woman had survived a life where so many others must have fatally failed.

The ambulance crew arrived and attempted to resuscitate Stanley before quickly transferring him out into the night. Martha walked out behind them, serene, head held high and something suddenly flashed inside Nathan. In a moment he was at her side.

'Does anything ever ruffle that cold exterior of yours?' he demanded as Stanley's pale, limp body was loaded into the ambulance.

'Oh, really, Mister King! I hardly think my falling to pieces would help the situation. Do you...?'

The cool cerulean eyes held his questioningly and he backed away as if he had been spat on by a rattlesnake. Martha climbed into the ambulance, ignoring the helping arm of one of the ambulance crew. The doors closed behind her. Nathan stood and watched the ambulance disappear down the lane then he wandered back inside, filled with fear and guilt.

Martha sat outside in the waiting area next to the Casualty Department. It was full and every three or four minutes the sliding glass doors to the outside world would open as more accidents and emergencies made their way in. In a staff side room a television was showing some light entertainment that held no interest for her.

Martha knew the recent traumatic events had played heavily on Stanley's mind. The emotional side had got the better of him. It was something she had never allowed. It was a battle between survival and death. There was the emotional side of life and the practical side. If one was to survive in what had been her line of work, the emotional side always had to be fought against. Martha had never found it that difficult. It was like being addicted to something, but deciding to give it up because it was not good for you. Once the choice was made, there was no going back. The practical side had always stood her in good stead because it had kept her alive. If she had led a normal life she would have chosen differently, but in her line of work the soul had to deal with the scars. As for the heart, it simply could not exist.

'Mrs Moore?' enquired a kindly-faced matron. 'Would you like to come through to my office?'

Martha stood up and followed her through double doors into a corridor with pale green walls that had a faint smell of disinfectant. Martha was shown into a small room with a desk and invited to sit in a small armchair to one side of it.

'The doctor will be with you in a minute,' the matron explained before leaving the room.

Martha sat waiting and it was only moments before a young, fair-haired doctor entered the room and enquired if she was Mrs Moore.

'Yes,' said Martha.

The young man sat down and tried to look sufficiently regretful.

'He's passed away, hasn't he?' smiled Martha reassuringly.

'It was a cardiac arrest, I'm afraid. We tried everything we could. I'm sorry.'

'It's all right,' she told him. 'When you get to my age, death is always a distant friend that constantly keeps in touch.'

'Do you have any questions?' he asked her.

'Did he gain consciousness at all?'

'No, he didn't.'

'No,' said Martha, 'then it was his time to go, wasn't it?'

The doctor nodded and smiled.

'There is one thing,' she said. 'I gave false details about the deceased. You see, it mattered when he was alive, but now he is gone, I think he should have the dignity of his own name, don't you?'

The doctor frowned and studied her carefully.

'Why did you give false details?' he enquired.

'Stanley Hoffman – for that was his real name – had rather got himself into hot water. There were people that had been hounding Stanley for a long time. Bad debts, you see. Stanley owed the wrong people rather a lot so I acted prudently. I hope you understand.'

'And his current address…?'

'Stanley was of no fixed abode.'

'Was he wanted by the police?' the doctor enquired.

'No, only the loan sharks: such callous people.'

The explanation seemed to satisfy the doctor.

'You were given as his next of kin…?'

'Yes, I am in a way. You see, Stanley had no living relatives. I shall be dealing with everything,' she said.

'Do we have a number for you, Mrs Moore?'

'Ah, now I have just moved house and I have yet to have the telephone installed. I will contact you the minute I do. Will there need to be a post-mortem?' asked Martha.

'As it was a sudden death, I believe there will.'

'Perhaps you would be so kind as to give me the number of the coroner…?'

'Yes, of course.'

The doctor left the room and nodded to the matron who was just outside the door holding a plastic bag.

'I'm so sorry for your loss, Mrs Moore. I have his things here,' she said, passing over the bag. 'Would you like to see him?'

Martha thought for a moment and then said, 'Yes. I would, thank you.'

They walked further along the corridor and the matron indicated a small room where Stanley's body was lying on a trolley. Martha approached slowly. The expression on his bloodless face did not look at peace, it looked strained. Martha took a couple of his lifeless fingers and wrapped her own around them, squeezing them gently.

'Farewell, Stanley,' she said to the corpse, 'and I'm sorry if I asked too much of you. It's a failing of mine, I'm afraid.'

Allowing the fingers to drop she turned and left. Outside, the matron handed her a piece of paper.

'This is the number for the coroner's office.'

'Thank you. I'll contact the undertakers and ring with the information. Thank you for all you have done,' smiled Martha.

Martha walked back along the corridor and through the double doors to the Casualty waiting area. Glancing round, she noticed a picture on the television screen in the staff room and she caught her breath. It showed the face of a young soldier and she stopped to listen to what was being said. The newscaster was announcing that the Chinese had captured the British soldier who, they claimed, had been captured near Lhasa following an accident on a British military airship. The soldier was shown again, clearly speaking under duress and the direct orders of the Chinese military.

'My name is Geoff Hains. I am a guest of the Chinese. My country has been experimenting with a new airship that invaded Chinese territory. I was badly injured but have received medical attention…'

The picture switched back to the newscaster who continued his report by saying the incident had led to a serious strain in relations between the British and Chinese who claimed the airship had been sent to spy. As the picture switched to the British Home Secretary and the Defence Secretary arriving at Downing Street, Martha made her way to a cubicle the other side of the Casualty Department where there was a public telephone.

It was Nathan who answered the call.

'Nathan, it's Martha. Turn on the news,' she directed him.

'What? How's Stanley?' he enquired.

'Turn on the television to BBC 1. Quickly!' she told him and replaced the receiver.

In front of her, four mini cab cards were stuck to the wall and she dialled the third one's number.

Outside it was dark, cold and damp where there had been a light downpour of rain but she preferred the fresh air to the cramped and suffocating atmosphere inside. As she waited for the cab to arrive, she focused on what had to be done. For the time being, Stanley Hoffman was already forgotten.

CHAPTER THIRTY-FOUR

THE MOGUL

'What does it mean?' enquired Leo. 'Do you think this soldier captured by the Chinese could be part of the experimental programme?'

'He has to be,' said Nathan. 'Lhasa. It's too much of a coincidence. What happens now?'

'This changes everything,' said Elling. 'We have a live witness.'

'But for how long?' asked Leo. 'The Chinese have him, for pity's sake!'

'He will feel greatly intimidated but he's clearly misled them with the information he's given. The Government will want him back urgently. I'm sure they will try and do some sort of deal with the Chinese,' Martha assured them.

'Even then, how would we get access to him?' asked Leo. 'He'll be placed into the hands of our police or military and the whole thing could be covered up again.'

'We have to blow this open now,' Nathan told Martha.

'I agree,' said Martha. 'This soldier has rather precipitated things. We need to approach someone with what we have now, but under no circumstances must the essential pages be produced or *anyone* be told the full nature of the experiment. Is that clear?'

'Yes, I believe we all realize the consequences of that,' said Elling. 'I'll have to doctor further pages.'

'Leo, who should we approach?' Martha asked.

'There's only one man. He's powerful enough and he's rich enough and he doesn't mind shaking a few cages – Sheridan MacKenzie.'

'The media mogul?' enquired Nathan.

'Yes. The best thing about MacKenzie is he can afford the best security. I've got his number here somewhere,' Leo told them as he sifted through a wad of business cards he had taken from his pocket.

Martha had seen MacKenzie on television and he had struck her as a grandiloquent individual but one who, nevertheless, knew his speciality.

'Contact him from a public phone,' instructed Martha.

'I'll go with him,' said Nathan.

Once Nathan and Leo had left, Professor Elling sat carefully regarding the sage seated at the table.

'I'm sorry about Stanley,' he said, 'even if he did almost kill me,' he added with a sorrowful smile.

'Yes,' said Martha. 'It's a shame he won't get to see the end of the story.'

'Where does this really leave me now?' Elling enquired. 'Will I still be hiding for the rest of my life?'

'No, but I would always remain vigilant. Even though we will manage to disband TIDI, some other body will quickly take its place. It has to for the continuing research. One has to hope that exposure will make the next organization more morally conscious and the Government more aware that these organizations can be quick to go their own way if left unchecked. It is imperative they keep a close eye regarding research and defence matters, but the danger will be forever present.'

'Do you think TIDI had broken away from the original blueprint?' asked Elling.

'I certainly think they kept a certain amount under their armpit. It's surprising how little details in the small print can be furtively manipulated. It's a stark lesson in the danger of giving certain individuals too much power. How much the Government know regarding the military strategy and how much some of the military know is open to question. Like rock formation, these things have many layers.'

'What of the essential pages from the book? What am I to do with them?' Elling enquired.

'When TIDI is disbanded, which it has to be, Price's full work must be personally handed to the Home Secretary with a copy to the Defence Secretary. Another copy must be kept in a secure place as insurance for your own protection,' Martha instructed him.

Forty-five minutes later, Nathan peered behind the curtain as two black Mercedes pulled up outside the flat and two burly men left the cars and made their way to the front door. Nathan opened it and the first man flashed an ID card and addressed him.

'Mister MacKenzie says there are four of you. Is that correct?'

'Yes, that's right. I'm Nathan King...'

'No need for introductions,' said the man brusquely. 'Follow me to the car, sir.'

Nathan and Martha followed their minder out. The other security man gave a perplexed glance at the little rodent pushing its pink nose through the cage held by Martha, then motioned to Jeremy and Leo. Two other security men stood by the cars, keeping a sharp watch. Nathan and Martha were ushered into the first car while Jeremy and Leo were placed in the second. The minders were quick to put their feet down and get away.

The whole journey was taken in silence.

MacKenzie owned an impressive mansion in Surrey. As they approached it, a minder confirmed their identity by giving a password over a walkie-talkie and the gates glided open to offer a wide, winding driveway up to the mansion. When they pulled up outside the building, one minder got out of the car and told Martha and Nathan to wait a moment. They watched him as he ran up the steps to the door and spoke into an intercom. Moments later he came hurrying back and all four were escorted from the cars to the entrance. Here they were welcomed in by a butler while the minders slipped away.

The mansion was Italian style and smelt of oranges. They were shown into a large room with a white, stone fire surround above which hung a portrait of sunflowers in a vase. Jeremy assumed by the name that MacKenzie may have a Scottish accent and red hair, Leo already knew what to expect because he had met MacKenzie once before at a media conference and Martha and Nathan had seen him, briefly, on television.

The white double doors opened and in walked a hefty man with dark wavy hair, green cords, white shirt, gold medallion and a number of thick gold rings on his fingers. MacKenzie spoke with a cockney accent.

'Found your way all right then,' he laughed, approaching them and offering a hand in greeting to each in turn.

'Now I hear you've got a major story. Is that right? Something about a secret organization and the murder of British soldiers? Let's have drinks all round. Make yourselves comfortable and you can tell me all about it...'

MacKenzie had remained unruffled, attentive and in command. The photographs of the monks caused a raise of his eyebrow but did not shock him. This was his area and his questions were sharp and intrusive. Not only did he appear to believe them without question, but he reassured them and put them at ease. They were provided with comfortable rooms in his home and each were given a personal minder. Although MacKenzie had assured them of their safety, Martha still suggested they keep away from the windows at all times.

Later, when the four of them were alone, except for one minder outside the television room where they sat after dinner, Leo again produced the photographs of the monks. Jeremy Elling studied them with interest, Martha with a distance of emotion.

'They still disturb you,' Leo observed as he saw Nathan wince.

'I was just thinking of Yeshe, the old man at the hotel in Lhasa. I'm guessing he must have known Price and that he must have talked to the Chinese or someone from TIDI. Those monks are dead because of him and that dog knew it.'

'Dog?' enquired Elling.

'It's another story,' smiled Nathan wearily.

'Animals have an amazing perception,' agreed Martha.

'I wonder if those monks would have been so keen to honour Price if they'd known the true nature of his work?' Nathan mused.

The room fell silent as they each became lost in their own thoughts and it was then that Martha felt an overwhelming sadness that one of them was not present. How angry she felt that Stanley could not have seen this through to the end. It was only Jeremy Elling who noticed the misting over of those cold blue eyes.

The following morning a reporter from The Daily Envoy arrived at MacKenzie's mansion. After the meeting, the journalist left to check certain facts before returning later with a photographer.

Rene was in Liz's flat thinking about the news report that had left her feeling perturbed. Somehow, she sensed that this could have been what Richard had been caught up in. Did that soldier know Richard? Was Richard alive or dead? There was a ring on the doorbell. Rene clicked her tongue irritably, squashed out her cigarette in a nearby ashtray and went to open the door. A dark-haired man of slim stature stood with one hand leaning on the wall. Rene looked him up and down and wondered who on earth he could be.

'Yes?' she enquired.

Before she knew what was happening, the man had grabbed her, forced her back inside and slammed the door behind him.

That evening's newspapers carried the front page story with the headline 'Our Guinea Pig Soldiers'. The following morning, a very embarrassed Home Secretary attempted to answer the questions thrown at him from members of the House of Commons as well as the media. Downing Street, Palais Schaumburg and The White House all flatly denied the accusations of any such experiment having taken place.

Subsequently some media took an alternative view and began to demand more tangible proof, accusing Leo of wanting to further his career and Nathan of falsifying the photographs of the monks.

That afternoon Nathan, Martha, Leo and Jeremy sat at a media conference facing the world's press.

'Mister King, how do you hope to prove that David Spontiak and Edward Price's bodies are where you say they are when the Chinese authorities will not allow anyone within the Tibetan square mile?' asked Julian Straker from ITV.

'Obviously I can't prove it if the bodies are never given up but I'm hoping that situation will change,' Nathan replied.

'It's doubtful, though, isn't it, considering the current situation between China and the West?'

'I can't say what's going to happen in the future, I'm not Nostradamus,' Nathan came back at him.

'Silvie Gurnson from CNN,' another journalist introduced herself. 'Miss Kemp, you have refused to say who you approached about the missing Richard Paulton. Will you tell us now? Was it a member of MI5?'

'I have never mentioned MI5. That is pure supposition', Martha replied calmly.

'Which organization are we talking about then, Miss Kemp?'

'The organization was a complementary branch to the Special Operations Executive and was disbanded after the war. A remaining contact was still in a position to be of assistance.'

'Do you think Richard Paulton was murdered in a degaussing experiment, Miss Kemp?'

'Yes, I do,' said Martha decidedly.

'Yet the British, American and German Governments have all denied this,' Silvie Gurnson argued.

'I am sure they have,' smiled Martha calmly.

'Cain Jeffreys from the Universal News,' said another journalist taking the microphone. 'It seems to me you have a story involving a lot of characters who are either dead or unable to testify, a half-baked theory about a degauss experiment and some wild accusations about some dangerous organization that nobody can prove exists. Where, exactly, is your tangible proof?'

'You're a journalist. Read between the lines and work out what's going on here,' Leo barked at him.

From the corner of her eye, Martha spotted a security man approach MacKenzie and whisper in his ear. MacKenzie nodded. Nathan was fending off a particularly aggressive American journalist, who was claiming Nathan's photographic career was on the wane and this publicity stunt might put it back on track, when a door at the back of the room opened. A host of security men escorted two people up the centre of the room. Nathan stopped speaking and seconds later the media that had gathered followed his gaze and turned their attention to the visitors. Lowered whispers suddenly filled the air.

One was a middle-aged woman, nicely dressed, if a little Bohemian, with brown hair in a French roll. Next to her walked a slim, dark-haired man with sharp features looking gaunt and nervous. They stopped just before they reached the media and MacKenzie indicated for the man to be passed a microphone. The man took it and in a high-pitched American accent announced, 'My

262

name is Bruce Toony. I was with Richard Paulton and Geoff Hains aboard a navy vessel that was used in an experiment jointly carried out by the British and American military...'

For a brief moment, there was a complete stunned silence and then a storm broke out as the media left their seats to swamp Toony. Martha closed her eyes, Leo hung his head, Jeremy leaned back and let out a deep breath. Nathan stood up and amid the mayhem and flashing of camera lights, found Rene's face turned towards him. For a long moment they stared at each other then Nathan mouthed 'Thank you' and she nodded at him before her face was screened by the arm of one of the security men.

Alistair Milestone stood looking out of the window at the falling leaves of the oak trees. A message had just come through to him that British Diplomats had left for China to open talks with the Chinese about the release of Geoff Hains. The phone on his desk rang and kept ringing, but he did not answer it.

THE CONCLUSION

A week later, Nathan sat at a table, glancing out at the sky beyond a small, kitchen window framed by red and white chequered curtains. A clock ticked in the stillness of the room. In his imagination, Nathan visioned Martha Kemp alone in her room at MacKenzie's mansion and heard the bang as she placed a gun to her temple and pulled the trigger.

Once again, he slowly, respectfully, opened the letter and began to read:

My Dearest Nathan

I discovered Henry dead in his cage this evening and now would seem as good a time as any to join the loved ones that death has stolen from me.

I enclose the key to my cottage. Everything I have is yours for there is no one else. All I ask is that you notify my solicitors who are Rochester and Vaughn in Dorchester and complete arrangements for Stanley's funeral.

Forgive my rather abrupt departure from this world but I have always lived on my terms and must die on the same. I have seen a story through to its end.

It has been an honour to work alongside you. You see something wrong and you want to put it right, which is how I started off in my career. Unlike me, you sometimes allow your heart to rule your head, which means you will never be a complete success but you will always be a very decent human being.

For that reason, I salute you – Sign of the Light.

Yours in friendship
Martha Kemp